AB

Rachael Lucas has written fifteen novels for adults and teenagers, including the Carnegie nominated *The State of Grace,* which was selected as an Outstanding Book for Young People with Disabilities by IBBY. She lives on a beautiful stretch of coastline in the north west of England with her family and two very enthusiastic spaniels. When she's not writing at the kitchen table with a cup of coffee by her side, she's out walking the dogs on the beach or in the nearby pinewoods.

Keep up with Rachael - follow her on Facebook @rachaellucaswriter where you can join her VIP reader group and hear the latest book news and behind the scenes updates.

ALSO BY RACHAEL LUCAS

The Winter Cottage

The Flower Farm

Midsummer House

Christmas at Applemore

Sealed with a Kiss

Sealed with a Christmas Kiss

Wildflower Bay

The Telephone Box Library

The Village Green Bookshop

Finding Hope at Hillside Farm

Coming Up Roses

The State of Grace

My Box-Shaped Heart

Writing as Rosie Curtis

We Met in December

THE COTTAGE BY THE SHORE

RACHAEL LUCAS

PRAISE FOR RACHAEL LUCAS

Absolutely delightful - The Winter Cottage is ROMANTIC and FUN and like a big, squishy hug.

— MARIAN KEYES

Rachael Lucas has created an irresistible world to disappear into once again

— LOUISE O'NEILL

A gift to anyone in need of comfort, calm, and a deep breath of Scottish fresh air. Charming, tender and funny. (Also: nice dogs, hot men, and big houses!)

— ELLA RISBRIDGER

The most deliciously wintry, sizzlingly romantic hug of a book - the perfect Christmas comfort read

— CRESSIDA MCLAUGHLIN

PRAISE FOR RACHAEL LUCAS

Full of comfort and joy

— ALEX BROWN

I loved it - a snuggly hot chocolate of a book

— HOLLY MARTIN

Wonderfully warm, brave and wise

— MIRANDA DICKINSON

A perfect cosy romantic treat

— CATHY BRAMLEY

A romantic, atmospheric read about fresh starts and second chances

— TASMINA PERRY

Published by Rachael Lucas in 2023

ISBN (Mass Market Paperback) 978-1-7398040-4-6

Cover design by Diane Meacham at dmeachamdesigns

To my dear friend Jax, with much love.

PROLOGUE

Sophie had been driving for hours. The Highlands looked a lot smaller on Google Maps, and not only was it getting dark outside, but it had started to rain. She leaned forward slightly, peering at the overgrown sign as she put her foot on the brake, earning herself a blast on the horn from a black car behind her which – flashing headlights in annoyance – overtook her at speed, leaving her at a crossroads, none the wiser. The irony wasn't lost on her. It had been the only car she'd seen in well over an hour, so she took a guess that she was safe enough to stop. Flicking on her hazard lights, she pulled up to a halt and climbed out to investigate.

The sign had been knocked out of place and the metal post had a huge dent in it. Chips of red paint indicated the colour of whatever had crashed into it. She smiled to herself, thinking about Tabby and her love of real-life crime shows. She'd have made up a complicated scenario by now, and would be wondering what had happened to the culprit. But Tabby wasn't here, and Sophie was running out of time. So, climbing back into the car, she took a guess at which one led to Applemore. Hopefully she wasn't making the second-worst mistake of her life.

CHAPTER ONE

Two months earlier

'She got off okay then?'

Sophie's best friend Bea passed over an unbleached paper napkin from the neat stack which sat on the counter next to pottery bowls full of misshapen brown sugar lumps.

'Not a glance back over her shoulder.' Sophie blew her nose loudly, stuffing the napkin in the pocket of her blue-spotted raincoat, and then took another and began dabbing at the corner of her eyes.

'You're supposed to be proud that she's independent,' said Bea, pushing a steaming mug of coffee towards her friend.

'I am,' said Sophie, disconsolately.

'I can tell.' Bea's fair eyebrows arched upwards in amusement, but her expression was gentle. She reached over, closing her warm hand over Sophie's still cold one, and squeezing gently. 'You're doing an amazing impression of a mother who's just sent her only daughter on a plane back to the USA.'

Sophie gave a gusty sigh and tucked her hair behind her ears, looking at her wrist for the elasticated hairband that was normally sitting beside her watch. She remembered with a little jolt of despair that it was currently tying up Tabby's hair, and was probably making its way across Iceland.

'I'm really proud of her. You know I am. It's just...'

'I know. It's a long way, and she's not back now until the summer.'

'She's not back for the summer.' Sophie's heart contracted at the thought. 'She's already been snapped up for a summer job coaching kids at a camp. She was utterly over the moon when she told me.'

'I assume you did your best impression of not minding at all?'

'Exactly.' Unlike now, when she was giving in to the sadness she felt, her cheeks rigid and her eyes red-rimmed from crying all the way home from Manchester airport. Sophie picked up the mug and took a sip, gazing out of the window at the rainy January street. An almost empty bus splashed past on the sleek wet tarmac, and an elderly couple – him in a flat cap, his wife in an old-fashioned rain-hat – peered into the window of the café, looked at each other and without exchanging a single word, headed inside. A blast of chilly air made the hairs on her arms stand on end as they made their way in, taking off coats and hats and making a long performance of finding somewhere to sit. Bea, who had infinite patience with people, picked up a menu and headed over to welcome them with her habitual smile. Sophie turned back to her coffee, leaning against the counter and watching as her friend put the couple at their ease, making them laugh as she took their order.

'Sorry, you came in for a chat and I've been run off my feet. Give me ten minutes to sort this lot out and I'm all yours.'

The door swung open again as another group of customers came in from the rain. The air filled with the sound of chatter, along with the clatter of cups and dishes behind the counter as Bea and her co-workers got to work. Steam clouded the mirror behind the shelves. Sophie, realising she was in danger of getting under her friend's feet standing by the counter, made her way down the little side passage to sit in her favourite battered leather armchair, trying very hard not to think about all the times in the past when she'd been here after school with Tabby, and failing quite spectacularly.

She pushed aside a copy of the local newspaper which had been left on the table by a previous customer, feeling the usual sense of revulsion tinged with fear that she experienced whenever she caught sight of the sensationalist headlines. On second thought, she didn't want to share space with it at all. She picked it up and dropped it with disdain into the recycling bin under the noticeboard.

Half an hour passed. Bea, who had the best of intentions but always forgot how busy the café got on rainy days, had managed no more than a brief apologetic wave and several *I'll be with you in a moment*s.

Tabby's words on the journey to the airport were still echoing in Sophie's ears. Her daughter was moving on with her life, having been brave enough at eighteen to take the opportunity of a soccer scholarship at a US university where – thanks to some talent-spotters at a national girls' football tournament – she'd been offered what was known as a *full ride*, which meant that everything from travel to university fees to accommodation was covered.

It would have been an opportunity too good to miss for anyone, but under the circumstances, Sophie had bitten back her desolation at the thought of losing her baby and encouraged her to go for it. Nearly ten hours away by plane would be far enough to keep her out of harm's reach.

Not that Tabby had any inkling about any of that, of course. No, because Sophie had spent all of Tabby's life teaching her to be brave, go for what she wanted, have big ambitions. The irony wasn't lost on her.

'So what are you going to do now, Mum?' Returning for the Christmas break, Tabby had looked around the little house where she'd grown up. Tall and sporty, after a semester in the states she somehow seemed to have grown six inches taller, tanned from the Atlanta sunshine and broad-shouldered from working out in the gym every day. Sophie had been so desperate to get her daughter back that she'd made sure everything was exactly the way she remembered it – the familiar things in the fridge she loved to eat, the same old pizza ordered from the little shop along the road the first night home.

Bea had asked how it had gone after Tabby had been home for a couple of days.

'Oh great,' she'd replied, brightly. 'Yeah, it's so lovely to have her back.'

The truth that Sophie didn't want to admit – the truth which hung in the air as they sat on the same old sofas watching the same crime show ('I saved them all for you so we can have a big binge with pizza') was that Tabby had gone to the USA to spread her wings, and while Sophie had been busy trying to cope with empty nest syndrome, her little bird had grown so big that the nest simply wasn't the right fit any more, no matter how much she hoped it might be.

Sophie picked up her coat and the coffee mug and headed back to the counter. 'I'm sorry,' said Bea, leaning over to give Sophie a kiss with a huge plate of lemon meringue pie in her hands, 'I think I need to admit defeat. It's just far too busy today. Let's catch up properly later in the week. Maybe a drink? Dinner? Mark can cook and we'll have wine by the fire.'

'Sounds perfect,' said Sophie, fastening her coat and wrapping her scarf around her neck as she prepared to head out into the rain. She blew her friend a kiss and left the cosy warmth of the café for the chill of the January street, car keys jingling in her hand as she walked.

Ten minutes later, she was driving through the traffic in Crosby towards the veterinary surgery where she'd worked since Tabby was at kindergarten. She pulled up outside, managing to sandwich her little blue Citroen between a white van containing two men in high-vis vests who were eating sandwiches and looking at their phones, and her boss Nick's sleek black Range Rover. The ugly, flat roofed building housed not only the surgery, but also a rather depressed looking charity shop full of second-hand clothes and leftover junk from house clearances, and a newsagent which had a tattered sign outside promising that someone would be the winner of this week's lottery. Unlikely, thought Sophie, as she did every time she saw it, then smiled to herself, thinking of the ever-positive Tabby, who'd reprimand her and say, '*someone* has to win it'.

The brass plate by the door of the surgery was freshly polished. She paused for a moment on the threshold, noticing it when normally she passed it by.

'Nick Kouros MRCVS,' the sign announced. Normally she passed it by, but today for some reason the absence of her name – and identical qualification – rankled. She shook herself, putting a hand to the door.

'Waiting for something?' Hattie, the new receptionist, bustled up behind her, unfastening her jacket as she shook out an umbrella, taking up space so Sophie automatically shrunk slightly. She looked at Sophie and lifted an amused, perfectly shaped eyebrow. 'Or someone?'

Sophie hadn't warmed to Hattie when she'd arrived a couple of months ago. She'd never been exactly glamorous, dressing for work every day in a practical uniform of black jeans and a polo shirt with the surgery logo embroidered on the front. She'd always nodded and smiled politely when the others were chatting about hair and make-up – both things that she'd never really managed to work up enthusiasm about, but somehow the uber-glam Hattie had changed the atmosphere in the surgery. Now Sophie had the uncomfortable feeling that she was the punchline to a joke that was going to happen as soon as she walked out of the room, and she didn't like it very much.

'Not waiting for anything – or anyone,' said Sophie, finally. Hattie tipped her head upwards in a nod of acknowledgement with a little amused twist to her mouth, as if – despite having only been there for a month or so – she'd already established that the chances of Sophie having any sort of romantic entanglement was so unlikely as to be laughable.

'Didn't think so somehow.' Hattie gave a tinkly little laugh. 'You coming in?'

Sophie pulled a face behind Hattie's back as she bustled inside, which wasn't very grown up but made her feel slightly better.

Afternoon surgery wasn't due to start for another ten minutes, but already the waiting room was filling up. In the corner, a long-legged woman sat with a cat box on her knee, hugging it tightly and shooting disapproving looks across the floor at a short balding man in a pair of unseasonal Bermuda shorts, who was stroking the ears of his Boxer dog with one hand, and rubbing his stubbled chin anxiously with the other. A fair-haired woman with two brown and white Cavalier spaniels stood to one side reading the notice board while her dogs sat obediently with their tongues lolling. Hattie adjusted the collar of her uniform shirt and sat down at the reception desk, already wise to the fact that the best way to deal with clients was to avoid catching their eye at any costs until you were ready to deal with them. Despite this, when her computer chirruped a note of welcome everyone surged forward at the same time. Meanwhile, Sophie, who had taken off her coat and hung it up, looked through the client list for the afternoon and was now heading towards her room, smiled to herself. Sometimes being the sort of person who flew under the radar had its advantages.

The afternoon rushed past in a blur of the usual routine vaccinations and health checks. Only when her four o'clock appointment was a no-show did she grab a moment to head out to the loo and to make a quick coffee. She'd just taken a scalding hot sip when she sensed that she was being discussed on the other side of the surgery. Lisa, the older receptionist, pushed her blue glasses up on her forehead and sat back in her office chair behind the desk.

'You'll do it, won't you Soph? I bet you're free.'

'Do what?' Sophie made her way across the waiting room, smiling at a little girl who was holding on tightly to her pet gecko.

'Nick's been held up and can't do evening surgery.' Lisa took her glasses off and started cleaning them on the hem of her polo-shirt.

Katy, the vet nurse, gave a snort of amusement. 'Held up my backside, I bet he's out for lunch with that glamorous sales rep from the drug company that was in the other day. He'll be halfway down his second bottle of red.'

She looked at Hattie and they giggled.

'Anyway,' said Jenny, replacing her glasses. 'You'll do it,

won't you? Be a love. It's not like you have to rush home for Tabby now she's in America.'

Ouch, thought Sophie. Nice way to make me feel completely redundant.

She opened her mouth and then closed it again a moment later. She'd never been very good at making up excuses on the spot. The truth was she had an appointment with a hot bubble bath and the new book she'd downloaded on her kindle, which was about as exciting as her life got these days.

'I –' she began.

'You are an angel,' said Kirsty, 'I promise we'll be done as soon as we can. I've got a hot date this evening with that girl I met at the club on Saturday night, and I've no intentions of keeping her waiting.'

'Good for you,' said Lisa, putting down her pen and turning around to look at Kirsty with a nod of approval. 'Nice to see you young ones getting out and about. How about you, Hattie? What happened with that boy you went for a drink with the other day?'

Hattie made a face. 'Oh he was awful,' she laughed, exchanging glances with Kirsty. 'I made a run for it after I'd finished my cocktail.' Hattie gave Sophie a sideways look. 'How about you, Soph? We never hear anything about your love life.'

Jenny shot Hattie a look and Kirsty raised her eyebrows.

Sophie turned, hearing the door opening. A woman with a worried expression and her hair hanging in damp tendrils around her face was dragged into the surgery by an overweight brown Labrador Retriever.

'So sorry I'm late. I got off the bus at the wrong stop - I'm here for Hector's jabs.' The woman's mouth puckered in anxiety.

Saved by the bell. Sophie dropped to the floor on one knee,

greeting Hector the Labrador with such alacrity that he looked slightly startled. The woman's shoulders dropped in relief and she allowed herself a small smile as Sophie looked up at her.

'Don't worry at all,' Sophie said reassuringly. 'Come on, we'll get you sorted. It's been horrible all day, hasn't it? It's so easy to get off at the wrong stop when it's raining this hard. It always seems to happen to me when I have to be somewhere on time.'

She opened the examination room door and beckoned them in. It was such a relief to get back to the safe predictability of work, and away from the conversation between Jenny, Hattie and Kirsty, which increasingly seemed to feel like she was being led into some sort of trap. The last thing she wanted to get into was a conversation about her relationship status. She'd managed to keep things under wraps for this long, and somehow Hattie seemed to have upset the balance.

'So you'll do this evening?' Kirsty called after her as she made to close the door. Sophie heard Hattie mutter something and the two other women laugh and then shush each other.

'Okay,' she conceded. 'Seeing as I'm not busy,' she added, a moment later.

'As if she's ever busy,' muttered Kirsty, not quietly enough. Sophie pulled the door closed, feeling a horrible, creeping sense of shame. The back of her neck prickled uncomfortably.

Later that evening, when the last clients had gone and she'd kindly suggested that Kirsty get off home to get ready for her date (mainly so she didn't have to make awkward conversation) she made her way around the surgery doing the last checks – wiping down her examination table and logging off the computer system, turning off the lights and securely locking up the meds room and making sure everything was safe. She hated the dark, and had worked out a system whereby she could edge out of the back door, flicking off the last light as she pulled the door closed, and then dash around past the corner shop to her car, dodging the circling teenagers on their bikes who congregated there every evening, drinking energy drinks and looking for trouble.

She climbed into the car and switched on the radio, then turned it off again a second later when she felt a stab of sadness on hearing Tabby's favourite song. In an hour she'd be landing and texting to say she was safe. Sophie looked once again at the flight tracker app, watching as the tiny airplane slowly moved down towards its final destination. Funny to think that her only child was currently suspended in the air in a tube of metal. Sophie shook her head. Funny wasn't the word. Terrifying was more like it. She puffed out a long breath, which clouded in the chilly evening air.

The house echoed with emptiness as she flicked on the lights and checked the sitting room and the little back dining room out of habit, closing the curtains. The night lights she had plugged into sockets in each room glowed, taking the edge off the darkness.

Ten minutes later, a bath run and a clean towel and her dressing gown folded on the top of the loo seat, she climbed out of her clothes, leaving them lying where they fell before slipping into the scented water.

There, she told herself, it wasn't so bad. She had chocolate, and she had a nice bath and a warm house. Lots of people didn't have that. She was talking to herself, which wasn't great, but that was a minor detail.

The trouble was that work had been tolerable – only just, she grudgingly conceded – when Tabby was still at home. Back then she'd get back from the surgery and make her daughter laugh with stories about her day. Nick, who owned the practice, had been a friend from their time at Liverpool Vet School. Loud and confident, with his parents' backing, he'd invested well and now owned a string of vet surgeries across the North West of England, owned a massive house in an exclusive village in Lancashire, and two daughters who attended an expensive private school near Liverpool which was packed with the offspring of footballers and self-made millionaires.

Sophie hadn't had parental backing, and – she slid under the water, closing her eyes – because of what had happened she'd nothing in the bank, a re-mortgaged house, and a car payment which took a hefty chunk out of her wages every month. There was no way she'd ever be in a position to invest the sort of money she'd need to start up her own practice. Maybe, she thought, I should start buying lottery tickets. Your life could be changed in a moment, the adverts said. Chance would be a fine thing.

CHAPTER TWO

Made it!

Sophie woke at 2am to the sound of her phone vibrating on the bedside table. Awake immediately she scooped it up and gazed at the screen. The message showed Tabby grinning back at her from the arrivals hall of Atlanta's airport, rucksack on shoulder and her hair tied back from her face, which looked ridiculously bright and enthusiastic after an almost ten-hour flight.

She hit the call button, but the phone – complete with the now-familiar foreign ring tone – rang out.

Sorry, just getting into the mini-bus with the others. Shouldn't you be sleeping? Will ring tomorrow. Love you! x

The reply was instant. Sophie started to compose a long message reminding her to make sure she got some rest, remembered to take her vitamins, and a million other motherly urgings, then she hit the delete button so the words disappeared backwards before her eyes. Tabby was more than capable – and the last thing she needed was Sophie banging on. She started again.

So glad you've made it safely! Love you lots, give me a shout when you're settled.

She added a heart emoji and a row of kisses and hit send, closing her eyes as she did so. That would do.

She tossed and turned for the rest of the night, willing sleep to come and watching the hours tick by on her bedside clock, painfully aware that she was in clinic from 8.30 and would have to leave an hour before that to get organised. Eventually she dropped off, and what felt like a minute later the alarm woke her with a jolt.

Armed with a travel mug full of industrial strength coffee, she locked the door and watched as Mino scampered back in via the cat flap, his black and white tail disappearing as he headed inside for a day of snoozing on his favourite cushion. Sophie suppressed a yawn. She had three cat spays to get through this morning, and she needed to be on the ball, not wishing she could curl up in a patch of sunshine and doze the day away.

'Ah, there you are, lifesaver.'

She hadn't even made it through the door when Nick pounced. His dark hair was flopping in carefully-tended curls over his forehead and his teeth gleamed white against the tan he maintained with regular trips to the spray booth between foreign holidays. He gave her a wolfish grin and followed her inside.

'Thanks for having my back last night. I couldn't get away from the meeting with the rep – you know what it's like, they start talking and the next thing you know...'

'It's fine,' said Sophie, automatically. She unfastened her coat and hung it up on the hooks inside the staffroom.

'You're such a sweetheart,' Nick began, and she recognised the wheedle in his voice immediately 'That I know you won't mind if I ask if you'll cover me again this evening?'

Sophie folded her arms and looked at him with eyebrows raised. 'Isn't it Claire's turn to do evening surgery?'

He nodded. 'It would be but she's got parents evening for Violet and George. I told her she could have the evening off –'

Without checking I could cover, thought Sophie, but didn't say anything out loud. As usual. If she looked in the mirror she'd see the word MUG stamped across her forehead.

'- and of course tonight's my golf evening and I can't let the boys down, they're expecting me at the driving range.'

'I might be busy,' said Sophie, but they both knew she was weakening.

'But you're not, are you?' Nick gave her the full puppy-dog eyes treatment.

'I'm not, no,' she conceded. 'But that doesn't mean I want to do evening surgery every blooming night while you lot all gad about doing stuff.'

'You know as well as I do that parents evening is hardly gadding about.'

'True.' To be fair, Claire was pretty hard-working herself. She'd joined the practice nine months or so ago, so there were now four vets working together, all focused on small animal practice and constantly busy. Nick was the star of the show, the vet that all the clients wanted to see – years before, when they'd been students, he'd been one of the main characters in a fly-on-the-wall tv show which had shown six students as they worked their way through their veterinary science degree, and the resultant glamour had meant that he'd segued smoothly into owning his own practice – which had rapidly grown into a group – and was raking in the profits as a result.

Sophie had been part of the same cohort but never anything more than a fleeting figure behind the scenes. As a consequence, nobody seemed particularly excited to see her when she opened the examination room door to welcome their pets inside. Nick, on the other hand, only had to flash a grin and give that familiar hearty chuckle while he ran a hand through his floppy black locks – helped with a regular treatment of Just for Men dye these days - and he had clients eating out of his hands.

'So you'll cover?' He picked up a pile of trade catalogues and magazines that were heaped on the table, flicking through the Vet Times for a moment and making a face as he threw it back down in the direction of the table, whereupon it slid off and landed face down on the floor.

'Yes,' sighed Sophie.

'Excellent,' he said, flashing her the well-worn grin which had absolutely no effect on her and hadn't for years. Long ago, when she was a student, it had made her go weak at the knees. She suspected that Nick still thought it did, given the frequency with which he employed it.

Sophie bent down and picked up the magazine. As she straightened up, Nick cleared his throat and then casually, as he paused for a moment with his hand on the door of the staffroom, dropped the bombshell.

'Oh, by the way, about the promotion thing.' He couldn't quite meet her eye, rubbing his nose and flicking a glance down at the floor as he spoke. 'She's got more surgical experience.'

'I- ' Sophie's mouth dropped open. Before she'd had the chance to gather her thoughts, Nick had disappeared out of the room, leaving behind only the faint hint of Givenchy for Men and his vaguely apologetic Cheshire Cat grin, which seemed to hang for a moment in mid-air.

She flopped down onto the beaten-up leather sofa in a heap of furious despair. Claire, who was married to a GP and completely rolling in it, probably wouldn't even notice the extra money going into her account each month.

Don't be mean about Claire, she heard the little voice in her head say, *it's not her fault and she's lovely.*

Stop being such a pathetic wimp, said the other, rather more strident voice which she tried to keep quiet most of the time. *You mightn't have the range of experience Claire has but you know this place back to front, not to mention the clients. You've given everything for years.*

'And for what?' Sophie said aloud.

'For what?' echoed Kathryn, who walked into the room at exactly the wrong moment. 'Talking to yourself is the first sign of madness, you know.' She chuckled at her own joke.

'Taking the same crap day after day is the second,' muttered Sophie, pushing herself back out of the sofa.

Sensing gossip, Kathryn's expression switched from mild amusement to curiosity in a split second. 'Have I missed something?'

'Nothing,' said Sophie. Still holding the Vet Times magazine, she strode out of the room.

She shoved it on the side table of her exam room and scrubbed up for the morning's surgeries. The vet nurses had been hard at work getting everything organised so all she had to do was back into the room – gloves held in the air – and with the still furious expression on her face obscured by a mask, she got to work.

Lunchtime came around before she knew it and she tossed her gloves and mask into the bin, loosening her hair which had been pulling tightly on her scalp all morning after she'd tied it back too tightly in her fury at the news she'd been passed over for the promotion.

'Coffee?' said Kathryn, who was filling the kettle.

'No thanks, I'm going out for lunch,' said Sophie, grabbing her coat. She was almost out the door when she turned back and grabbed the copy of Vet Times she'd left lying on the table. She'd been a bit lax when it came to keeping up with the news – maybe it was time she actually took a bit of notice of what was going on in her professional world.

Armed with a coffee and a pre-packed sandwich from the corner shop, she jumped into the car and drove two streets down, parking opposite the primary school playground where children were skipping and jumping around in brightly coloured anoraks. Suppressing the pang of longing to text Tabby – who would be fast asleep, hopefully – she picked up the magazine and started leafing through the pages.

With everything in her personal life taking up her time, she'd let her professional development slide. Sophie was completely absorbed, catching up with the latest research news, flicking through the pages and sipping her coffee. It was only when she went to toss it away that the recruitment ads caught her eye. She'd been part of the furniture for so long at Nick's practice that she'd given up thinking about moving on. Her situation meant she couldn't exactly buy into a partnership, but she'd thought that eventually she'd be recognised for the work she'd put in.

She could tell without even speaking to Bea what she'd say.

Sack it off, get something new. You're not beholden to him because he gave you a job when you were in a sticky situation.

It was true. She'd told herself often enough. But some sort of misplaced loyalty had kept her tied to the practice, doing more than her fair share of cover work, always bending over backwards to make sure everyone else was okay, even if it meant she had to rely on favours from friends to collect Tabby from school when she was younger or missing out on parents' evenings and having to make do with a catch-up telephone call. Honestly, the situation was ridiculous. She'd always been a pushover, that was the problem.

And now here she was, alone, with Tabby setting off into

the world to live her own life. Something had to change. She glanced at the pages. *Senior vet wanted for busy London practice... Clinical Director for a mixed animal group based in Hampshire... Vet Nurse wanted in Dubai.* She didn't have much experience with camels. The thought of it made her laugh. And then she saw one advert, just as she was about to toss the magazine back onto the passenger seat and head back to work.

Vet wanted for small Highland Practice
Applemore is a wonderful place to live - with lochs, glens, and mountains on your doorstep you'll be looking for the perfect work/life balance to enjoy the surroundings. We've got an award-winning adventure centre on the doorstep, and you can indulge your passion for running, hill walking, mountain biking, wild swimming, paddle boarding, skiing, not to mention genuine Highland culture – everyone loves a Ceilidh! Our farmers and crofters are friendly, and we believe variety is the spice of veterinary life. We see a lot of interesting cases! We always encourage our vets to develop any interests they may have.

Her heart thumped unevenly against her ribs in a way she hadn't felt for a long, long time. Sophie folded the page back, and looked at the advert again. She couldn't, could she?

A million reasons why not popped into her head, and yet all she could hear was Tabby saying 'why not?'. She imagined for a moment how it would feel to wake up and look out of her window and see the beautiful Highland landscape and not the overflowing green wheely bin of the neighbours on the other side of the street, which they left outside their front door because it was easier than taking it round from the back garden every Thursday morning. What would it be like to have to pull on wellies and deal with gentle Highland cows in a barn instead of the routine cats, dogs and gerbils? Alright, maybe not so much the cows. She pulled a face.

You need to do something for yourself now, Mum, Tabby had told her as they walked on the beach on New Year's Day.

Sophie threw the magazine onto the back seat, and fastened her seat belt. She'd been longer than she meant to and someone would no doubt be wondering where she'd got to. Glancing in the rear-view mirror, she turned on the engine and indicated, heading back along the familiar streets to the place she'd worked for most of her adult life.

'And I said to him I wasn't interested in seeing a photo of *that* sort of thing,' Hattie was saying, her little nose wrinkled in disgust and amusement, as Sophie walked into the surgery. A silence fell.

'Oh hi Sophie,' said Kathryn, with a slightly artificial cheeriness. 'How are you?'

'Fine thanks,' Sophie said, puzzled.

'Are you sure?' Kathryn cocked her head slightly to one side. 'I wondered, you know, under the...' she trailed off.

'With Claire getting the promotion and all, she means,' said Merry matter-of-factly. 'We all thought you'd get it, of course.'

Everyone nodded in sympathy, which somehow made her feel even more inadequate. There was nothing quite like having it underlined that you were – literally – not up to the job.

'It's fine,' said Sophie, trying to sound carefree and taking a pen from the pot on the desk. She slotted it into the pocket on her polo shirt. 'Honestly.'

She headed for the examination room, uncomfortably

aware that nobody was saying anything. As the door closed, she heard them all burst into conversation once again.

All afternoon as she worked she found her thoughts circling back to the advert in the Vet Times and how it would feel to do something completely out of character. It wouldn't hurt to apply, she decided. She resolved to talk it over with Tabby when they had a Facetime chat that evening, and sent a message to Bea.

I could do with your advice about something, she typed between clients. *It's a bit bonkers, but...*

Bonkers ideas are my favourite kind, Bea typed back. *If I hadn't had one, I wouldn't have taken over the lease for the café.*

Sophie put the phone down and thought. Bea's life had been transformed when she'd taken over the café from the old owners. She'd been grieving the loss of her parents, lost and miserable – the cafe had given her a purpose and a reason to get up every morning. It wasn't likely that a new job was going to do the same for her, but – well, maybe that old cliché about a change being as good as a rest was true.

CHAPTER THREE

'I can't believe how much *stuff* one person can acquire.'

Bea threw another black rubbish bag onto the almost-full skip.

'Believe me, if she'd been here I suspect we wouldn't have gotten away with binning half this stuff. As it is I've had to declutter and pack up Tabby's room via Facetime, with dire warnings.' Sophie gave an old, chipped mirror a final glance then tossed it decisively onto the top of the pile where it cracked and slid down into the depths.

'I thought she was all for the move?' Bea stood back, putting her hands in her back pockets and assessing their work so far. A tiny starling flew out of the rowan tree nearby and hopped onto the top of a pile of old newspapers, looking at them beadily, his head cocked sideways.

'She is.' Sophie wiped her hands down the front of her jeans. She'd been cleaning and tidying for ages, and it seemed that the cleaner the flat became, the grubbier she was, as if the dirt and grime of almost twenty years was determined to stick to her one way or another. She flicked a clump of cat hair off her sweatshirt. 'She said to put her stuff in storage because there was nothing she'd miss.' Sophie grimaced. 'How's that for a reminder that she really does feel like she's left home.'

'You'll be so busy with your exciting new job you won't have time to miss her.' Bea brushed a lock of hair out of her face as a sudden breeze blew down the street, lifting the newspapers from the pile and ruffling them so the little starling hopped away and flew off in disgust.

'That is the general idea,' Sophie's eyes met those of her oldest friend. She made a rueful face. 'It was that or sit around here for the next thirty years waiting for something to happen.'

Bea headed inside and Sophie followed her. The hall was full of neatly taped up cardboard packing boxes, each one labelled and stacked against the wall ready to go into storage. She wasn't ready to commit to moving everything she owned to the Highlands – instead she'd been ruthless, selected the bare bones of what she needed and decided that she'd approach it the way she would if she was packing for a long trip. It made it easier, somehow.

She thought back to the day she'd picked up the copy of Vet Times that had changed everything… it was funny how life could turn on a sixpence. If she'd been offered the promotion, she wouldn't have even considered applying for the job at Applemore Vets. The whole thing, though, felt as if it was meant to be.

'I'm calling about the – about the job,' she'd said, a catch in her voice as she stood in the sitting room gazing out of the window and onto the street.

'Are you really?' The woman on the other side of the phone had sounded both delighted and surprised. 'Are you sure?'

'Quite sure,' Sophie had said, faintly puzzled by her response.

'Well that's a turn up for the books. Give me two seconds and I'll put you on to Fiona.' There was a brief pause and some scuffling before she heard the woman yelling. 'Fiona! You'll never guess what – someone's on the phone about the job!'

'Hello,' said a brisk, clipped voice a moment later. 'Are you coming to save our bacon?'

'I – um, well – ' Sophie had faltered. 'I – might be?'

'Might is a good start. How can I help?'

It had been a strange start, Sophie thought as she watched Bea vacuuming the sitting room rug almost two months later. Fiona, who owned the practice, had been brisk and slightly eccentric on the telephone.

'I'm sure you don't want to come all the way up here for an interview,' she'd said, quite firmly. 'Let's be modern. We can do it on Zoom, if you're happy with that?'

'Right, that's the sitting room sorted, and the bedrooms are done.' Bea perched her bottom on the edge of the sofa. 'If you grab your bag, we can lock this place up, and get back to our place for dinner. Mark's making a beef bourguignon with dauphinoise potatoes.'

Sophie's stomach growled. 'That sounds amazing.' She'd been so busy all week getting things organised in the hours she had between finishing work and falling into bed exhausted that dinner had been a Pot Noodle or a something that she shoved in the microwave. She'd fallen off the cooking wagon a bit since Tabby went to America in any case, finding it depressing and a bit pointless to cook for herself.

'Right, come on then, let's go. We'll get this stuff loaded up with Mark tomorrow and taken over to the storage unit, and then you can head off on your magical mystery tour to the Highlands.' Bea shook her head, laughing. 'Only you, Soph.'

'...Only you, Sophie,' Mark echoed, an hour later, as he carried a huge Le Creuset dish through and placed it reverently on the long scrubbed pine table in the middle of the kitchen where he and Bea spent all their time together. He whipped the dishtowel off his shoulder and used it to protect his hands as he turned back to their high-tech silver range cooker, pulling out another identical dish, this one without a lid and full of a deliciously-scented creamy potato side dish. Sophie slid to one side to let him pop it down beside her on a brown cork mat, inhaling the smell of garlic as the steam curled up towards her nose.

'Only me what?' She reached out to pick a little curl of crispy cheese topping which had fallen onto the table, popping it into her mouth with a blissful sigh. 'This is amazing, Mark.'

'Only you could end up taking a job in the depths of the Highlands without even visiting the place. What if they're all awful?'

'Have you met the staff at Sophie's work? To be honest, you'd be hard pushed to find worse.'

'They're not that bad,' said Sophie, stoutly, trying to defend them.

Bea's nostrils flared in derision and she raised both eyebrows to the sky. 'Come on, they're not exactly the colleagues of a lifetime. You said yourself a million times that you've always felt they're waiting for you to leave the room so they can start talking about you.'

Sophie shifted uncomfortably, aware the conversation was moving onto shaky ground. She shot Bea a warning look.

'Anyway, I'm sure these new people will be lovely,' said Bea quickly, covering her tracks.

'Well they seemed it on Zoom.'

Sophie chewed her lip. When she'd had the interview, she'd

sort of been caught up in the excitement of the whole thing and the idea of taking control of her life. Fiona, the practice owner, had said briskly that she was more than happy that she'd do a good job and offered her the position on the spot. Some sort of mania had made Sophie say yes. Ever since then, somehow, she'd felt slightly shell-shocked, as if the whole thing was happening to someone else.

'Soph?' Bea nudged her gently.

'Yeah,' she said, absently. 'I'm sure they'll be fine.'

A couple of hours later Sophie lay in the spare room bed, eyes wide in the darkness, unable to sleep because her mind was going round in circles. How on earth had she ended up in this situation? One minute she'd been peed off because Nick hadn't offered her the promotion. Instead of fronting up to him and dealing with the problem face on, the next thing she knew she'd been on the phone to some random veterinary practice in the far north-west Highlands. And now here she was, having handed in her notice to a stunned Nick and agreed to start in six weeks' time.

'This is a bit out of left field,' Nick had said, sitting on the desk in his office, a pen rattling against his teeth.

Sophie had shaken her head. 'I can't stay here forever, Nick. And with Tabby gone there's nothing to keep me here. It's not like I have family ties.'

'You've got me.' Nick had frowned. 'We've been friends since university.'

And you passed me over for promotion even though you knew my financial situation, she thought, but didn't say out loud.

'We have, and that won't change,' she said calmly. 'I've spent all Tab's life telling her she should be brave and take chances when they're offered to her and in the meantime I've been sitting here in the same job for the whole of her life.'

Nick had shrugged slightly, admitting defeat. 'Well, I must

hand it to you, Soph. You don't mess about when you do decide to go for it.'

He could have made it awkward for her, insisting on a long notice period, but instead said he was happy to let her go and that he'd find it easy enough to get someone in, even – he said with a grin - if he had to poach one of the disaffected vets who worked at the university vet hospital, luring them over with the promise of a decent car and a package that would make the lack of glamour worthwhile.

She'd arranged to rent the house part-furnished to a young mother and her two daughters, delighted to be able to give something back by telling her that no, she didn't mind one bit if she was on benefits and that of course they could have pets. The mortgage payments would be covered by the rent, and she'd sorted out all the practicalities like gas and water cover in her lunch hours as she worked out her notice, spending long hours on hold listening to awful music as she waited to get through. And now it was all sorted, and she had nothing to worry about, and yet here she was lying staring in the darkness at the ceiling of Bea and Mark's spare room, wondering what the hell she was doing and convincing herself she was making the biggest mistake of her life.

Guess who got an A+ in her statistics exam?

Her phone screen lit up the room as a message from Tabby came though at exactly the right moment.

Oh well done darling, you clever thing. Was it hard?

No, easy actually.
Oh and guess what? I scored twice in the game yesterday night.

Amazing! I'm so proud of you. I've got Mino here, he sends a kiss and a nose-rub

Is he being good at Aunty Bea's house?

An angel. She's going to look after him until I get settled in the new place. He's a bit old to be dragged all the way to the Highlands.

Are you excited? I can't wait to see it. Promise you'll video call me as soon as you get to the house?

I promise.

I... she started to type, then wiped it away. Tabby didn't need to be worrying on her behalf.

What were you going to say?

I love you, Sophie typed, which wasn't a lie, *and I can't wait to show you it. It's a big move but I think it's exciting.*

And a bit scary.

Sophie looked at the words, remembering how Tabby had felt the night before her flight to Atlanta last September. She'd crept in to see her daughter curled up under the covers fast asleep for the last time only to find her lying flat on her back, Mino curled up on her stomach, her eyes wide open. She'd shifted over silently, making space, so that there was room for the two of them, and together they'd lain in the darkness, not speaking, the only sound that of Mino gently purring as he slept.

The good kind of scary, Sophie replied.

That's the best kind.

They chatted back and forth for a little while longer, and then – worn out from all the hard work, her muscles aching and her head still spinning with everything she had to do – Sophie fell into a dreamless sleep.

CHAPTER FOUR

Ben Lewis placed the final log on the top of the stack he'd created and stood back with his hands on his hips to admire his handiwork. When the old oak had fallen in a storm two years before he'd logged it up with a chainsaw, hefting each chunk of wood onto the back of the trailer and bumping up across the field to the yard behind his little croft cottage, splitting it up once again into pieces which would eventually fit perfectly into his wood-fired range, and stacking them in neat piles so they could dry out. Now, having been weathered over the seasons, the wood had faded to a pale silvery brown, all the moisture driven out by the wind which whistled up the valley and whispered through the pinewoods of the forestry that surrounded his two hundred year old stone cottage. It was hard work, but it was the sort of work that he'd chosen when he'd moved from Lancashire to live in the Highlands of Scotland, close enough to the little village of Applemore that he could find company over a pint of beer in the hotel if he fancied it and pick up whatever he wanted from the little farm shop outside the village, but far enough away that he could keep himself to himself and get on with his woodcarving in peace.

A cool wind whistled through the distant pine trees, and the two dogs scampered in circles around him. He headed back towards the cottage with a basket under one arm, logs heaped up to the top, ready to stoke up the fire and make himself a coffee after a long morning's work.

The house was simple inside – when he'd first bought it a few years ago he'd stripped back the yellow-painted wood panels which had decorated the sitting room and pulled off the fussy curtains which obscured the view. Now the walls were plain – whitewashed with lime to show off the paintings he'd done and the windows unadorned with any form of dressing at all, so the view outside was an ever-changing landscape painting. Today it showed the moorland covered in faded heather, grazed down by the sheep after a long winter, and in the distance the deep green of the pine trees which clad the hills, rising to a bruised grey-purple sky which promised rain later. The fire in the wood-burner in the sitting room had almost burned out, and he opened the door, shoving in a couple of logs and leaving it ajar for a few minutes, watching as the oxygen coaxed the flames back to life so in a few moments bright orange flames licked around the sides of the wood he'd chopped and dried, catching it alight.

He clicked the wood burner door shut and headed for the kitchen, where he repeated the same sequence, opening the air vent at the top so the range cooker would heat up quickly and the kettle would come back to the boil. He was bloody freezing after being outside working all morning. The sweat that had gathered on the back of his t-shirt was cold against his skin now, and he turned, warming himself against the woodburning stove until the kettle started to whistle, letting him know it was time for a break before he got to work for the afternoon. Having made a coffee, Ben kicked off his boots and put his feet up against the bar of the range and let his eyes close for a moment as he thought about his plans for the afternoon.

He was working on a huge new commission from Harry and Rob, business partners who ran the Applemore Hotel together. The new restaurant was up and running and had been getting rave reviews from food writers who'd come from all over Scotland to try the new menu. After a fire that had taken place during the renovations, they'd altered their plans and decided to remodel the restaurant slightly, and Harry and Rob – pouring him a pint of the beer made by Lachlan Fraser who lived at the Applemore, the castle nearby from which the village took its name – had suggested that he might like to create something which would be a conversation point.

'Like a naked woman, that sort of thing?' Rob had roared with laughter at his own joke.

Harry, polishing glasses behind the bar, had shaken his head in despair. 'I was thinking more something abstract – something that'll get people talking? We've done the place up to try and get away from the whole tartan and shortbread tourist look.'

Ben had scribbled as they bickered good-naturedly and passed over the beermat he'd sketched an idea on. 'Something like that?'

'You did that just now?' Rob was open mouthed.

Ben nodded, catching Harry's eye and laughing. 'Also available for weddings and bar mitzvahs,' he'd said, with a grin.

'Alright.' Rob, still business-like despite having given up his job in the city to come and live in Applemore a couple of years before, dusted off his hands on the front of his jeans and reached across, extending a hand towards Ben.

'It's a deal. How much are we talking?'

Ben made a face – he always found it awkward putting a price on his work, even after all this time – and named a sum.

'That's way too cheap.' Rob had looked at Harry for confirmation and they exchanged a look before he added a few hundred pounds to the price. 'Let's say that and we've got a deal.'

'You're on. I'll get started asap.'

That was a couple of weeks ago. Since then he'd spent all his time working – first on a smaller prototype so he could get an idea of the dimensions, and now on what would be the finished piece – a huge abstract piece which (he hoped) spoke of the wild scenery and the emotions that life in the Highlands evoked. It was something that meant a lot to him. Being a newcomer wasn't always easy, and especially when you were – well, of course he hadn't planned on being here alone, but here he was. He looped the heavy leather apron he wore over his neck and tied it at the waist, pulling on his work boots which he'd left drying by the stove while he drank his coffee.

'Knock knock,' called a familiar voice from the hallway. Ben plonked down the empty coffee cup and headed for the door. Standing there, flat cap on and an old tweed coat buttoned up tightly against the wind, was Annie, his closest neighbour. Her grey hair was coming loose from its habitual bun and loose tendrils waved in the breeze. She gave a wink and for a moment he caught a glimpse of the young woman she'd been years before.

'I come bearing gifts,' she said, and waved a foil wrapped parcel at him.

'Who could resist you,' he said, laughing.

'Fruit cake,' she explained, putting it down on the wooden bench in the hall as she unwrapped her scarf and hung it on the metal hooks he'd made. 'I made double and thought you might like some.' She looked him up and down. 'Looks like I caught you at the right time, too. Have you come in for a break?'

He looked down at his loose bootlaces and didn't have the heart to tell her he was on the way to get on with some work.

'Just about to make a coffee,' he said, giving her a smile. She beamed back at him.

'Well, that's what I hoped. I've had family visitors this morning and I could do with a chat to talk things over. You know what they're like.'

He poured more water into the kettle and placed it back on top of the stove.

'Go on then, what's been happening?'

'My daughter-in-law Diane came over – nine o'clock this morning she was on the blooming doorstep. I was barely conscious.' Annie chuckled to herself. 'Anyway I told her she'd need to get herself a cup of tea while I got myself organised, and when I got through to the kitchen, I found her sitting there at the table with a pile of paperwork from the estate agent, all set to pressurise me into selling the cottage.'

She unwrapped the silver foil to reveal a delicious-looking fruit cake.

'Knife?'

'Just a sec.' Ben took two dry plates from the draining board by the sink, fished a bread knife out of the drawer and retrieved a second mug to make Annie a coffee.

'Anyway, I told her that just because I didn't want the hassle of holiday lets any more didn't mean I was planning on putting it on the market.'

Passing her the knife, he watched as she cut two thick slices, passing one over to him as he poured milk into their mugs and stirred the coffee. His spaniels, Otto and Bear - resigned to the fact that they were stuck inside for a while longer – had flopped onto their bed on the stone floor beside the range and seemingly dozed off instantly. Otto, the younger of the two, lifted his head hopefully with one eye half open, checking to make sure there definitely wasn't any food on offer.

'Nothing for you,' Ben said, leaning back to rub Otto's long, silky ears for a moment. The dog gave a gusty sigh and drooped back onto his bed.

'Why would she want you to sell?'

Annie gave a wry laugh. 'I suspect she's thinking if she gets that place sorted, it's one less thing to deal with when I pop my clogs.'

'Surely not?' He'd so far managed to avoid meeting the infamous daughter in law, but he'd heard enough about her from Annie's frequent visits after she'd come around, often marching the half mile down the road on foot rather than driving in her neat green Mini. Inevitably fuming and muttering under her breath, Annie would turn up with a cake of some sort – over the years he'd worked out that she took out her stresses in the kitchen – and plonk herself down at the bench by the kitchen table and offload her latest family drama.

'I wouldn't be in the least surprised,' said Annie, darkly.

'She might just be thinking that you've got enough on your plate looking after your own place without worrying about the cottage.'

'Pfft.'

'What *are* you going to do with it?' He looked out of the kitchen window, down the long stretch of rough moorland that led down towards the shore. The white cottage sat looking out over the beach, protected by the sea winds by a long ridge lined by trees in the distance.

'Well, as you know it means a lot to me. I can't just sell it to any old person that wanders by.'

The cottage had been in Annie's family for years, passed from her parents to an uncle and then to a distant cousin who'd lived there for years with her children until they'd all grown up and she headed to Inverness, wanting to live somewhere less isolated. Annie hadn't wanted to sell the house then, so she'd renovated the whole place herself, stripping back the old wallpaper and removing the tired old patterned carpets so the wooden floors could be sanded and varnished. Once the redecoration was done she'd grudgingly accepted that replacing the bathroom was beyond her and allowed Kenny, the local builder, to come in and renovate the kitchen while he was at it (scrutinising his every move, Kenny had told him one night in the pub with a wry chuckle). Since then, she'd let out the cottage to holiday visitors over the years, but only those she'd self-selected and who passed her somewhat eccentric vetting procedures. Whatever she did, though, seemed to work – there were guests who'd come back year after year. Ben had met a family with almost-grown teenagers who were in tears as they stood at the gate on their last day, telling him sadly that they couldn't believe they'd never come back again after Annie had decided that that summer would be the last one as 'I'm getting too old for all this nonsense'.

'You could always get Charlotte to add it to her holiday cottage portfolio. She's got loads of places, and from what I hear she's always looking to add more.'

'Pfft,' said Annie again. 'Charlotte Fraser has more than enough holiday cottages. She doesn't need to add mine to her list, and anyway she'd be letting any Tom Dick or Harry stay there. You know I only like certain people.'

'You don't like anyone,' he laughed.

'I don't mind you,' Annie raised her mug to her lips, a tiny smile twisting at the edges of her mouth.

'High praise indeed.' He broke off a piece of cake and looked at it thoughtfully. 'So what are you going to do?'

'Well, as it happens – not that I was going to tell Diane – I've solved the problem myself. Not that it was a problem, I should add.'

Ben felt his eyebrows raising slightly. Keeping up with Annie's mental gymnastics was a feat. 'Go on?'

'Well, it turns out that Fiona has a new vet starting next week. She promised her the flat above the surgery, then told me the roof needs work and there's a problem with the plumbing. I said it sounded like an easy way to lose a perfectly good new employee before she even gets started, and suggested she use the cottage.'

He sat back in surprise. 'You don't even know what this new vet's like. How do you know they're going to pass your stringent tests?'

'I don't know what you're talking about,' said Annie, beadily. 'I don't have any tests.'

'You said yourself you had strict criteria and you wouldn't let it out to just anyone.'

He looked out of the window at the cottage, trying to imagine what it would be like to have someone living there full time when he'd taken for granted having the beach to himself from September until May. It was an odd thought, not that he had any right to an opinion. He shook himself and looked back at Annie, who was brushing cake crumbs off her tweed coat onto the floor. Bear, realising there was a whisper of a chance of some food, sprung into life and started sniffing around at her feet.

'I have feelings about people,' Annie said, with an enigmatic smile, 'That's all. And I have a feeling that this new vet will be just right for the place.'

His eyebrows were now in danger of heading so far north that they were disappearing into his hairline.

'Let's hope you're right.'

'Oh, I will be.' Annie cupped her mug with both hands and looked at him over the top of it with her hooded periwinkle-blue eyes. 'I will be. Now never mind me, what's happening in your life? Any sign of Esther coming up to stay?'

Unthinkingly, he looked over at the black and white pictures that hung on the wall. One showed a much-younger Esther dressed as a fairy in her first school nativity play, and the other, the most recent, was his daughter in a pair of sturdy work boots sitting on an oak log outside the cottage, hair tied back from her face and one hand up shading her eyes from the sunshine. It felt to him like there were minutes between the two pictures, not more than a decade. Now she was in Bristol studying civil engineering at university, and promising that she'd come and visit in the holidays. But one holiday slipped into another and she was busy seeing friends and working and the Highlands were so far away and life working in a beach bar in Cornwall was far more exciting... he didn't resent it, because he knew how it felt to be caught up in the novelty of student life, but he missed her like mad. Video calls made up for it – he loved seeing her face lit up with excitement as he walked around the steading with his phone, showing off the latest artwork he'd created or the vegetables growing in the raised beds she'd helped design.

'I'm hoping she might make it up at Easter,' he said, after a moment.

'Well that would be a turn-up for the books.'

'And how's her mother?' Annie said artlessly.

'Oh, still the same I imagine. Haven't spoken to her in a long time.'

'I should imagine that's a relief.' Annie scanned his face, her eyes narrowed slightly. 'Of course you shouldn't tar all women with the same brush.'

He felt the muscle in his jaw tighten as it always did when he thought of Liz, his ex-wife. They'd made plans – or so he thought – to travel to a new life in the Highlands, selling the house and giving up their jobs, when she'd chosen what was supposed to be a get-together to tell their friends about their plans to move to Scotland into an opportunity to tell them – and him that she wanted a divorce.

'I thought it was easier to let everyone know as they were all in the same place,' she'd shrugged, as if she'd been passing on a bit of casual village gossip. The guests had looked shocked, not quite knowing what to do with themselves as the news registered and they took in the stricken expression on Ben's face and realised that he'd been as much in the dark as they had.

Liz had always seen the world differently. He'd known that – even admired it – when they first got together. Back then, straight out of art school and working together in the warehouse studio where they'd met she'd seemed exotic and unusual. She took risks with her work and lived as she painted – huge, abstract, and colourful. If she hadn't made the most conventional of mothers, well, life was never dull with her and he couldn't deny that she adored Esther even if she'd proved to be less than ideal wife material...

Annie had winkled the whole story out of him not long after he'd landed – bruised and determined to keep himself to himself – in the old croft house. Bringing cake and flasks of hot tea when he was working hard on the renovation, she'd slowly earned his trust. Now they were firm friends, despite the decades between them. But until now, Annie hadn't ventured onto the subject of the women – or lack of – in his life, and he had been quite happy with that.

'I'm not tarring everyone with the same brush,' he said, after a moment.

'Glad to hear it,' said Annie, looking at him directly.

Shifting his cup, he rearranged some of the cake crumbs on the table until they formed a tiny pyramid. When he looked up, Annie's eyes were still on him.

She chuckled to herself and took a sip of her drink.

'What?' Ben protested.

Annie shook her head. 'Nothing at all. Just wondering if there might be room at this big table for someone else one day.' She waved her arm in a vague gesture. He'd found the old table at a farm sale after he'd moved to the croft, and spent long days sanding it back and waxing it so the grain of the wood could glow gently in the pale Highland light that filtered in through the window.

He shook his head. 'Definitely not. Been there, done that. I've got enough with work and running this place.'

'Hmmm,' said Annie.

CHAPTER FIVE

After setting off at six in the morning, Sophie had the whole journey planned out. She'd set the route on the maps app on her phone, clipping it into place so she could keep an eye on it as she drove north. It had all gone spookily well for the first three-quarters of the trip. Bea and Mark had kissed her goodbye, making her promise to message en route when she stopped for coffee, lunch and loo breaks (all of which had been scheduled) and she'd set off, driving up the empty motorway in the pink glow of an early spring sunrise. But after hours of driving, even with the huge coffee she'd picked up from a drive through Starbucks, she was starting to flag. She missed a turning on the twisty road and ended up driving down towards the sea with a nagging suspicion that she was going in completely the wrong direction. The map seemed to have frozen, as well, which didn't help. She pulled over into a handy stopping place and tapped at the screen, trying to work out what was going on.

'Oh hell,' she said, as she realised that there was no reception whatsoever. The map wouldn't load. And then a white van drove past, blaring its horn at her for no reason she could fathom. She started up the engine again and headed back the way she'd already driven, hoping that the phone would pick up signal and the map would start working.

An hour later, the sky now turning pink again, she finally worked out where she'd gone wrong, and took the right turning at the crossroads, relieved a couple of miles later to see a sign telling her the village of Applemore – and her new life - was three miles away.

Butterflies were crashing around in her stomach, fuelled by the vast amounts of coffee she'd drunk on the journey. She turned left down a steeply banked lane flanked on either side by high hedges and slowed, cautious about the blind bends which seemed to appear with alarming regularity. A few minutes later, and she saw a white painted cottage on the side of the hill, and then her heart started to thud with nerves and excitement as the village came into sight. She pulled over once again to get her bearings, this time outside a row of white-painted cottages rather than a passing place on a single track road, pulling her phone off the holder and scrolling through her emails to find the message with directions in it. She'd been expecting a long, detailed list of instructions, and instead when it had finally arrived – taking so long that she'd started to wonder if they'd had second thoughts about the job offer which had arrived by post – it had been a brief couple of lines which had left her not much the wiser.

'It's easy to find us,' Fiona, the practice owner, had written. *'Just follow the road along and you'll see us on the right. If you pass the Applemore Hotel you've gone too far. F.'*

She shaded her eyes and looked down the road. The sky was ablaze – a riot of pink and gold streaks which surrounded the setting sun, which hung low over the dark shapes of some distant islands out to sea. She could see a long white building with some wooden tables and chairs outside and colourful bunting hanging from the lamp-posts and strung around a hanging metal sign which clearly stated ***Applemore Hotel***.

She looked at the row of cottages with their brightly painted doors and window-boxes stuffed with yellow and cream narcissi. An old man with a cardigan over his shirt twitched back his curtains and looked out at her with a curious expression on his face. None of these looked like a vet surgery. She looked again at the map on her phone, relieved to discover that it had finally come back to life with – miracle of miracles – a full signal. It started chirruping vigorously as a stream of delayed messages appeared one after the other. It was already half past four. She didn't have time to send replies – they'd have to wait. There on the map, clearly indicated, was Applemore Vets. Confusingly, it was very definitely *after* the hotel. Sophie shook her head and tossed the phone onto the empty passenger seat, setting off slowly along the main street of the village.

She pulled up on the side of the road beside a little mini-supermarket, slotting her car in behind an enormous bright red tractor. As she climbed out of her seat a red-haired lad of in his early twenties, clad in a set of mud-covered overalls, emerged from the shop with a bottle of lemonade under his arm.

'Alright?' He nodded a hello at her and clambered into the cab of the tractor, surprising her when he turned on the engine and rock music started blaring out.

Sophie took a deep breath, squaring her shoulders and bracing herself before striding forward and putting her hand on the door of the surgery.

'DON'T COME IN!' A voice shrieked at her through the gap and she stepped back, startled, as someone on the other side slammed it closed.

She blinked in surprise. It wasn't quite the welcome she was hoping for.

A few seconds later, the door cracked open slightly and a face peeked out.

'Sorry,' said a mousey-haired girl with huge black glasses. 'We've got an escapee.' She narrowed her eyes for a moment. 'Sophie?'

'Yes,' said Sophie. 'I'm here for the – I mean I've got a – '

The door opened fleetingly and the girl beckoned her in, quickly slamming the door closed again.

She recognised Thea, the red-haired vet who she'd spoken to via video call on her interview. Then she'd been cheerily practical, taking five minutes out of her day to have a word with Sophie, which had clearly been part of the vetting procedure to make sure they'd get on in person. This time, though, Thea was on her hands and knees underneath the reception desk. She looked up for a second and grinned before reversing back out, narrowly avoiding the office chair which rolled backwards and crashed into the filing cabinet behind her.

'Gotcha,' she said, standing upright and opening her hand to reveal a tiny peach-coloured gerbil.

'Close your hand before he buggers off again!' The girl leapt forward with an anxious expression on her face.

Sophie spotted a cardboard box on the desk and reached across, handing it to Thea who deposited the tiny creature inside and closed the top with an over-exaggerated sigh of relief.

'Welcome to the madhouse,' she said with a chuckle of amusement. 'Nice to meet you in real life, though.'

'Sorry for slamming the door on you,' said the girl, puffing out a breath in relief. 'I'm Mhairi,' she said, putting out her hand in welcome. Sophie looked at the name badge, which bore no relation to the name she'd just said.

'Oh, I always forget how much it confuses English people. It's pronounced Varrie, but it's spelt Mhairi. It's Gaelic.'

'It's a lovely name.'

'Thanks.' She beamed, showing dimples on her freckled cheeks. 'Believe it or not we're quite common up here. You can't move for falling over Mhairis and Morags.'

'Not many Theas, though,' said Thea, who picked up the box and reversed through a door. 'If you want to follow me, Sophie, I'll give you the guided tour. Hopefully now we've got this miscreant back under lock and key we can make the rest of the evening a bit calmer.'

She led Sophie down a passageway and into the recovery room where a metal cage was waiting, bedded down with a layer of soft fleece and with a little hideaway in the corner. She tipped the cardboard box gently onto one side and they both watched as the tiny gerbil scuttled out of sight.

'And we'll close the door securely this time, mister, to keep you in one piece.'

'What's he in for?' Sophie looked around to see if there were any other residents but the room was empty.

'Owner said she felt a lump on his abdomen. She dropped him off earlier on her way in to work at the hotel, and I said we'd have a proper look after surgery because she didn't have time to wait. Only someone left his cage door open for a microsecond and he made a run for it when my back was turned. That would have taken some explaining.'

'Easy mistake to make,' said Sophie, reassuringly.

Thea snorted. 'Given the choice I'd take large animal practice any day. A herd of cattle don't run away the second your back's turned.'

'No, they just cover you in manure and stand on your feet and break your toes.'

'I've never had to crawl around on hands and knees

looking for one though.' Thea laughed again. 'Right, with that drama over, let's see if we can get you organised. Did Fiona send you an email with the news about the flat?'

'No,' Sophie shook her head, following Thea back into the reception where Mhairi was now typing up reports on the computer, her fingers flying over the keyboard as she frowned in concentration.

'Ah,' said Thea. 'Between you me and the gatepost Fi has started checking out already. I had a suspicion she'd forgotten.'

Sophie shifted from one foot to the other, watching as a glance was exchanged between Thea and Mhairi. Whatever the news was, they were clearly not that keen on passing it on.

'Well, Fiona was supposed to be here to see you this afternoon, but she got called away to Inverness at short notice. Her mum's deteriorating faster than she expected.'

'She mentioned something about it at the interview.'

Fiona had touched on it, briefly alluding to the fact that her mother, who'd once run the practice alongside her husband, had recently been diagnosed with dementia.

'We've been struggling along here, but we can't manage with her back and forth all the time. We've got locum cover, but while things are the way they are, we need all hands on deck.' Thea ran a hand through her fox-coloured bobbed hair, which settled neatly back into place. 'Anyway, I digress.'

Mhairi looked up for a moment and met Sophie's gaze with an amused expression, lifting one eyebrow in a look which suggested that going off the topic wasn't an unusual situation for Thea to find herself in.

'Are you making faces behind my back?' Thea turned around, waggling her eyebrows in mock-disapproval.

'I'm merely suggesting that keeping to the point isn't your

strong point.' Mhairi tapped a pen against her teeth and gave a cheeky grin.

'Right,' said Thea in a business-like manner. 'Well, just to confound Madam here and to break the news and get it over and done with...' She started rummaging in a drawer, pulling out an envelope and checking the contents, peering inside and frowning for a second.

Sophie felt herself going cold inside. For one terrible, irrational moment, every terrible scenario spooled through her head. What if they'd had second thoughts? She'd burnt her bridges back home, and her place was rented out. She curled her fingers into her palms, feeling the nails pressing into her skin.

'Fiona said the job would come with the flat upstairs, but it turns out that the place needs some fairly major renovations. Unless you're into the whole survival thing, and you like creeping damp and no central heating, in which case it might turn out to be your idea of heaven.'

Sophie opened her mouth but no sound came out. Of course it was all too good to be true. When she'd parked outside the cottages and looked at the tiny boat bobbing around in the little harbour and the sun setting over the islands, she'd felt a moment of sheer delight at the idea that this place was going to be where she worked.

'Anyway, you've dodged a bullet there and fallen on your feet. The only trouble is you're about ten minutes out of the village.'

'Oh that's okay,' Sophie's heart, which seemed to have stopped for the whole time that Thea was talking, started hammering loudly in her chest. 'It's fine, I don't mind at all.'

'Are you sure?' Thea glanced at Mhairi and Sophie could see that they'd been dreading this conversation.

'Of course not! I'm just glad to be here.'

'Well that makes things a bit easier. Fi's arranged to let a cottage from a friend of hers – I've never been in, but I've driven past and seen it in the distance and by all accounts it's very pretty inside.'

'I'm sure it'll be fine,' said Sophie, who was so relieved that she would have said thank you to a cardboard box or a space next to the errant gerbil. 'After the drive I've had, I'll be glad to get there and put my feet up.'

'Uh-oh,' said Thea, shaking her head. 'Tea. Or coffee. I don't drink it so I always forget the niceties. You've been driving for ages. Shall I put the kettle on?'

'That's lovely of you,' said Sophie, shaking her head. 'But honestly, I've drunk so much coffee that if I have any more caffeine today I'll be awake for about a week.'

'Right. Well, in that case, why don't I give you the keys and you can get out there and get settled before it gets dark.'

'That sounds perfect.'

CHAPTER SIX

Sophie tossed the keys and the envelope onto the back seat and headed back out of the village, this time taking the road which she was clearly supposed to have taken in the first place. Climbing up a hill, she passed a little village hall and some more houses, newer ones this time, with children playing on bikes on the pavement outside. She felt a sudden stab of longing for Tabby as a child, remembering her learning to ride her bike without stabiliser wheels, but shook it away. She had to find this cottage before night fell and she ended up driving round in circles in the dark with no idea where she was going. Miraculously this time the phone map behaved itself and she turned uphill, along another lane lined with gorse bushes and fields dotted with black and white cows, before turning right down another single track road and bumping over a cattle grid. A long white-washed cottage sat in the middle of a field, surrounded by old dry stone walls.

Turn left, instructed the voice on her phone. The road petered out into a rocky, bumpy track which curved round between two fields and led down towards the sea, and then a moment later she spotted it – the most perfect picture-postcard cottage, which sat on some rocks so close to the sea that for a moment until she drew closer it looked as if it was almost floating on the water.

She stopped the car, turning off the engine and stepping out in wonderment.

'I was beginning to think you weren't coming today,' said a voice.

Sophie turned in surprise to see a grey-haired woman with a long, gnarled wooden walking stick standing looking at her.

'I-' Sophie began, looking around to see if there were any other people about to emerge from thin air.

'There's just me,' said the woman, stepping towards her with a hand extended. 'I'm sorry, I didn't mean to startle you. I'm Annie. I thought I'd come down and start a fire for you – it gets cold down here even in the daytime by the sea – and make sure everything was tidy. It's been a while since the cleaners came.'

'Thank you.' Sophie took her hand and shook it, surprised at how firm the old woman's grasp was. 'Are you…'

'This is my cottage,' said Annie. 'Fiona was in a bit of a pickle, as you will no doubt have gathered. And she's got enough on her plate thinking about her mother, and sorting out the surgery, and all the rest of it. I needed a tenant, and – well, the rest is history, as they say. Come on, I'll show you around.'

Sophie obediently headed towards the cottage, hardly having time to take in the beauty of her surroundings. The place looked like something from a Visit Scotland brochure. Gulls whirled overhead, calling as they swooped down towards the white sand of the beach. White-crested waves crashed against slick black rocks in the gathering dusk.

'Here we are,' said Annie, opening the door.

They stepped into a hallway with a woven rush mat covering stone flagstones. It led through to a kitchen which was pale cream with oak worktops and a sparkling white Belfast sink, and a surprisingly modern stainless steel oven and hob.

'You'll be rattling around a little, with three double bedrooms, but I'm sure you'll fill the space if you're anything like me. I find clutter seems to follow me wherever I go.'

Sophie swallowed. She had everything in the back of the car.

'It's lovely,' she said finally, after her brain and mouth had managed to reconnect.

'I expect you're tired after such a long drive. I hope you don't mind, but I thought you might not have time to get some food in, so I've left you some milk and bread, and there's a fruit cake and some soda bread in the larder.'

Her stomach growled at the thought. She'd nibbled on sweets and crisps for the first part of the journey, then been so busy trying to navigate her way through the winding Highland roads for hours that she hadn't eaten anything.

'That's so kind. Thank you so much.'

'Well, I'll let you get in and get organised. I must get back and feed the cats in any case. They'll be protesting if I'm five minutes late.' Annie chuckled. 'If you need anything, my number is on the noticeboard on the wall in the utility room and I'm not far.' She waved her arm in the direction of the hills. 'About half a mile up that way, as the crow flies.'

'I'm sure I'll be fine,' said Sophie, immediately wondering if she sounded ungrateful. 'I mean thank you – I'll let you know if I do need anything. Sorry,' she added. 'I've been driving for ages. I think my brain has run out of steam.'

'I'll get out of your hair.' Annie gave a little smile. 'Enjoy exploring. I love this place. I hope you do, too.'

'Oh I think I will,' said Sophie, following her to the door and outside to where her car was parked at a jaunty angle across the gravel drive.

'Oh, and the internet password is on the noticeboard as well, in case you need it. All mod cons, you know.'

Annie headed off into the twilight on foot. Sophie peered after her, wondering if she'd left a car parked somewhere out of sight, or if she lived nearby. Carrying her bags inside, she felt a shiver down her spine as for a moment she wondered if Annie was some sort of village spectre that haunted newcomers to Applemore, then laughed at herself.

For goodness sake, she told herself, you're an adult. Pull yourself together.

She drew all the curtains and checked all the cupboards and under all the beds just in case, a hangover from Tabby's habit of watching real crime documentaries. There were none, thankfully. She wandered into the sitting room, where the logs were glowing orange behind the glass of the wood burner, and picked up her phone.

'Hi mum,'

'Oh darling, I didn't expect to get you, I was just going to leave a voicemail. It's lovely to hear you.'

Sophie could have burst into tears at the sound of Tabby's voice.

'I'm running to class in a moment or I'd hang up and video call you. Have you arrived? What time is it with you?'

'It's six thirty. I'm here, it's amazing.'

'I want loads of photos.'

'I promise, I'll take tons in the morning.'

'What's the flat like? Is it weird that you're going to be living above work?'

'Ah,' said Sophie, smiling, 'About that...'

So let me get this straight, replied Bea ten minutes later.

You're not living above the shop after all, you've landed on your feet in a holiday cottage that looks like something from a destination holiday brochure?

Pretty much, typed Sophie, opening the kitchen cupboards as she investigated the cottage properly.

And three bedrooms. So you don't mind if we come for a visit this weekend?

I would love that so much, Sophie replied, laughing at her friend as she did so.

Seriously, I'll be up asap. I mean, I was planning to come and see you anyway, but if you've got a spare room and the place is amazing...

Anytime, you know that. You don't even need to say the word, just turn up on the doorstep.

I'll be there with bells on, came the reply.

Sophie sighed. It would be lovely if she was, but the reality was that Bea was always flat out with the café, and finding the time for holidays had never been her workaholic friend's strong point.

Once she'd sent messages to Bea and Tabby, Sophie curled up on the sofa in front of the log burner and picked up the tv remote control. Her eyes were drooping in about half an hour, and despite the coffee she'd drunk, she realised that there was no chance she'd stay awake if she tried to watch something. She headed upstairs to the bathroom, brushed her teeth and got ready for bed.

It was only once she climbed under the covers that she realised what was missing. Noise. The place was weirdly silent. She opened the window to check outside and realised that all she could hear was the swish of the waves on the sand just below the garden, and the occasional hoot of an owl. She pulled the window closed and climbed back into bed, lying there in the uneasy silence, not daring to turn off the bedside light, eyes wide open. At this rate she'd be awake all night.

She woke with a start as the light peeked through her curtains. Picking up her phone she realised with relief that she hadn't spent the entire night owl-eyed with terror as she'd feared. It was half six in the morning and – she pulled back the curtains – a new day was dawning in the cottage by the shore. It was time to explore.

The bathroom was furnished simply with wooden panelled walls and a huge deep cast-iron bath, over which a shower stood. She fiddled with the taps for a moment, working out how to get it working, then jumped back as steaming hot water splashed down on her, soaking her hair. She stood under thundering hot water for ten minutes, feeling the ache in her shoulders being soothed away as she washed her hair with the lavender-scented shampoo and conditioner which was sitting on the edge of the bath. Clearly Annie had left the supplies that were meant for holiday guests for her, and she was thankful that she had. She'd completely forgotten – or not even thought about the fact – that a tiny Highland village wouldn't have a supermarket close by, and that she'd forgotten about supplies of just about everything, chucking it out or passing it on to Bea in her mission to take only the bare minimum with her. She'd have to sort that out today, along with getting some food in – delicious as Annie's cake had been, it wasn't really going to keep her sustained until she started work in a few days' time.

Towelling herself dry (the airing cupboard was packed with a stack of huge white cotton bath sheets, which was a lovely surprise) she got dressed and headed downstairs, pulling her dark hair back into a ponytail as she went.

She pulled open the curtains in the kitchen and jumped about three feet in the air in shock.

Outside the window, so close that she could see the curl of her long lashes, stood a dark eyed Highland cow. Sophie closed her eyes then opened them again. No, she wasn't seeing things. The cow blinked in a leisurely manner, her jaw working as she chewed steadily.

She went to the next window, winding up the blind to discover another two cows grazing quite happily on the stretch of lawn outside, making themselves completely at home. Waves rolled in on the sand on the beach and the gulls from last night were still whirling overhead. Nothing had changed, except for her three new bovine companions.

She went around the cottage, opening all the curtains, wondering what she might find next. Satisfied that there was no lurking wildlife, she pulled on her boots and headed outside. The sky was bright blue and cloudless and the sea mirror-glass calm. The islands she'd seen the night before which had seemed dark and ominous looking were now a soft hazy purple, lit up by the rising sun which glowed golden behind the cottage. She headed over to her car, grabbing her coat and a scarf – it was chilly despite the sunshine – and wandered down the stony path towards the beach.

It could have been a tropical island, were it not for the weather. The sand was the same pale white she'd seen a hundred times before on the front cover of holiday brochures, and the sea sparkled turquoise, the white waves splashing against the rocks in the distance. Sophie set off along the shoreline, heading towards the rocks to see what was beyond their bulk. As she drew closer she realised with surprise that some of the rocks were in fact grey seals, who watched her with curiosity as she walked towards them. The rocks were fringed with vibrant green seaweed and contained pools which looked as if they'd been designed for a child's storybook. In the first one she saw a tiny crab sat perched by the side, grooming its face with outsize claws. In the bottom of the water, half-hidden by the waving tendrils of dark orange and gold weed, a starfish lay peacefully. She thought of Tabby as a toddler and how much she'd have loved this place, and then turned away, not making space for the pang of loss she felt in her chest. The gold rays of the early sun warmed the rocks, which had been worn smooth after hundreds of years of waves far fiercer than these crashing against them. Scrambling up to the top, Sophie gasped in surprise when she saw that beyond the little beach there lay a longer, wider one which stretched out as far as she could see, and in the distance a crumbling castle stood outlined against the sky. She shivered with excitement, turning back to look at the little white cottage which nestled by the beach, surrounded by the dip of the land which protected it from the worst of the elements. It was almost impossibly beautiful. Now all she had to do was come to terms with the fact that she'd upended her life in her forties, and was standing on a heap of rocks with no idea what on earth she was doing.

CHAPTER SEVEN

'I'll be with you in half an hour. Just on my way out to give the dogs a run.' Ben pocketed his phone and fought his way to the front door. Otto and Bear jostled each other, weaving around his legs until he shoved them back, laughing, and opened the big wooden door so they could hurtle out, their plumy spaniel tails waving in the air as they shot down the field towards the road.

'Idiots,' he said fondly, closing the door behind him. He didn't bother with their leads – they knew the route all too well, and the chances of anything besides a lumbering tractor coming along the lane at this time of the morning were slim to non-existent.

Mel's call at seven hadn't woken him – he'd been sitting in the kitchen with his feet up on the woodburning stove catching up on the news on his laptop when she'd rung to say she'd forgotten the plumber was coming first thing and asked if he'd be an angel and open the gallery first thing.

'I know, I know, I should write these things down. But you know what I'm like,' she'd wheedled. He'd pictured her sitting there with a begging expression on her heart-shaped little face and – as they'd both known perfectly well from the moment he'd picked up the phone – he caved, despite his plans.

'I'm supposed to be working,' he'd said, with a groan, folding his laptop closed and standing up even as he'd carried on talking, pressing down the coffee in the cafetiere as Mel had explained that there was a tourist group coming in first thing.

'You mean can I make sure I look halfway respectable?' He'd glanced at his reflection in the mirror over the fireplace, running a hand through the thick dark spikes of his hair which was overdue a visit to the barbers. The beard needed a trim as well. 'I can't make any promises,' he'd said, with a wry laugh.

'Looking like an artist will do,' Mel had said, thanking him effusively.

That wasn't difficult, he thought, looking at the thick navy sweater he was wearing, still covered in wood shavings from his work yesterday. It had been a while since he'd picked up a brush, but between the mad hair, the beard and the general demeanour, he suspected that he'd pass the artist test with flying colours.

He vaulted over the gate at the bottom of the field and whistled the dogs, who'd shot off in the wrong direction in hot pursuit of a pheasant, and set off towards the beach.

It had been a few years since he'd arrived at the steading, which back then had been dilapidated and freezing cold, with a collapsing roof and damp blooming up the sides of the grimy walls. The first year – angry with himself for believing that he had a chance of making a future up there with Liz, he'd focused on rebuilding the place, and in the process of doing so had slowly rebuilt himself. He turned to look at the old croft, which stood alone on the hillside, low and solid, a curl of smoke twisting out of the chimney like a child's drawing. He'd built the door that kept out the wild winds that blew off the sea almost every month of the year, and planted the hedge that now provided a home for the birds and wildlife that returned there every spring to raise their young. As he'd returned to working on his art and his daughter Esther had come to visit in school holidays he'd settled into the life he'd found himself in – it might not be the one he'd have chosen, but it was as close as he could get. When Annie had told him about a gamekeeper friend she knew who had a litter of spaniel pups looking for homes a couple of years ago, he'd suspected that she was meddling – worried he was lonely, no doubt – but the two dogs had proved to be the final piece that was missing. He'd made a friend in Andy, the keeper, too, who often dropped by if he passed by. Andy was quiet and easy-going, and didn't expect much other than a chat over the gate and a chance to check up on how his pups were doing.

He watched them gallop past, tongues lolling, and grinned to himself. On a day like today, when spring was making itself known and the dogs were full of joy, it was hard to feel anything but positive, even if his plans had been knocked sideways by Mel. He brushed past a gorse bush covered in yellow flowers, inhaling the familiar coconut scent as he walked and thought, as he did every morning.

'Otto,' he shouted, as the smaller of the two circled away in pursuit of a fresh scent. Otto ignored him for a moment then jack-knifed back, lolloping towards him with an innocent expression. Of the two he'd been the harder to train. Even now he had a habit of taking himself off, finding employment if his brain wasn't getting enough entertainment. Despite their sweet-tempered nature the two of them were effective guard dogs, barking in a surprisingly intimidating manner if they felt their territory was being threatened.

Not that there was any chance of that today. He had the place to himself, which was exactly how he liked it. Overhead a hawk circled, looking for a spot of breakfast. A moment later it shot down like an arrow, bringing a sudden end to the life of a field mouse or some other tiny creature.

He loved his peaceful existence out here. It gave him the chance to watch nature at work – birds were already bustling back and forth making their nests outside his kitchen window, and soon the tiny fledglings peeping with impatience as their mother returned with food for them. Andy popped by in the shooting season and brought him a brace of pheasant now and again. He'd learned (thanks to YouTube) how to pluck and dress the birds, and the freezer was well stocked with stews he'd made in the log burning stove in autumn. He'd always been the cook at home, and even after all these years he'd found it hard to adjust to cooking for one. Many the time Annie turned up with a cake she'd baked and returned home with a container of something he'd made for dinner. It was a good deal for both.

The track dropped down and the cottage came into view again. Outside, a little Citroen was parked by the side wall. A split second later he heard a short alarm bark and then both dogs raced past him. In their mind, this track and the path down to the beach counted as their territory, and they hurtled down the hill, barking furiously. Ben called them back, but they showed no sign of stopping.

He broke into a run as the dogs disappeared round the side of the cottage, still barking.

'Otto! Bear!'

He could hear furious barking. Turning at the corner of the cottage, he encountered a tall, good looking woman of around his age with dark hair and a distinctly unamused expression on her face. Despite the early hour, she too was dressed for walking, her hair tied back in a pony-tail but with long strands blowing around her face. Her hands were balled into fists on her hips. The dogs danced back and forth, darting out of reach, hackles raised as they made their feelings quite clear.

'Are these yours?'

'Otto, get here.' The smaller of the two spaniels – clearly knowing he'd stepped out of line – slunk towards him, tail wagging and an apologetic look on his face. His brother, Bear, was still standing four square. His legs were planted firmly and the expression on his face suggested that he wasn't going anywhere soon. Ben marched over and grabbed his collar, pulling him back.

'Sorry, they're –'

'It's fine,' said the woman, with an expression that suggested it was anything but. 'Perhaps keep them on a lead when you're passing next time.'

'Of course,' he said, straightening up and releasing their collars, giving them a hard stare as he did so. They seemed to get the hint and pootled off meekly, leaving him standing there opposite what he presumed must be his new neighbour.

'Is this some kind of a footpath?' she said, a moment later.

He looked at the cottage and the track that led down to the beach. 'It's – well, I – normally I walk the dogs here on the beach. It's not normally a problem.' How many times could a man say the word *normally* in one conversation?

'Oh. Right.' She looked at him, then tucked one of the loose strands of hair behind her ear. 'Well, I'll let you get on with your walk then.'

With that she turned and went back inside. Ben's eyebrows shot up towards his forehead and he rubbed his chin in bemusement. Annie's new tenant didn't exactly seem like the friendliest person on the planet.

He carried on down to the beach, gathering a couple of pieces of faded driftwood from the water's edge, letting the dogs run free along the sand but feeling a nagging sense of discomfort. He glanced up at the cottage, where he could see a light on in the kitchen window. She might be undeniably pretty, with dark hair and curves he couldn't help but notice, but his misgivings about having a full time neighbour after years of relative solitude seemed pretty well founded, if their first meeting was anything to go by.

Half an hour later, with the dogs fast asleep on the back seat of his battered pick up truck, he pulled up in the courtyard outside the collection of white-painted buildings which housed the gallery and an assortment of other local businesses.

A few years before they'd been transformed by Polly Fraser, youngest of the four Fraser children who'd grew up in the once-grand Applemore House. The house had not only lent the village its name but once upon a time had been the main employer of the locals who lived there, working on the land and in the house and as tenant farmers. Over generations the Frasers had been stung by inheritance taxes and the cost of running a huge old house - until they'd had a change in fortune when Lachlan, Polly's older brother, had come into money after selling his brewery business. Now Applemore House had been renovated to its former glory and Lachlan and his partner Rilla ran a wild camping site in the remaining thirty acres of woodland that surrounded their home. Charlotte, the oldest Fraser sister, ran the holiday cottage business, and Polly's other sister Beth ran a thriving flower farm from the old walled garden in the grounds.

Polly had started off by renovating the old stable buildings by the lodge. A coffee shop run by Gavin and Tom had soon followed, and then the gallery and an artisan bakery had been created from more old buildings, along with a workshop where Beth gave classes in floristry. Polly had recently moved out of the cottage and into the house above the Applemore Hotel to live full time with her fiancé Harry.

'Morning Ben,' she called as he climbed out of the car, giving a wave as she headed into the Farm Shop with a cardboard box under her arm. She was in her usual jeans and a checked shirt, with her long blonde hair swinging loose. She doubled back a moment later, the door to the shop held ajar by the box she'd been carrying.

'Hang on, I thought Mel was in this week?' Polly scratched her head in confusion. 'In fact she said last night she'd be in early. I thought she'd be here by the time I arrived, especially when I'm running late.' She put a hand to her mouth as she tried to suppress a yawn. 'Sorry, we had a bit of a late night last night at the pub. I'm worn out.'

The dogs were worn out after their misdemeanours earlier on, both now flat out asleep. He'd leave them in the truck while he opened the gallery and got everything sorted.

'She's double booked herself with the plumber, so I've been roped in.'

'You know we've got a busload of tourists coming in first thing?' Polly's expression was amused, her eyebrows quirking as she flicked a glance over his shoulder towards the gallery.

'Ohh yes,' he groaned. 'I can hardly wait. I'm on top social form this morning, as it turns out.'

Polly folded her arms and leaned back against the door of the shop. 'How so?'

'Took these two down to t'beach,' he began, nodding in the direction of the car, 'And they took it upon themselves to set upon the new resident like a pair of prize security dogs.'

'These two softies?' Polly giggled. 'What were they going to do, lick her to death?'

'I was surprised at them. I think they must've got it in their heads it was their territory and of course it's off season so I didn't even have the leads. Had to grab them by the collar and look like I actually had them under control while looking like a prize idiot.'

'Who's the new resident, anyway - I thought Annie wasn't having any more holiday guests? I thought she might sell the place to Charlotte but apparently she sent her off with a flea in her ear when she suggested it. You know what Annie's like, she doesn't suffer fools gladly.' Polly rolled her eyes. 'Not that I'm suggesting Charlotte's a fool, obviously.'

Ben chuckled. 'Course not. I'm surprised you haven't heard, village gossip being what it is. It's the new vet that's taking over now Fiona is retiring.'

'The new vet? Surely she wouldn't mind a couple of dogs barking at her?' Polly looked surprised.

'Morning, lovies,' said a Welsh voice from behind them. They both turned to see Gavin, one half of the couple who ran the café, beetling towards them at speed. 'I sense hot gossip from the way you two are standing chatting when you should be getting on with work. What's going on?'

Polly caught his eye and smiled. With Gavin and Tom the village gossip flowed as freely as the delicious coffee they served. Folding his arms, Gavin joined them, with an expectant look on his face.

'Spill,' he said, tapping a finger on his well-muscled bicep.

'Apparently Ben gave the new vet a bit of an unexpected welcome – or rather the dogs did. She's moved in to the cottage by the shore, you know, the one Charlotte had her eye on?'

'The pretty one down near your place?' Gavin looked at him sideways. 'That'll put the cat among the pigeons. I thought you liked living out there being all arty in splendid isolation.'

'Hardly.' Ben snorted. 'Anyway, now the dogs have gone full attack mode when she's just stepped outside of her new front door I suspect she'll be giving me and them a wide berth.'

'She's a vet, she'll be used to far worse,' said Polly, reassuringly.

'I dunno, she didn't seem particularly impressed.' Ben shrugged. 'Not that I can do much about it, though, and thankfully these two have recently had their booster jabs so I won't be at the surgery for a good while. I'll keep my fingers crossed that the next time she bumps into me they don't try and take her arm off.'

Gavin peered inside the window. Sensing people, which meant food and fuss, both dogs had now woken up and had their noses pressed up against the glass of the back window.

'These two are so soft I can't see you having any trouble winning her round.'

'I don't want to win her round,' Ben said, 'I'd just like her not to think I can't control my animals.'

They all headed off towards their respective workplaces. Ben flicked on the gallery lights and straightened up a couple of the tiny miniatures that Mel painted which were so small and light that they were habitually knocked sideways by visitors. He straightened up the stacks of colourful business cards which gallery artists left on the counter in the hope of commissions or selling private pieces, and put on some music to play in the background as the place started to warm up as the heater took the chill off the air. He glanced out of the window, checking for signs of the promised busload of tourists who were on their way this morning. They tended to go one way or the other – sometimes they'd turn up and clear the place out, others they'd wander in, put their grubby fingerprints all over everything then clear off with not one of them having put their hand in their pocket. He crossed his fingers it would be the former – he'd recently finished off a few new pieces and they were hanging on the walls of the gallery waiting for homes. He ran a hand along a driftwood sculpture of a horse's head he'd created last month. It had been a commission which hadn't made it in the end – the couple he'd been making it for had split two months before their wedding. He'd felt so bad for the bloke that he'd offered to return the deposit he'd paid when he turned up at the gallery, ashen faced with dark shadows under his eyes, his jaw marked with a week's worth of stubble. He'd refused to take it, but Ben had felt for him, remembering how he'd felt when he'd arrived in the Highlands alone.

'It'll get better, mate,' he told the man, giving him a brief nod of reassurance.

'Hope so.'

'It will.'

He looked at the horse. Hopefully it wasn't cursed with bad luck. He shook his head, laughing at himself, and got back to work.

CHAPTER EIGHT

'Hello-oo?'

Sophie was standing in the kitchen making a shopping list when she heard a knock at the door and a voice calling. She headed out into the hall in her socks. Standing by the door with an apologetic expression on her face was Annie, clearly dressed for a trip out. Her hair was tucked neatly in a bun and she had a flower-patterned scarf at her neck, which brought out the colour of her unusual blue eyes.

'Now I don't want you thinking I'm going to be turning up at all hours of the day and night, but I wanted to say that I was going into town and it struck me that you might not know where the best place to get your shopping was, and normally I leave a little guidebook with all that sort of thing for my guests, but – well, you're not a guest, and –' she stopped mid-sentence and looked at Sophie, then gave a low chuckle.

'I'm sorry, I'm getting ahead of myself. I just – well, I was thinking about you last night when I was watching the television and thinking it was a big change coming from England all the way up here and then ending up out in the sticks.'

Sophie, who'd been standing thinking pretty much the same thing, tried to think of the right thing to say in response. In all the time she'd lived in Crosby, she didn't think she'd ever had more than a brief conversation about the weather or the surprising lack of bin collection with her neighbours. Now she was here and they seemed to be all over the place. It was a bit disconcerting.

'I do need to get some shopping, now you mention it,' she said, after a moment's thought. 'That's very helpful.'

'Oh well, that is good news. Right then. Do you have a pen and paper?'

Sophie shook her head. 'I'll remember, don't worry.'

'There's a little mini market in the village – you'll perhaps have seen that when you were in the surgery yesterday getting the keys?'

Sophie nodded. 'I did, yes. I was thinking of going to a big supermarket to get a load of shopping in so I don't have to think about it when I start work tomorrow.'

'And then there's the Farm Shop on the other side of the village as well,' continued Annie. Sophie wondered if she hadn't heard. 'If you're looking for bread, there's a little bakery there at the Farm Shop as well, but if it's a big supermarket you're looking for, you'll need to drive ten miles to go to the Co-Op.'

'That sounds ideal.'

'You slept well, then?' Annie looked at her closely. 'Not too quiet for you?'

Sophie gave a laugh of surprise.

'It was quiet, yes. How did you guess?'

'My late husband came from Glasgow. When he first moved up here he couldn't get a wink of sleep for all the quiet outside. He was used to the sounds of the shipyard nearby and people working and the rumble of traffic on the road outside his window. It takes a bit of getting used to, the silence. But if you listen closely, you'll soon hear that there's a lot more going on than you realise.'

'That sounds a bit like vet practice. I always remember one of my tutors at university telling me that you learned most about your patients by observing quietly.'

Annie gave a little smile. 'Yes, well, that's the thing, isn't it? You can't very well ask them how they're feeling. When are you starting work?'

'Tomorrow.' Sophie felt a wave of nerves. She'd lain awake last night worrying that she'd somehow have forgotten everything she knew and that she'd mess up in her first morning. It was ridiculous that she spent so much time geeing up Tabby and making her believe in herself and yet here she was a bag of nerves and self-doubt underneath. It didn't help that Fiona had all but admitted that they'd struggled to recruit someone. Vets were leaving the profession at a rate of knots, stressed out and overworked and under intolerable pressure. The lack of challenge was – she was almost afraid to admit to herself – was one of the real reasons she'd never moved away from Nick's surgery. Well, that and – well, he'd always been there for her when she needed him. He was a bit of a knob, but his heart was in the right place. She'd discovered a text from him on her phone when she got back from her walk, wishing her luck and telling her she'd knock 'em out of the park.

'Better to just jump in at the deep end, I expect,' said Annie, adjusting the scarf around her neck. She didn't seem to be showing any sign of departing, and Sophie wavered for a moment, not sure what the etiquette was on inviting the owner of the house you were living in.

'Would you like a… some tea?'

'Och no,' said Annie with a shake of her head. 'I must get

off. I don't want to be getting under your feet. Just wanted to check you were alright down here, as I said.'

'It was kind of you to think of me,' said Sophie, as Annie turned to leave. 'I did bump into – well, there was a bit of an incident this morning with a couple of springers who appeared in the garden. I'd just got back and they appeared out of the blue.'

She didn't add *and I thought one of them was going to take my arm off* but the words were hovering in her head.

'Ah, Otto and Bear,' Annie beamed. 'And I'm taking it you met my pal Ben, in that case?'

'He didn't introduce himself,' said Sophie, slightly stiffly. Again she didn't add that she'd been distinctly frosty with him, but he'd hardly been a ray of sunshine himself.

'I don't think he was expecting me to be here.'

'Oh, he knew you were arriving last night,' said Annie, looking surprised.

In that case, thought Sophie, he must've been doing some sort of territorial posturing. Spaniels weren't exactly the first dogs you'd think of when it came to the whole Alpha Male thing, but it took all sorts.

'I didn't realise. But no, we didn't get a chance to say much. He shot off with his dogs, and I was just on my way inside.'

'Hmm,' said Annie. 'Well, I'd better get off. Good luck for tomorrow. And don't forget to let me know if you need anything.'

Sophie closed the door and stood in the hallway for a moment, nonplussed. People up here were different, that was for sure. She pocketed her phone, picked up her car keys and decided to head into the nearest big town and the security of the familiar aisles of a supermarket. If nothing else, she could fill the fridge and that would be one less thing to contend with. Somehow the thought of walking into the village shop and getting the third degree from someone else who probably knew everyone was a bit beyond her.

At least this way, she told herself, she'd get to know the roads around Applemore before she started working. Parking at the supermarket, she was about to pop her phone into her bag when she saw Bea's face pop up on the screen a second before it started to ring. She hit the answer button in a second.

'Wow, that was quick. I thought you'd be off hiking up a hill or something on your first morning. How's it going?' Bea sounded bright and cheery.

Sophie scratched her forehead and grimaced, glad that she wasn't on a video call.

'It's… a lot.' She puffed out a breath. 'I survived the first night though, that has to be worth something.'

'You're not on I'm a Celebrity,' laughed Bea. 'I thought you were all mod cons in your posh holiday cottage. Is the hot water not working or something?'

'No, the place is amazing. I can't wait for you to see it. It's just…' she stalled and then thought of what she'd say to Tabby – what she *did* say to her daughter when she arrived in the states and everything was new, unfamiliar and terrifying. She was eighteen and she'd managed. 'Ah, I'm just feeling a bit at sea. It's all new. Give me time.'

'You sure?' Bea's voice was kind. 'It's a massive leap going from having Just Eat at the end of your fingertips and a corner shop twenty metres away to living in the middle of nowhere in the Highlands. I was saying to Mark this morning it's hard to believe you're really there.'

'I'm really here,' said Sophie, looking out of the window at the car park. A woman in a green Barbour jacket walked past, hand in hand with a tiny blond-haired child in a pair of pink wellie boots who was carrying a colourful comic. It felt like five minutes since she'd been doing the same with Tabby. But there was no point in harping on about that and feeling sorry for herself. She'd got herself into this situation, and she was going to make the best of it. 'I'm going to be fine, I promise. You'll see when you come to visit.'

'I'm working out dates as we speak. I want to see this cottage for myself.'

'Play your cards right and you might meet Annie as well. In fact scratch that, I suspect she'll appear on the doorstep with some spurious reason and a cake, if the last twenty four hours are anything to go by. It seems to be her thing.'

'I'm totally fine with random old ladies turning up with cake,' laughed Bea. 'You can tell her to send some my way, if she likes.'

'Noted.' Sophie smiled to herself. Just speaking to Bea seemed to have given her the tiny injection of confidence she needed to get going. All she had to do now was keep it in mind until she walked through the surgery door in the morning. 'Right, I had better get going. I've got a hot date with the Co-Op.'

'Not Tesco?'

'Apparently not, no. The nearest one is in Ullapool and I'm not driving forty miles to get my fix of chicken tikka ready meals. I'm going to have to branch out.'

'Well look at you. You've changed already. Happy shopping –' Bea blew kisses down the line '- I'll text later for updates. Let me know if you meet any hot farmers on your travels.'

'I think that's hardly likely,' said Sophie, saying goodbye and pocketing her phone.

Inside the supermarket the clientele suggested that her suspicions were correct. The only men she saw were a slightly anaemic looking checkout operator and two old men in flat caps with walking sticks who stood on the end of the bakery section having a long conversation which lasted the duration of her shopping trip. They were still there chatting away when she left the shop with her bags. As she pulled out of the car park she noticed with a laugh to herself that they were only just wandering out, still talking, at last.

Without the panic of thinking she was going to get lost she was able to take in the scenery and appreciate just how beautiful it was on the way home. She opened the window for a moment, letting a blast of bracingly cold air rush in and wake her up – she was sleepy after getting up and rushing out first thing – and caught a whiff of cow muck which reminded her of her time doing large animal work when she was training. She'd told Fiona at the interview that she was out of practise but happy to muck in when needed, crossing her fingers and hoping she wouldn't *be* needed often – if at all. It wasn't that she didn't like cows or sheep, and she wasn't precious about getting mucky or getting her hands dirty… it was just a confidence thing. Large animal vets always seemed so hearty and direct and alarmingly straight-talking. Give her a waiting room full of dogs and cats, gerbils and even the odd parrakeet any day.

CHAPTER NINE

'There now, that wasn't so bad, was it?' Polly said at lunchtime. Ben looked out of the long window of the coffee shop and watched as the last of the tourist visitors disappeared out of view, wandering back to their bus which was parked on the side of the long drive that led to Applemore House. He smiled to himself, watching an elderly couple - who'd bought the horse sculpture, to his delight – as they rounded the corner, still chatting and smiling as they'd been every time he saw them.

'Cute, aren't they?' Polly followed his gaze. 'They bought t-shirts for all their great-grandchildren, and a ton of stuff from the shop. I don't know how they're going to fit it all on the bus home.'

'I should have taken it off their hands and shipped it along with the horse,' he laughed.

'Ooh, they bought it?' Polly's face lit up with delight. 'Ah, that's really good. You must be really pleased.'

Ben nodded. He didn't mention his completely ridiculous secret worry that the thing might be cursed – a couple who'd been together that long and were clearly still as happy as that clearly didn't have any worries on that front.

'It's so cute,' Polly went on, taking a sip of her coffee. 'They told me they're on their thirtieth wedding anniversary trip, and they wanted to come back here because they met on a wildlife trek on the islands, so they've been all over the Highlands on this bus tour.'

'Thirtieth wedding?' Ben frowned. 'Sure you heard that right? They must've been eighty, at least.'

'Oh yes,' Polly turned to look at him with a mischievous twinkle in her eye. 'They got married when they were fifty apparently, so there's hope for you yet.'

'Very funny,' he said drily, rolling his eyes.

'Just saying,' teased Polly. 'They do say there's someone out there for everyone.'

'I'm quite happy by myself, thanks very much. Just because you and Harry are all loved up, and everyone's got wedding fever after Matt and Anna's do...'

'It was a gorgeous wedding, you have to admit,' Polly put a hand to her chest and gave an over-dramatic sigh.

'It was a lovely wedding,' Ben acknowledged. Matt had made a roaring success of the artisan bakery in one of the old outbuildings next to the gallery, and everyone had watched as he and Polly's friend Anna – who baked delicious sweet treats for the farm shop and the café – had fallen in love.

'Well, like I say, it's never too late. The perfect woman might be right around the corner.'

'Whatever you say,' Ben said, finishing his coffee and handing the cup to a passing Tom, who was clearing tables. 'Thanks, mate.'

'No probs. Looks like this bus tour thing is a winner. We've made a fortune.' He looked at Polly hopefully.

'Yeah, I think we can all agree it's been a hit. As long as

nobody has any objections to busloads of tourists coming through once a week, I think we might be onto something.'

'I'm sure Dolina will have words to say about it,' said Tom, grinning. 'You know what she's like.'

'That's fine, we'll just keep it between us and she'll never know. Oh, wait.'

They all laughed at the idea of Dolina, village busybody and repository of every piece of gossip ever known, not knowing about something. There wasn't anything that she didn't notice.

'I won't breathe a word,' promised Tom, tossing the dish-cloth he was holding over his shoulder and wandering off. Polly and Ben, who knew that was extremely unlikely, exchanged looks but said nothing.

'Anyway, I better get back. I've left Jenny on the till and I said I'd only be five minutes. Are you here for the whole of the day?'

Ben shrugged. 'Well, I wasn't planning to be – '

'No sign of Mel?'

'Not a word. Maybe the plumber didn't turn up on time.'

He spent the next hour or so tidying up the gallery and hanging some artworks that were stacked up in the back room, filling the spaces that had been taken when several pieces had been sold that morning. The dogs – by this time getting bored and ready for a decent run, not just a quick wander around the courtyard of the farm shop – bumbled around the gallery, getting under his feet as he worked. The other artists would be pretty chuffed to find out how well things had gone – he'd been run off his feet dealing with customers and answering questions about the artists, handing out their colourful business cards and wrapping up the smaller paintings that were easily transported home on the bus.

The others had been decorated with the much-longed-for red dot, the sticker which indicated that the piece was sold. He snapped photos of the walls and sent them to the gallery group chat, causing a flurry of delighted replies. Next time there was a bus tour, he suspected, they'd be fighting to be there in person. It was always easier to sell something you'd created yourself – he'd wrapped up a load of his smaller pieces and taken payment for them, which would keep the wolves from the door for a decent while. Now all he had to do was wrap and box the horse head sculpture, and he'd get it in the back of the car and taken down to be picked up by the couriers at the shop later in the week.

He felt a bit like an extra from The Godfather as he unreeled a roll of bubble wrap round and around the horse's head before placing it carefully into the reinforced box he'd used to transport it to the gallery and surrounding it with packing chips. This head wasn't destined for the pillow of a gangster, though, but for a little Victorian house by the seaside in Grimsby, where it would – the couple had told him delightedly – take pride of place in their bay window.

'That way people can enjoy it as they go past,' the man had told him, with a smile at his wife. She'd squeezed his hand and looked at him fondly.

He shook his head, remembering Polly's not-so-subtle hints about marriage. For the last few years it had been one couple getting together after another in Applemore, and he felt a vague sense that choosing to be single was going against the grain. The truth was that they were all first-timers, rosy cheeked and full of naïve hope. He'd had his fingers well and truly burned when it came to relationships, and now – with a daughter about to finish university and his career ticking along quite nicely – he didn't see any reason whatsoever to upset the status quo.

Talking of work... if Mel actually bothered to turn up at any point, he might have half a chance of getting something done in the latter half of the afternoon before the light went. She was supposed to be here getting things organised for this art course she was running in the workshop, if nothing else. A couple of huge boxes of supplies had been tripping him up every time he went into the back room, and several of the bus tour visitors had noticed the signs on the wall, saying how much they'd love to try something like that. It was his idea of hell, teaching a class of newbies how to rediscover their creativity – no doubt Dolina would be there with her cronies, just in case she missed out on any scandal, and the whole thing would be full of the usual village suspects. He shook his head, laughing at himself. He sounded like a cantankerous old sod sometimes. It was lucky nobody could read his mind.

The dogs circled him, tails waving hopefully. He was kidding himself. He really needed to get them out for a decent walk – this morning's had been truncated by their unexpected run-in with the new resident, and they were used to a good hour or so galloping freely along the beach and scrambling around the rock pools or heading out over the moors.

He pulled his phone out of his pocket, feeling it vibrate as a call came through.

'At last,' he said, seeing Mel's name come up on the screen. 'Have you had the whole place re-plumbed?'

There was a scuffling sound on the other end of the line and then 'Hello? Ben?'

He felt his eyebrows rise in amusement. 'Yep, it's definitely me. Are you alright?'

'Not – well, not really,' said Mel, and he realised that her voice sounded strained, as if she was breathing carefully between each word.

'You okay? Mel?'

'I'm in the car with Fee,' she said. There was another scuffling noise and he could hear Fee, her partner, talking distantly in the background for a moment.

'Is it on speaker? Put it on speaker. Ben, that you?'

Fee boomed into his ear.

'Yep, it's me. What the hell is going on?'

'We're on our way to x ray to get Mel's arm checked out. She fell off the kerb as she was leaving for the gallery and – shush, I'll sort it, you just hold the phone – I think she's probably done her wrist, by the looks of it.'

'It's fine,' said Mel, 'I bet it's just a sprain. She's fussing over nothing.'

'We're going to go into that patch down the glen where there's no reception in a moment,' said Fee, shouting now as if that would make a difference. 'I'll keep you post...'

And then the line went silent, and he stood for a moment and looked out of the window, not quite sure what to do next.

He packed the car up with the box and switched everything off in the gallery, popping into the shop to tell Polly he was heading home.

'I've just spoken to Charlotte,' she said, biting her lip and looking worried. 'She said Mel's on her way to the hospital.'

'That didn't take long.' Ben dug his hands into the back pockets of his jeans, casting a glance around to see who else was in the shop. 'By the time I get back through the village the rumour mill will have her in traction with four broken limbs.'

'Fee was at the office when it happened,' Polly went on.

'Ah, of course.'

Fiona, Mel's partner, was the office manager of Charlotte Fraser's holiday cottage business. It made sense that Charlotte would know. Of course it would be all over the village in no time – not that it mattered. But sometimes, even after living up in Applemore for years, he found the rapidity of the village rumour mill made his head spin. Back home in Lancashire he'd lived a completely anonymous existence, which had suited him down to the ground. It was one of the reasons he loved living slightly apart from Applemore, and one of the reasons that he didn't mind Annie as a friend and neighbour. She'd always kept herself to herself to a degree, and he'd known instinctively he could trust her with a confidence. Having someone else on his doorstep irked him more than he liked to admit.

'Anyway, fingers crossed she'll be okay,' he said gruffly, after a moment's reflection.

'I'm sure she'll be fine.' Polly's smile didn't quite mask the concern in her voice.

'Right, well, I'll get off. See you soon.'

A call from Esther distracted him when he got back to the croft. Shoving his headphones in his ear and his phone in his pocket, he grabbed the dogs leads – he wasn't taking any chances this time – and headed back down the field to give them a decent leg stretch as he caught up with his daughter, who was ringing from the side of a motorway.

'How's it going?'

'Not bad. This placement's actually really interesting. I have to send you a photo of the work we're doing. I'm in the welfare van just now, waiting for traffic management to get organised so we can get out and have a look.'

'You sound like a professional,' said Ben, impressed. He got to the end of the road, still listening to Esther chatting animatedly about her third year work placement working with National Highways on a motorway improvement scheme. He glanced at the road down towards the cottage by the shore and made a split second decision, turning away and calling the dogs to follow him as he climbed the stile that led down the footpath towards the old castle. After this morning, he was going to steer clear of any chances of bumping into his new neighbour.

'What's happening with you?' said Esther, eventually. He grinned.

'Oh you know, the usual. Sold a few pieces this morning so if you want to tap your old man for money, now's the time.'

'Funny you should mention it,' Esther laughed in his ear.

'I'll transfer some over when I get home. Remind me if I forget.'

'Oh, it looks like things are moving,' she said, and he waited as he heard her chatting to a couple of men about closing traffic lanes. 'Yep, we're on. I need to go, Dad. I'll text you later.'

'Don't get squashed by any lorries when you're wandering around the side of a motorway,' he said, trying to keep his tone light.

'Don't worry, that's what the helmet's for. Love you,' she said, and was gone.

He grimaced at the thought of her out there. She might be almost twenty one and a fully grown adult but there was a part of her that would always be the tiny gap-toothed five year old who loved to build complicated structures with her wooden train track. Crazy to think that it had led to a degree in civil engineering, and now she was dreaming of a job working on the highways network. It couldn't be further removed from her parents and their respective careers as artists. Maybe all children rebelled against their parents occupations – after all, his dad had worked man and boy in a factory in Manchester, starting out at fifteen and ending up manager. He'd tried his hardest to push Ben in the same direction, and had been horrified when he'd turned around and said that no, he was off to art school.

'What kind of job are you going to get as an artist,' his dad had scoffed. 'Nowt that you can do with a degree in art but be a teacher.'

'I can promise you one thing,' he'd told his father, 'I will never be a bloody teacher.'

Broken in two places, said the text from Mel he read when he got home an hour later. *You know I wouldn't ask you if there was any other choice, but the art class starts two weeks on Thursday...*

CHAPTER TEN

Despite her nerves the day before, Sophie woke up looking forward to going into work. She looked at herself in the mirror – she'd chosen her favourite grey trousers which were well-worn but still smart, and soft-soled black boots which made standing up all day comfortable which was no mean feat. She pulled down the hem of her navy sweatshirt so it covered her bottom – Fiona, who'd handed over the uniform, had confided that she hated things that didn't cover what she'd called with a chuckle *a multitude of tums*. Sophie gave a silent sigh of relief. Once again her New Year's Resolution to become a lithe over-forty yoga goddess had taken a tumble at the first hurdle. The lifestyle of a busy town vet hadn't left her much time for cooking dinner and the old ice cream and ready meals diet didn't really lend itself to hip-skimming jeans and crop tops. Not that she had any desire whatsoever to wear either – ironically, given she had an athlete's figure, neither did Tabby. Her daughter had always tended to dress for comfort in baggy sweats and jeans, and that hadn't changed now she was living in the warmth of Atlanta. She'd sent a video overnight of her new friends from university all having dinner together, identical in huge colourful hooded sweat-shirts with their hair tied back from their face after a football game. Sophie smiled at the thought as she slicked on some coloured lip balm and a quick swipe of mascara. That would do. It was work, not a fashion show.

She drove into Applemore, half-expecting a flurry of last minute butterflies to come marching in and take over, but as she parked the car outside the surgery none materialised.

'Morning,' said Mhairi as she opened the door. 'Just making drinks for everyone. D'you want a tea? Coffee?'

'Coffee would be amazing, thanks. Sophie hung up her scarf on the coat hooks.

'I'm Evie,' said a voice, emerging from under the reception desk. 'You must be Sophie. I'm the other receptionist, and I'm training to be a vet nurse.'

'That's a juggle,' Sophie smiled a hello.

'I know, my poor wee brain gets tired from all the studying at nights, but I love it. But between that and getting to grips with the new software we've just installed sometimes I think I live sleep and breathe this place.'

'Don't talk to me about that flipping software,' growled Mhairi. 'It's supposed to be intuitive and I swear it's got a mind of its own. I've been trying to update patient records for about a month – or at least that's what it feels like.'

'What are you using?' Sophie leaned over to look at the screen. 'Oh, we had that at my old place. I can give you some tips if you like?'

'Seriously?' Mhairi and Evie exchanged a look of relief. 'That would be amazing.'

'You're taking your life into your hands sitting there,' said Thea ten minutes later, walking into the surgery to find Sophie sitting in the receptionists' chair with her hand on the mouse. 'These two guard this desk like a couple of rottweilers.'

'Not when Sophie knows her way round this ridiculous new software,' beamed Mhairi. 'In fact I'm happy to hand over the reins to her and let her get on with it.'

'I wouldn't say that if I were you, I have a suspicion this morning's going to be busy.' Thea headed for the kettle. A short woman with close-cropped grey hair appeared, seemingly out of nowhere, giving her a little wave of welcome.

'Nice to see you,' she said, with a cheerful smile. 'I'm Grace. I see they've got you straight to work.'

'Just helping out with the new computer software,' explained Sophie. She looked over at Mhairi. 'Hopefully that'll help a bit.'

She pushed the chair back and the wheels slid on the floor so it crashed back against the wall, knocking over a stack of delivery boxes which Evie caught with a practised hand.

'I'd better get organised before the doors open.'

She headed into her room, noticing the sign on the door with her name on it and smiling to herself. It felt like being home, despite the newness of her surroundings. She wiped down the examining table and tossed the paper towel in the bin, turning to the computer screen a moment later to check who was first on the books.

'Taco Jones,' she said, opening the door to peer out into the waiting room which had miraculously filled up in moments. The name was so unusual that she half-wondered if it was a wind-up by the reception staff, which is the sort of joke that used to happen all the time back at the old place. But no, as she peered around, a fair-haired woman was standing up, pulling an uncertain-looking little terrier out from under her chair.

'Come on in,' she said, waving an arm in welcome. A fair-haired woman followed, having scooped the little dog into her arms.

'Hello there, little one.' Sophie squatted down and let the little dog come towards her, sniffing her hand cautiously. 'Here for your injections, are you? Do you want to pop him up on the table for me?'

Sophie waited as his owner did so.

'Right then, let's get you sorted.'

The morning passed by in a flash. Grace, the other vet nurse, popped back and forth giving her a hand between her own jobs, clearly wanting to make sure she wasn't feeling out of her depth with a whole collection of new clients, which was sweet of her. The usual run of routine appointments, one huge soft-eyed German Shepherd dog who'd managed to get a piece of stick caught across the roof of her mouth, and a guinea pig who wasn't eating took her right up to the end of surgery. Mhairi closed the door and slid the bolt across, turning to look at Sophie with a triumphant grin.

'Well, it looks like you're a hit.'

'That's just as well,' said Thea, 'Or we'd be in a bit of trouble. How did it go?'

'Great,' said Sophie, smiling broadly. The clients had been friendly and welcoming, some chatting away and asking where she was from when they heard her northern accent. 'I had a really good morning.'

'I think that deserves a bit of lunch, don't you? Pub, everyone?'

Sophie felt her eyes widen. She'd been so used to disappearing off at lunchtime with a packet of sandwiches that the idea of being invited out was completely new. But where the team at Nick's place had always somehow made her feel like a bit of an out of place oddball, she seemed to be – welcome. It was a nice surprise.

'You're on,' said Mhairi, pushing the computer mouse away with relish. 'I could go a steak pie and chips after wrestling with that thing all morning.' She scowled at the computer.

'I thought you had it under control?' Thea's mouth curled into a smile. 'Well, relatively so. I didn't mention to Mrs James when she came in with her cat for a post-spay check-up that the screen was telling me that her budgie had an infection in one of his claws...'

Mhairi put a hand to her forehead. 'I thought I'd switched that round before anyone noticed.'

'Let's just call it teething problems,' said Thea, picking up her coat from the hook. 'Come on, lunch is on the practice.'

'In that case, I'm having sticky toffee pudding as well.' Mhairi pulled a grey and white striped fleece over her head.

The Applemore Hotel was warm and welcoming. A log fire was lit by their table and a window looked out onto the little harbour where a white-painted boat rocked gently on the waves.

'Take a seat,' said a tall, sandy haired man in a black apron, 'And I'll be with you in a sec.' He looked at Sophie for a moment and smiled. 'Aha, the new vet.'

Grace joined them at the table, having finished up some paperwork in the office before she left.

'Have a look at the menu,' said Thea, passing Sophie a freshly-printed sheet of paper. 'The burgers are amazing, but I warn you you'll need a napkin or you'll be greeting clients with melted cheese and sauce all down the front of your top this afternoon.'

Mhairi went up to the bar and got them some drinks while they scanned the menus. An old man in a green utility-style waistcoat looked over at Sophie and nodded a hello as she looked around, taking in her surroundings. He was sitting with his newspaper spread out at the bar, looking very much like part of the furniture.

'No Fiona,' he called across to Thea.

'No, she's down looking after her mum.' Thea tipped her head towards Mhairi. 'While the cat's away, and all that.'

'So I see,' he chuckled, returning to his paper.

'I'm Harry Robertson,' said the sandy haired man a moment later, arriving at the table with a sheaf of paper menus and a pen tucked in the pocket of his polo shirt. 'Nice to meet you. No doubt your arrival will be all round the village thanks to the jungle drums after a morning in the surgery. How's it going?'

'Good thanks,' said Sophie. 'Really good.'

The food was amazing. Heeding Thea's warning, she plumped on Mhairi's recommendation for the famous steak pie and chips which was huge, and utterly delicious.

'It's a shame Fiona isn't here. Anyway, she's treated us to lunch which is something.' Thea said, wiping her mouth with a napkin. 'And Sophie hasn't headed for the hills yet, which is another.' She grinned.

'Were you all expecting me to?' Sophie laughed.

Thea shook her head. 'No, but it's a bit of a shock to the system I expect, coming from a big town practice to a place like this. It was a bit of a struggle to get anyone interested in the job because there are so many preconceived ideas about what a small village practice will entail.'

'In what way?' Mhairi said, looking interested.

'I think a lot of people are intimidated,' explained Thea. 'They assume that with only two full time vets they're going to be run off their feet. It's an easy mistake to make.'

'Ah,' Sophie moved sideways to allow a pink-haired girl to take away their empty plates, smiling a thank you as she did so, 'I think you did quite a good job of explaining that wouldn't be the case when we were doing the interview.'

'Yeah, we're lucky to share on-call with the other two practices nearby. I was reading an article about a vet on one of the islands who operates on a solo basis. She's on call 24/7, every single day of the year.'

Grace tutted and shook her head. 'No way on this earth you'd get me signing up for that. My husband does the on-call fire work and that's enough. I tell you, that pager only ever goes off if we've got something planned.'

'Talking of plans,' said Mhairi, finishing her orange juice, 'There's an art class starting up at the gallery soon. I've tried to persuade Grace to come along, but she said that she hasn't picked up a pencil since school and that must be about ninety million years ago.'

Grace swiped jokingly at Mhairi's head. 'Watch your cheek, lassie.'

'Do you fancy it?' Mhairi looked at Sophie, her expression eager. Sophie shook her head.

'I'm with Grace on this one.' Sophie made a face.

'You're not that old,' said Mhairi, artlessly.

'You're not helping yourself,' said Thea, shaking her head as she laughed. She glanced up at the clock over the bar. 'We'd better get a wriggle on, or it will be afternoon surgery before we know it.'

'Seriously though,' said Mhairi, young and enthusiastic, as they walked back along the street towards the surgery, 'Have a think about it. It'd be nice for you to have something to do in the evenings.'

'You make it sound like she needs a carer, like Fiona's mum,' Grace snorted. 'Honestly you young things. Sophie's hardly over the hill, and I'm perfectly sure she's got more than enough to keep her occupied in the evenings.'

'Something like that,' said Sophie, never more grateful to have made it back to the surgery than she was that moment. She unwrapped her scarf and put it back on the hook again, heading for the computer to type up her notes from the morning's surgery. She checked her phone and replied to a couple of messages from Bea and Tabby asking how her first day was going, relieved that she could answer truthfully that it was going pretty well...

Back home at the cottage that evening, she kicked off her shoes and flopped down on the sofa. She'd got home and switched on the lights, turning on the television for some company and background noise as she shoved a ready meal in the oven to warm up. Laying her head back against the striped navy and white cushions, she watched the flames dancing in the log burner, feeling quite impressed with herself that she'd managed once again to get it to light. The room was spacious and tastefully decorated in pale creams and shades of blue, with heavy navy curtains which skimmed the varnished wooden floorboards. It was all very lovely, if a little over the top in size just for one person. She closed her eyes for a moment. It had been a long day, but she'd made it to the end in one piece.

CHAPTER ELEVEN

Sophie woke with a start. It was freezing cold – the log fire had long cooled, and the television show she'd turned on hours before had reverted to the shopping channel with a notification asking her if she was *still* watching and informing her that if she didn't click the button the screen would go into sleep mode in a matter of minutes. Jumping off the sofa, she headed for the kitchen where the ready meal she'd chosen had turned into a dried out, blackened disc in a foil tray. Well, it was lucky that she was too tired to be hungry. She switched off the oven, tossed the burnt offering into the pristine Belfast sink and headed up to bed, making doubly sure she'd set her alarm for the morning.

'No surgery today,' said Thea, cheerily, when she walked into work. 'We don't do a huge amount of large animal work really, because most of it is scooped up by Parker and Maclaren in town. But there's an old guard who've been with the practice since it was owned by Fiona's dad, and they've stayed loyal.'

Sophie suppressed a yawn and rubbed her face. The alarm

had been a bit of a rude awakening, and she'd had to drag herself out of bed and into the shower, feeling a bit like Tabby must have done every day when she'd been extracted from bed and lured downstairs with the promise of coffee and her favourite almond croissants. There was no such luxury for Sophie, though – she'd had to make do with an instant coffee mixed in her travel mug and shoved in the cup holder as she drove the five miles back into Applemore from the cottage. She'd looked up the hill as she'd reached the end of the track, seeing a plume of grey smoke twisting into the air above the chimney of the white cottage that belonged to her neighbour with the unruly dogs.

'So I thought it'd be a good chance for you to come out with me,' Thea said, bringing her back to the present moment. 'Fiona's on her way back this afternoon apparently, so we can have a proper catch up then – and meanwhile it'll be good for you to get to know some of the large animal clients, just in case you end up dealing with them if I'm off sick or whatever.'

Sophie tried to arrange her face into a suitably enthusiastic impression. She could have done with a nice morning doing what she did best, i.e. treating small and manageable animals, and not having to fake it in large animal practice.

'That sounds great,' she said, hoping the smile she was displaying was less of a rictus than it felt.

'Here you are,' said Grace, a moment later, returning from the stockroom with a couple of plastic wrapped packages. 'Another practice sweatshirt and a fleece – you'll need that today, mind, it's chilly out there. Feels more like winter than spring to me.'

'Thanks.' Sophie unwrapped the sweatshirt and pulled it over her head, then tossed the packaging into the bin under the desk. 'Are we going now?'

Thea nodded. 'No time like the present. We'll go to Kirsty's place first,' she instructed Mhairi, 'If you want to give her a ring and let her know we're on the way?'

Thea's Land Rover was splattered with mud and the inside was covered in dog hair. A black spaniel was lying belly up on the driver's seat wagging his tail.

'In the back, you.' Thea rubbed him on the tummy and he jumped upright, tail end wagging furiously as he wriggled forward to meet Sophie, who rubbed his ears and let him sniff her fingers and lick her on the nose.

'This is Ted.'

'Oh hello,' Sophie said, laughing. 'Very nice to meet you.'

'He's ridiculous,' said Thea fondly, 'But he comes everywhere with me. Keeps me company when I'm working. My husband says there are three of us in our marriage – and I have to admit when I wake up in the middle of the night with a spaniel's bum in my face I do wonder who rules the roost. Wouldn't be without him though.' She posted Ted through the middle section of the car, clipping his harness into place.

'Have to be seen to be following the rules,' she explained. 'Last thing I need is a massive fine for having an unsecured dog floating about in the back.'

Sophie climbed into the passenger seat and followed suit, fastening her seatbelt as well.

Thea looked at her sideways. 'Reading between the lines – regardless of what you said at the interview – I get the feeling large animal isn't your thing?'

Sophie's eyes widened slightly in surprise and she looked out of the window as Thea pulled away, turning to drive her car back along past the harbour and turning by a little patch of grass where a couple in walking gear were sitting on a wooden picnic bench.

'I don't mind it,' she said. 'I'm just a bit out of practise, that's all.'

'Give me the back end of a cow over Mrs Jones's neurotic cat any day.' Thea grinned. 'Don't worry, I bet you'll be back in the swing of it in no time.'

'I'm sure I will,' said Sophie, trying to sound more convincing than she felt.

'Nice easy start anyway,' said Thea. 'It's jabs time up at the stables. Do you ride?'

'I haven't for ages, but I used to before I had my daughter.'

'Well, you've got loads of time now,' said Thea, turning up a hill which was flanked on either side by tall banks. 'You can have a word with Kirsty while we're here.'

Art classes last night, riding lessons today. Bea had jokingly suggested she sign up for an evening class so she didn't get bored. It felt like the universe was playing tricks.

She looked out of the window as the banks dipped away to reveal wooden post and rail fencing and a field full of sturdy grey Highland ponies.

'Here we are.' They parked in a neat gravelled space beside a stone barn. A black and white cat sat on a gatepost, watching them as they climbed out of the Land Rover and Thea handed Sophie the vet case, which was surprisingly heavy.

'You take this, I'll take the laptop and I can do the paperwork while we're going along. It's so much easier with two. I could do with my own PA, really.'

Sophie laughed. 'I think we all could. This job would be fine if it wasn't for the paperwork.'

'And the clients.' Thea pushed up her sleeves. 'Present company excepted, I should add. Kirsty's lovely.'

'Hello!' A girl in her thirties came towards them, parking a wheelbarrow outside a stone stable and brushing straw off her black jodhpurs. 'Beth, can you make sure everyone's ready?' She called across the stable yard and a moment later a tall black-haired girl scuttled past with an armful of colourful headcollars.

'I'm Kirsty. You must be the new vet?'

'Sophie.' She put out her hand for Kirsty to shake in greeting. 'Nice to meet you.'

'That's not an accent we hear round here very often. Manchester?'

'Lancashire.' Sophie had been asked by several people already. It was funny that up here they couldn't seem to tell the difference – but saying that, until she'd arrived in the Highlands she hadn't realised there was such a difference between the soft northern accent, and the far stronger dialect you heard from people on tv who came from places like Glasgow.

'That's a long way to come,' said Kirsty, setting out in the direction of the stables. A line of ponies were tied up outside, munching contentedly on stuffed nets full of hay.

'Sorry, we got caught up and the babies are still out in the paddock. Beth can bring them in while we get started on this lot.'

Sophie didn't have time to let her nerves take over. Thea flipped up the lid of her laptop and started logging the vaccinations as Sophie made her way along the row of ponies, saying hello to each one, giving them a scratch on the withers in greeting before rubbing gently and administering their annual vaccinations.

'Can you have a look at Mickey's hock while you're here? He got a kick in the field the other day and I've cleaned it out but it's a bit close to the joint.' Kirsty put a hand on the rump of a particularly solid, steel-grey pony. He flicked an ear back in her direction in acknowledgement. Sophie ran a hand along his back, and then squatted down, close to his body, ready to spring out of the way if he kicked out or flinched in pain as she palpated the limb and checked the wound over for signs of infection.

'Looks fine to me. You've cleaned it up well. We could give him a jab of antibiotics to be on the safe side,' she said, glancing at Thea for confirmation – it had been a long time, after all. Thea raised her eyebrows and gave the briefest of nods in agreement.

'But I think it should be fine.'

Thea had already gone into the bag and drawn up the antibiotics into a syringe, passing it over to Sophie. 'Sorry, my lovely,' Sophie said, giving him another pat. 'One more, I'm afraid.'

Mickey tossed his head, his long mane lifting in the air, and he gave a snort of disapproval. Sophie rubbed the white star on his forehead as an apology.

'Oh he loves that,' said Kirsty. 'You'll have a friend for life, now.'

'I was just saying Sophie should get out for a ride now she's here,' said Thea, as they worked their way along the next row of youngsters.

'Oh any time,' said Kirsty, cheerfully. 'I've got all this lot to get fit for the summer season. I don't have enough hours in the day to ride them all, and even with the lassies that come up after school I'm still always looking for willing volunteers.'

'That would be lovely,' said Sophie, realising she meant it and wasn't just being polite.

Half an hour later, Sophie and Thea were loading up the Land Rover when Kirsty rushed over, putting a card in Sophie's hand.

'Here,' she said, brushing her hair out of her eyes and squinting in the low sunlight. 'Give me a shout any time. I mean it.'

'That wasn't too painful after all,' said Thea as they headed down the single track road a while later. She looked over at Sophie who was holding the card in her hand, the other patting Ted on the top of his head as he poked his head between their seats, tongue lolling.

'It was lovely to get out,' agreed Sophie. 'Where next?'

'We've got a lamb with a broken leg at the Bannach Steading, then I promised Old Jimmy we'd drop by and check how he's doing for calving.'

The lamb was adorably cute, and the owners of the steading – a couple who'd moved from Inverness to start a little regenerative farm – were delighted to meet her. It was all going swimmingly.

'Jimmy's place next and then we can head back.'

Old Jimmy's farm turned out to be the sort of place that had terrified a younger Sophie when she was on her placement during her vet degree at university. They parked in a farmyard which was covered in a layer of thick black muck, and squelched through a narrow passageway between two massive dilapidated barns to a byre where what looked like about forty black and white cows were standing, their breath clouding, watching her with huge liquid brown eyes. The bottom dropped out of Sophie's stomach as she felt an enormous wave of impostor syndrome hit.

'Aye, this must be the new vet I've been hearing about,' said a voice behind her. Sophie turned to see a short, round man with grey hair which poked out from beneath a flat cap of indeterminate colour and age. His cheeks were ruddy and weather-beaten, as was his rather bulbous nose. He thrust his hands into a pair of dark work overalls and looked at her thoughtfully.

'Hello,' she said, trying to sound professional and confident.

'Cannae believe they had to bring you all the way up from

England,' he chuckled. 'Could you no' find a vet from round here?'

'Sophie was the best candidate for the job,' said Thea, stoutly, and in that moment Sophie could have hugged her. 'You took long enough to get your head around me starting, Jimmy. I thought you'd be getting used to new blood around here.'

Jimmy tutted. 'I swear the English are taking over. If it's no' Rob at Midsummer, it's Lachlan's other half – what's her name again? Ruth?'

'Rilla,' said Thea, shaking her head and laughing. 'And Rob's not even English, he's from Edinburgh.'

'Close enough,' said Jimmy, darkly. But as he narrowed his eyes and surveyed Sophie, she thought she could catch a glimmer of a twinkle in his eye, and a moment later he tipped his head in the direction of the cows. 'Right then, let's see what you think of this lot.'

All of the cows were due to calve imminently, and with any luck wouldn't need any help to do what nature expected of them. Once the checks were complete, Jimmy gave a brief nod and waved them off.

'Well, you've got his seal of approval,' said Thea, pretending to wipe sweat from her forehead.

'I have?' Sophie looked at her with eyes wide. 'That was approval?'

'Believe it or not, yes. I've had a text from Mhairi asking if we'll drop by Midsummer on the way back and check on Geoffrey. Apparently he's eaten something he shouldn't have.' Thea swung the vehicle round, taking a sharp left so they headed down a neatly kept driveway lined with nodding yellow daffodils.

At the top of the drive there was a gorgeous old Victorian house with blossom laden trees on either side. As they parked, a tall woman with long blonde hair tied up in a swinging ponytail emerged, an anxious expression on her face.

'Oh Thea, sorry, I know it's lunchtime.' She looked at Sophie for a moment and gave her a quick smile of welcome. 'But you know what he's like. I went out to the yard and discovered he'd eaten not just a tea towel but some of the washing line and probably a couple of pegs as well. I swear, that bloody goat will be the death of me.'

She led them round the side of the house, past a beautifully kept raised kitchen garden and through a rose arch into a gravelled yard where Sophie was surprised to see a huge set of adapted play equipment on a rubber-floored enclosure fenced with colourful wooden posts.

'Midsummer is a respite house,' Thea explained as the woman disappeared into a stable with a green-painted door. 'It's for families who have children with life-limiting illnesses to come and stay. Charlotte and her husband Rob run it.'

A moment later Charlotte returned with a slightly sorry-for-himself looking white billy goat on a lead rope. 'Here he is.'

Without thinking, Sophie took her stethoscope from round her neck and examined the goat, listening for gut sounds and then taking his temperature while Charlotte chided him for trying to nibble the lead rope.

'You've eaten more than enough already today, you monster.' She scratched him on the forehead and he butted her gently before shaking his head and looking at Sophie thoughtfully.

'What's the verdict?' Charlotte was chewing her lip, her pale freckled face tense with concern.

'It all sounds fine to me,' said Sophie, putting a hand on Geoffrey's jutting hip bones for a moment. She'd forgotten how coarse their hair was, and what an odd, ungainly shape goats were. 'I'd keep him in the stable for tonight, make sure everything's still passing through, but I suspect it's nothing to worry about.'

Charlotte gave a huge sigh. 'Well, that's a relief. I have no idea how this creature managed to worm his way into my affections, but I don't know what I'd do if anything happened to him. Even if he is a complete pest, and he absolutely honks.'

She led him back into the stable. Thea turned to Sophie and looked at her with a rather pleased-with-herself expression on her face.

'What is it?' Sophie adjusted the stethoscope around her neck.

'Oh, nothing.' Thea grinned. 'I had a feeling, that's all, and I've been proved right.'

Sophie scratched her head in confusion. 'About what?'

'One morning back on the field, so to speak, and you've completely forgotten your worries about large animal practice.'

'Oh!' Surprised at herself, Sophie burst out laughing. 'You're right.'

'You can't keep a good vet down, my dad always said. I guess he was right.'

'What are you two looking so happy about?' Charlotte reappeared a second later, hanging Geoffrey's collar on a peg outside the stable door.

'Oh, nothing,' Thea chuckled. 'Anyway, now we've got the goat based drama over with, I should introduce you. Charlotte Fraser, this is Sophie Jones, our new vet.'

'Ohh,' said Sophie. 'You're one of the Frasers.'

'For my sins,' said Charlotte, wryly. 'That sounds slightly ominous. Thea, have you been telling terrible tales about us?'

Thea shook her head. 'Not a word.'

'Grace the vet nurse said there were lots of you, that's all.'

Sophie tried to cover her tracks slightly. What Grace had actually said was that they once owned half the village and they were lovely and not at all posh, considering.

'Considering what?' Thea snorted with laughter as Sophie explained on the way back to the surgery.

'I have no idea.'

'Well, they've all been lovely in my experience. I mean I did jump the gun a bit and assume she and Rob were married when they'd only just met, but that's going back a few years now. And now they are married, so maybe I missed my calling as a psychic.'

Back at the surgery, Mhairi was swinging back and forth on her office chair, a pen in her mouth as she stared, lost in thought, at the computer screen. She looked up after a moment as Sophie and Thea took off their coats.

'Good morning?'

'Really good,' said Sophie, heading for the stockroom where she was going to have a good look around and get to grips where everything was while they were free of clients. She stopped halfway across the room and turned back to look at Mhairi for a moment. In for a penny, she decided.

'I've been thinking,' she said, 'And if you're still up for it I'd love to come to the art class. I might as well try something new.'

If she could get her head around a morning like that, she could manage to push herself out of her comfort zone and try something new. She didn't have to love it, after all, she just had to give it a go. After all, what was the worst that could happen?

CHAPTER TWELVE

Mel hitched herself cautiously up onto the sofa, wincing as she did so.

'Careful,' said Fee, looking at her girlfriend in concern. 'You see what I mean, though. She's hardly in a position to start giving a class when she can't even sit up without being in agony.'

'I'm sure I'd be fine,' protested Mel. She pushed her hair out of her eyes and looked over at them, the sling which was holding her arm in place dragging her shirt collar so she looked decidedly rumpled and untidy and not at all her usual chic, arty self.

Ben groaned and pushed a hand through his hair out of habit. He'd been to the barber so there was rather less of it than he was expecting, and when he ran a hand across his cheek the beard – which had been verging on reaching wild man of Borneo status – was close cropped and tidy under his fingers.

'Believe me, my desire to teach a load of pensioners about perspective is so small as to be virtually invisible. In fact I could take my desire and use it as an exercise in perspective.' He laughed at his own terrible joke.

Fee glanced over at Mel, who had shuffled herself up and was clearly trying to look as if she wasn't in tremendous discomfort - and failing badly.

'Don't worry,' said Ben, 'I'll take one for the team.'

'You are an angel.' Mel beamed up at him as he sat down on the edge of the sofa, shaking his head as Fee waggled the kettle at him to ask if he wanted a coffee.

'You're alright, thanks. I'm going to the pub for the quiz night so I'll save myself for the regulation pint of beer, unless I find someone willing to give me a lift home on their tractor.'

'Don't joke about it. Remember that night young Jimmy took you and Rob back on the trailer and Rob nearly fell out going round the corner by the fire shed?' Mel giggled.

'I assure you there will definitely not be a repeat performance of that night. I had a hangover for about a week. I'm too old for that sort of thing these days.'

'You're the same age as me,' scoffed Fee. 'Don't be ridiculous.'

Ben looked at Fee for a moment as she turned back to spoon coffee into mugs. Sturdy and sensible with salt and pepper grey hair, she seemed somehow ageless and at the same time as if she'd been middle-aged since she was about fifteen. She ran Charlotte's holiday cottage business with a brisk efficiency, which was in complete contrast to the way she doted over Mel, who was petite and elfin in contrast, and who would probably look about twenty-five when she was fifty.

'I'm not doing it all by myself,' he admitted, and suppressed a sigh of relief. 'I'm sure I can get someone roped in to help.'

'Told you,' said Fee, turning to her girlfriend and folding her arms.

'Oh Ben, you're brilliant.' Mel looked slightly damp eyed.

'Steady on,' said Fee, laughing. 'It's the pain relief,' she said in a mock whisper to him. 'It's sent her a bit doolally.'

'Excuse me,' said Mel, stoutly. 'I have all my faculties, thanks very much. And to prove it I'll send you through the lesson plans on an email later.'

'Lesson plans?' He raised his eyebrows.

'Of course. How were you planning to teach them?' Mel narrowed her eyes and looked at him for a moment before he replied.

'I – well, I dunno.' He shrugged. 'I think I was just going to wing it.'

'That sounds like a recipe for a complete disaster. Anyway, you don't have to worry. I'll zoom them over later. You can read them in the morning when you're nursing your non-existent hangover.'

Fee chuckled and strolled across the room, sitting down beside Mel and carefully handing her a cup of coffee into her non-bandaged hand.

'Right, well, I'd better get off. I've got a pub quiz to win.'

'First time for everything.'

'Too right.' Ben stood up and waved goodbye, heading out into the crisp spring evening. The moon was hanging in the sky, and beside it Jupiter was glowing brightly. Quiz night was always busy at the Applemore Hotel and he could see a string of customers heading inside. As the door opened, music leaked out – a band was playing a set of covers, and when he walked into the pub he was greeted by a shout from Rob, who was standing by the bar with a pint of beer in his hand.

'I'll get you one,' he shouted, 'Lachlan's here already. We've got the usual table.'

The tables had been reorganised as usual and he nodded hello to familiar faces as he headed to the far side of the room, tucking himself in at the back corner where he could see what was going on without getting caught up in a load of unnecessary chit-chat with people like Dolina, the village gossip, who'd be dying to know how Mel was and would no doubt have already heard that he'd been in to visit her.

'How's it going?' Rob returned, putting a tray of beers down on the table. 'The girls are on the way, apparently. Some problem over at the outdoor centre – a leak, or something. I swear everything goes at the same time. We should have been plumbers, we'd be making a fortune.'

'Not really one of your problems,' grinned Ben, teasing Jack, who came from a very well off family and had made a fortune of his own.

'The rate we're spending on the new hotel, it is.'

'How's it going?'

'Expensively.' Jack laughed. 'But with this place, the hotel gastropub, and the new one at least we can't say we're bored or short of things to do.'

Ben took a sip of his beer and watched as his friend Lachlan headed across towards them. Jack had settled into village life in his own way – very different from his. He'd been happy to live a low key, back to nature sort of existence, far from the big flat he'd lived in when he was with Liz. That had been a huge conversion in an old mill overlooking the town – the sort of place Jack had probably bought and sold in his old life.

'Is this one of yours?' Ben looked up at Lachlan. Lachlan made a face as he lifted the glass to his mouth to take a sip.

Lachlan ducked his head with a grin. 'Depends what you think of it. If it's amazing, yes, if it tastes like dishwater, it's nothing to do with Applemore Brewery.'

He pretended to choke. 'Kidding. It's great.'

'That's a relief. Harry said it was a new barrel and we've

had a couple of dodgy ones this week.' Lachlan, self-effacing and easy going, flopped back against the chair in mock-relief.

People fascinated Ben. If you hadn't known, you'd assume that Rob was the Laird of Applemore. He always looked well dressed, not in an over-the-top way – but there was something in the clothes he wore which just subtly suggested money and power. Lachlan, on the other hand, was wearing an old woollen sweater with a frayed sleeve, rips in his jeans and a pair of battered old work boots. Living in Applemore for the last few years had taught him that you couldn't ever judge on first appearances. Lachlan might not look the part, but he'd inherited the title, the old house and what was left of the estate when his father had died a few years back.

'So what's happening with you?'

Ben took another sip of beer and wiped the foam from his beard before catching them up on the news. He was touched by how delighted they all were to hear that the bus trip to the gallery had resulted in some decent sales.

'And one of the couples that was in liked the big piece I did so much that they've commissioned another.'

Rob nodded, impressed. 'How's our one coming on?'

'Another week I reckon and I'll be done.' Ben traced a finger along his lip, thinking.

'Excellent. I think it'll finish off the restaurant really well. So you guys did alright out of this bus trip thing?' Rob looked at Lachlan and Ben.

'I think it was a hit all round. Polly did well with the shop takings that day and the boys were over the moon about the café.' Lachlan sat back in his chair, raising an arm to wave a hello as he spotted his girlfriend Rilla and his sister Polly arriving. The pub was getting busy now, filling the room with a hubbub of chatter as locals gathered to catch up on the news and gossip before the quiz.

'No doubt we'll have someone grumbling about traffic on the village Facebook page but by all accounts it's been a hit all round.' Ben laughed.

'Talking of which, they're still going on about the mysterious driver who knocked into the crossroad sign.' Rob cocked his head, raising an eyebrow.

'Oh, this place loves a mystery. Probably someone who took the corner too fast. They're lucky they didn't end up in the field with Jimmy's cows.' Ben looked out of the window, raising a hand in greeting to one of the other artists from the gallery who was heading into the quiz.

'We need to get in on it too,' Rob said, thoughtfully. 'Once the weather is nicer, hopefully we can lure them down to the seafood shack.'

'Not a bad idea. We've got to keep finding ways to bring money into the area so we can keep people in jobs.' Ben looked up as the women arrived at the table. Polly ruffled her brother's hair, making him laugh. Rilla leaned over, dropping a kiss on the top of her partner's head before she sat down, tossing her coat onto the window ledge.

'Shove over,' said Polly, catching the end of the conversation. 'And tell me who are we keeping in jobs?'

'Anyone who wants one.' Rob laughed. 'Seriously though, if we don't want this place dying, we need young people coming here – or staying.'

'You came up here,' said Rilla, 'And me, too. And Ben.' She leaned over to give Lachlan another kiss, her dark curls falling over her face as she did so. She pushed them back, tucking her hair behind her ears and taking a sip of the drink that was waiting for her.

'Oh that's heaven. Yeah, anyway, as I was saying, we came up.'

'We're not exactly young blood,' grinned Rob.

'Speak for yourself.' Rilla giggled. 'Ben and I are in the prime of life, aren't we?'

'Something like that.' Ben rolled his eyes. 'It's not a bad idea to try and get some of the youngsters to think about coming to live here, or to come back after uni.'

As the quiz began, Esther, and what she was going to do when she graduated in a few months wasn't far from his thoughts. It was strange how kids left home by degrees – they disappeared off to university, and then slowly but surely never really came back. Her bedroom up at the croft had been sitting untouched since her last visit. He went in to tidy up and run around it with the vacuum – which had never really been his strong point, if he was honest – but other than that it felt like a shrine to the girl she'd been when he and Liz had split up. Maybe he needed to have a chat with her when she came up next, see if they could do it up a bit and make it somewhere she'd still feel felt like home. He took another mouthful of beer, just as Rob noticed his glass was empty and motioned to ask if he wanted another.

'No,' he shook his head. 'I'll just have a coke. I've got tons to do in the morning and I'm driving.'

'You alright, Ben?' Polly nudged him with her shoulder. 'You're quiet tonight.'

He shook himself out of his reverie. 'Just thinking about work,' he said, leaning over to look at the quiz sheet. So far, they'd managed to identify two out of the ten mystery faces so things were not looking good.

'Talking of work,' said Polly, in her clear, carrying voice, just as the quiz master stopped speaking so everyone in the room seemed to turn around and look at her. 'I hear you'll be teaching the art class now Mel's incapacitated.'

Lachlan gave a snort of amusement, knowing how he'd feel about it. Ben caught his eye and mouthed 'help me'.

'I bet you'll be amazing,' said Charlotte, who'd arrived a little while before and squashed herself into a gap between her brother and Rob. She was sitting with her hand on Rob's knee, laughing. 'I might come along.'

'Don't you dare.' Ben raised a finger in warning.

'Beth was saying she's doing some flowers for you,' Charlotte went on, a mischievous sparkle in her eye. 'We could make it a family affair and all come.'

'Don't be mean,' said Polly, giggling.

'If you lot turn up,' warned Ben, 'I swear I'll put you in separate corners of the room like naughty children.'

Polly echoed his words in a terrible imitation of his Lancashire accent.

'That is exactly what I'm talking about, Fraser.' He shook his head. 'I am no teacher, and I feel sorry for anyone who's subjected to me trying to show them how to paint anything other than a plain white wall.'

'You could always do that and call it modern art,' said Charlotte, helpfully.

He groaned. 'You lot are worse than useless.'

Driving home, though, he was glad he'd made the effort to go out. It was easy to get so caught up in the routine of work – home that he often found that when he did speak to Esther, she joked that he was going to wear a track between the croft and the gallery as that was all he ever did. Maybe, he admitted to himself grudgingly, teaching this art class might not be the worst thing he'd ever done.

CHAPTER THIRTEEN

Saturday morning surgery was a brief one. Sophie prescribed some worming pills for an elderly cat, caught up with some paperwork while Mhairi battled with the computer behind the reception desk and Grace cleaned the cage room as it was empty, and then just as they were about to close the doors the man in the green gilet who'd said hello in the hotel the other day rushed towards her, a worried expression on his face. He was carrying a small brown terrier who had a furious expression on his face. As soon as he stopped walking, the dog wriggled so vigorously that his owner had no choice but to let him down onto the ground where he shook himself hard and reasserted his authority by peeing on the door frame.

'Have you a minute to look at Jock?'

'Of course.' Sophie stepped back to usher him inside. 'How can I help?'

Mhairi looked up from the computer screen.

'Hello, Murdo, how are you?'

'No bad,' he said hurriedly, 'But wee Jock has had an accident or something and – well, you know how it is with dogs.'

Mhairi caught Sophie's eye briefly. It was funny how the gruffest of men could be reduced to a puddle when it came to their animals.

'He went down a rabbit hole this morning when I was up on the moor giving him a walk, and when he came back out, he was limping. I don't want to make a fuss but...'

'Don't worry,' said Sophie, kindly. She bent down on her knees to give the rough-coated Jock a scratch on his chest, and noticed that his owner had followed her down despite the fact that it was clearly quite an effort for him. He looked at her anxiously, his brow furrowed in concern and his mouth twisted sideways.

'Let's take you through to the exam room, little man, and we'll have a look at you properly.'

Jock was standing with his near foreleg up in the air slightly, and an expression on his face which suggested that he was far too busy for such nonsense.

'Do you want me to carry him?'

'I think he can make it on his own steam.' Sophie said with a smile. She opened the examination room door and waited as Jock was lifted onto the table.

'Right then, let's have a look at you.'

Sophie did the standard checks, looking inside his mouth and eyes, running a hand down his spine, checking for any signs of discomfort.

'All looks good there,' she said, to reassure him. She watched as his shoulders dropped noticeably. 'Let me have a little feel of this leg.'

She ran a careful hand down the little dog's leg, feeling through the thick fur for any signs of heat or swelling, and then –

'Ah, that'll be the culprit, I suspect.' She let go and went over to the side, selecting a pair of tweezers. With a gentle tug, she removed a large black thorn from just above his pad and held it out to show his owner. 'That'll feel a lot better, won't it, Jock?'

Jock wriggled under her hands and turned to give her a lick, as if to thank her.

'A thorn.' His owner shook his head. 'For goodness sake, I thought he'd broken something the way he was carrying himself.'

'I should think a thorn that big would be quite painful, wouldn't it, Jock?'

Jock's little stumpy tail wagged.

'Well now don't I feel like the prize idiot.'

'We're all the same when it comes to our animals,' said Sophie, laughing.

'Aye,' he said, 'I didn't even say hello properly. I'm Murdo,' he extended a hand, formally. 'How are you settling in?'

'Very well, thank you.' Sophie clipped the hair around the site of the thorn and cleaned it. 'Everyone has been lovely. I'm looking forward to having a chance to explore now it's the weekend.'

'You hit the ground running right enough,' nodded Murdo. 'I suppose that's better than getting here and having nothing to do.'

'Keeps me out of mischief,' she agreed, laughing. 'Keep an eye on that, and if it gets warm at all or he seems to be favouring the leg, come back and see me, but I can't see it being a problem. It was just a thorn, after all.'

'Don't rub it in,' chuckled Murdo. 'I'm going to look like a right Jessie when this gets out. Greta my wife always says I'm far too soft when it comes to this wee dog.'

'He's a lovely little dog,' reassured Sophie. 'And you were right to check. It could easily have been something far worse. That's the trouble with terriers, they have a habit of disappearing down holes and you've no idea what they'll encounter. I treated one that had been bitten by a badger, once. That was nasty. There you go, little one, that's you all done.' She rubbed him behind the ears one final time.

'Have you a dog yourself?' Murdo said, as Sophie motioned to him that he was free to take Jock back down.

Sophie shook her head.

'A vet needs a dog, I think. You need to speak to Janine who does the dog rescues, she's always looking for homes for the ones she gets in. She has some come all the way from Bulgaria.'

'Really?' Sophie paused by the reception desk where Mhairi was waiting. Murdo took out his wallet and paid.

'Mind and speak to Janine,' he said as she closed the surgery door behind him and locked it. 'A vet needs a dog.'

'That's you told,' said Mhairi, giggling. 'I'm cats all the way. I mean, I love all animals,' she added quickly, 'Obviously, or I wouldn't be working here, but I'm a cat person.'

'I'd worked that out.' Sophie indicated the Hello Kitty t-shirt Mhairi was wearing, and the postcards and photographs that were tucked all around the walls of her desk.

'Ah yes,' Mhairi giggled. 'They're a bit of a giveaway.'

'My old cat is down in England with my friend,' Sophie said, with a wave of sudden homesickness. 'I must give her a call and see if we can do a cat Facetime call. He wasn't keen the last time – she tried to get him on screen and he stalked off in disgust.'

'That's cats for you,' said Mhairi wisely.

'It really is.'

Once they'd locked up, Sophie headed back to the car. The sun was shining brightly and the sky was a vibrant cerulean blue. If you stood out of the wind, it almost felt quite warm. What she needed was to pick up some food, and then work out what she was going to do with herself for the rest of the weekend. It was weird to be so completely at a loose end, and the little wave of homesickness she'd felt was in danger of becoming a huge tsunami if she didn't do something to squash it. Maybe she'd head up to the Farm Shop and see what all the fuss was about. Everyone seemed to think it was amazing, but so far she'd only managed to pop into the little mini supermarket and wander down the high street of Applemore, such as it was.

She paused for a second, sitting in the driver's seat and watching people pass by. Saturday mornings were clearly a busy time in the village. A stream of small children wandered past with their parents, dressed in ballet outfits or football kit respectively, disappearing into the shop and emerging with colourful comics in hand or carrying a pack of crisps and a sweet after their busy activities. This wasn't helping the homesickness at all – now all she could think about was walking hand in hand with Tabby after her football matches on a Saturday morning, heading to Bea's café where they'd sit chatting and drinking huge cream-covered hot chocolates. Now Tabby was fast asleep half a world away, resting before the first big game of the season which was going to be streamed live online by the university football league. At least later that day she'd be able to see her, even if it was as a tiny figure on a computer screen.

She shook herself. This was ridiculous.

Starting the engine, she checked Google maps to see which direction she should be heading in, and set off for Applemore Farm Shop to see what all the fuss was about.

The road wound up out of the village. She slowed to overtake a woman on a huge bay horse who was leading a tiny pony beside her on a leading rein, with a very determined looking little girl on his back. The woman nodded a thank you and the little girl did the same, making Sophie smile. And then just as the sat nav instructed her to turn, she saw a big, beautifully hand-painted wooden sign which announced that she'd arrived.

Welcome to Applemore
Farm Shop
Wild Camping
Gallery
Café
Artisan Bakery

And lots more someone had scribbled underneath in chalk pen. The Fraser family really seemed to have cornered the market. It was the sort of place that Bea would have loved – the drive was neatly mown and covered in dancing daffodils and tiny colourful crocuses, with huge, shaggy rhododendron bushes dotted along beside old-fashioned metal fencing, behind which grazed some very pretty Highland cattle.

The car park was packed with a mixture of old bangers and some very expensive looking 4x4s which gleamed in the sunlight.

People were sitting at the tables, coats on against the chilly wind, but clearly enjoying the sunshine and the beginnings of spring. She parked the car and wandered into the courtyard. A huge archway, which had clearly once been for the carriages of the big house, was now glazed and decorated with tiny sparkling lights which shone in a welcoming manner. She caught a whiff of freshly baked bread and her stomach growled. It had been a long time since her coffee that morning, and she hadn't eaten. Maybe the first stop should be the café, to try some of the famous bagels that were baked on the premises.

Outside the door of the shop there was a wooden stand on which stood rows of aluminium buckets, each one crammed full of colourful tulips, narcissi and sweet-scented hyacinths which were wrapped in brown paper.

'Pretty, aren't they?' said a blond-haired woman in a blue and white striped Breton top with an apron tied around her waist. She smiled briefly, then bent down to reorganise the buckets, sprucing up the display and picking up a couple of discarded brown paper tags price which had come loose.

'Gorgeous,' agreed Sophie.

'Let me know if you need any help with anything,' said the woman, smiling again. She looked vaguely familiar, but Sophie couldn't think where she'd seen her before.

Inside the shop, she made her way past tumbling heaps of fresh fruit and vegetables and turned left in through the archway that led to the bustling café. For a moment the sound of the coffee machine steaming and the clatter of crockery made her feel a desperate homesick longing for Bea's place, but she squared her shoulders and headed over to the counter, joining the end of the queue and looking up at the menu, neatly written on chalk pen on a board above the counter.

'Hello lovely,' said the man behind the counter, surprising her with a strong Welsh accent, 'What can I get you?'

'I'll have a flat white, please, and a bagel with smoked salmon and cream cheese.'

'No probs,' he said, passing the order back to a teenage girl with shiny black hair and a ring through her eyebrow. 'Anything else? Can I tempt you to one of Anna's brownies? They're famous around these parts.'

'Funnily enough I've heard of them already,' laughed Sophie. 'Go on then, I'll take a couple – one for now and one for later.'

'Nice to see our reputation is travelling far and wide,' he

said, as he passed her a coffee a couple of moments later. 'I'll get Libby to bring your bagel over.'

A young couple with a baby in a pushchair were just leaving a little table which was tucked in a corner next to a window. Sophie helped by moving a chair out of the way as they manoeuvred their way through the narrow space between the tables, then sat down and took off her coat just as the bagel and brownie arrived, delivered with a smile by Libby.

'Here you are,' she said in the lovely soft Highland accent that Sophie was still adjusting to. 'Can I get you anything else?'

'No, but that's great, thanks.'

Libby tucked in the chair opposite Sophie and headed back across the café. Sophie smiled to herself at the fact that she must look so determinedly single that it didn't even occur to the teenager that there might be someone else joining her. It had been so long that she'd almost forgotten what it was like to have someone else. After last time, though – she tipped brown sugar from the little packet into her coffee – it was probably just as well.

CHAPTER FOURTEEN

Sophie spent the latter half of the afternoon glued to the screen of her laptop, watching coverage of the game which was being live streamed by the University football league. Over in Atlanta the sun was beating down on the football field – Tabby had texted on the coach across town to tell her that she was already melting and it was expected to reach 26 degrees in the afternoon.

Make sure you drink lots of water, Sophie had written.

Gallons. I feel sick with nerves and now I'm all sloshy. Better stop looking at my phone or I'll get car sick!!

Poor Tabby. She'd always been the same in anything with wheels. Goodness knows how she'd manage if she came up here to visit. Sophie hadn't really thought that part through. She'd been unpacking her few things after work on Friday, arranging them in the big white-painted wardrobe in the bedroom and putting her underwear into the drawers (thinking as she did so that at some point she really ought to splash out on some new stuff, instead of the greying scraps she'd had forever) and it had struck her with a wave of panic that she'd upended her entire life on a whim. She'd felt quite seasick at the thought, and only felt vaguely normal again after going outside into the strange pale light of the evening dusk and watching the waves crashing on the shore.

The first game was over – and no sign yet of Tabby's team. She headed back to the kitchen, making herself a cup of tea and unwrapping the chocolate brownie from its brown paper wrapping, hesitating for a moment before taking one of the pretty grey and white striped plates out of the cupboard and putting the brownie on it. Might as well make an effort to stay relatively civilised, even if she was living up here with no chance of visitors besides the occasional hello in passing from Annie, who had been true to her word and hadn't popped by or got in her hair at all.

She picked up her phone out of habit to check and see if there was a message from anyone – then put it down, shaking her head at herself. Tabby of course couldn't send her one, because her phone would be safely locked away with her things in the locker room. Bea would be right in the middle of the end-of-day rush, when shoppers always decided at the last moment that what they needed before they headed home was a quick coffee and something sweet to pick them up. She scrolled through the WhatsApp group for her old job, catching up on what had been happening – the usual teasing, in-jokes between the younger girls and haggling over shift swaps. She'd only done a few days but she was already more surefooted at the Applemore Vets than she'd been after all those years at Nick's place. Everyone seemed almost unnervingly nice, pleasant and positive. Maybe they'd all show their true colours next week and it would turn out to be a complete disaster.

She bit into the chocolate brownie and hit the volume button as the camera panned shakily across the field to two teams, one in green and white stripes (they looked rather like old-fashioned seaside deckchairs, she thought, with a giggle) and the other in Tabby's away strip of red shirt and black shorts. There she was! Her heart gave a huge lurch as she saw her darling baby girl – not a baby now at all, but long-limbed and tall all, 5 foot 10 inches of her. Tabby turned to the girl next to her who pushed a long braided ponytail back over her shoulder and gave a broad grin and looked directly into the camera. Somewhere out there her parents were probably feeling the same complicated mixture of pride and longing… or maybe they were out there sitting waiting to watch their daughter play.

Sophie hadn't had the first clue about football when Tabby had come home, aged seven, and informed her that she'd scored a goal at lunchtime and that she didn't want to go to ballet any more, she wanted to go to football on a Saturday morning like her friend George. She'd gone along and stood by the side-lines in the freezing cold, drinking coffee and listening to the raucous cheers of the other parents – mostly dads, it turned out. After the first couple of weekends she'd realised that the long padded coats that seemed to be some sort of uniform were in fact a defence against the freezing wind that whipped in off the Irish Sea, blowing the trees sideways and sending the ball off course and halfway into the next pitch at least once in every match.

Eventually she'd worked out the offside rule and even learned to love the game, supporting Tabby's beloved Liverpool FC alongside her and being accepted as one of the old guard as she moved her way up the ranks until she was talent-spotted and put forward for the chance to spend her university years in the US. And now here they were – Tabby had come home for Christmas full of stories of her experience living on campus and spending all hours on Facetime calling her new friends over in the states, while Sophie had hovered in the background trying not to feel sorry for herself because her little girl was growing up and away, which is after all exactly what she'd wished for. Being a parent was *so* confusing sometimes.

Still she had the promise of a trip to Atlanta in the summer to look forward to – and if the weather in spring was anything to go by, she'd better start stocking up on sun protection. It looked baking hot already, the players stopping midway through the goalless first half for a water break.

The second half flew by, with a win for the other team and Tabby's co-players trudging off the field looking dejected. It was nice to see the coach putting her arm around the shoulders of a couple of the girls and making a *chin up* gesture, then saying something that made them laugh.

You played really well, Sophie typed. *Message me later if you have time. Love you xxx*

The next morning she woke early. Lying under the pristine white covers, she looked around the room. There was a pretty line drawing of a couple of sleeping dogs – spaniels, it looked like – on the wall opposite, and a wooden carving sat on top of the chest of drawers, but other than her few bits and pieces the place looked like a show room. She'd unpacked, the house was clean – it was pretty hard to mess a place up when it was empty of belongings and there was only her in it – and it struck Sophie that if she didn't get out of bed and do something there was a distinct chance she might start wallowing – and that was never a good idea.

Showered and dressed half an hour later, she headed downstairs. She filled her travel mug with coffee and pulled on a fleece over her long-sleeved t-shirt. There was a whole new world out there to explore, after all.

She pulled the door closed and shoved the key in her

pocket, crunching down the stony path that led across the flower-sprinkled grass onto the white sands of the beach. On a spring day like today, somewhere as beautiful as this would have been packed with families playing and picnicking on the sand back home, but there wasn't a soul to be seen anywhere. She wandered along the beach towards the rocks, hoping that she might spot the seals again. Two were there, basking in the sunshine, far enough out to sea that she didn't seem to threaten them in any way. After a few minutes one plopped into the water with a splash, and a moment later she laughed as a little whiskered head popped up out of the water, seeming to stare straight at her.

'Nosy little things, aren't they?'

Sophie almost jumped out of her skin. She turned around, leaping to her feet, her sudden movement causing the other seal to splash into the safety of the water and disappear.

'Oh!' She put a hand to her chest. 'Sorry, you gave me a fright.' Her heart was thumping so hard that she thought it might leap out of her chest. Even after all this time, the old anxiety seemed always to be waiting to catch her out.

Annie was standing there, dressed somewhat incongruously in a faded purple cagoule and a pair of flowered trousers which looked like they'd come out of the ark. She gave a little chuckle. 'I thought you'd have heard me coming. You've gone native quickly.'

The confusion on Sophie's face must have been clear.

'Not expecting anyone else to be around,' Annie explained. 'I assume you're not used to having a place like this to yourself.'

'Not at all,' admitted Sophie. 'I was just thinking how busy this place would be back home. We've got a beach nearby, with an art installation on it – you might have heard of it, it's called Another Place?'

'Sir Antony Gormley,' nodded Annie. 'I've seen quite a few of his works. There's a lovely one in Winchester, where the figure stands in the crypt with his hands cupped. In winter, the crypt often floods so the water comes right up to his knees and his hands fill with water. It's a clever device.'

'I've never heard of that one. Is it the same as the figures on the beach?'

'Very similar. I like his work.' Annie put her hands on her hips, gazing out to sea. 'I haven't seen Another Place. I love the idea of all those figures looking out to sea,' she added.

'My daughter Tabby liked to take old clothes down – it's a bit of a standing joke in the area. The figures are often wrapped up in scarves or hats in winter. Sometimes they end up waist-deep in sand, depending on the tide. Tabby always giggled because they've got their willies on show.'

Annie chuckled again. 'I imagine that would appeal to a child's sense of humour.'

'Definitely in Tabby's case.'

'You must miss her.'

It wasn't a question but a statement.

'I do.' Sophie puffed out a brave breath. 'But I'm trying to find my way now she's all grown up.'

'That's how you've ended up here.'

Sophie nodded.

'I expect people have told you you're very brave.'

Together, in some unspoken agreement, they started walking along the water's edge.

'Some people have,' Sophie said. 'I suspect other people think I'm completely mad. But there was nothing to keep me down there – well, besides my friend Bea, of course, but she's recently re-married and I didn't want to feel like I was getting under her feet. You know what I mean?'

'Oh yes, I do. There's nothing worse than being – what is it the children call it these days? A third wheel?'

'That's what Tabby says, yes. Apparently the worst fate that could befall a person.'

'I could think of worse.' Annie bent to pick up a pretty piece of sea glass. 'Lovely, isn't it?' She held it out on her flat palm.

'It's really pretty.'

'I collect it when I'm out walking the beach, and give it to Ben. He uses it in his pieces – he's an artist, talking of Gormley and the like.'

'That makes sense.' He'd looked the sort. That or some sort of mad prepper, living out here in the wild with his mad hair and overgrown beard and plaid shirt. He probably had a YouTube channel where he talked about making his own beer from rosehips or seaweed. She had to suppress a giggle at the thought.

'Something tickling you?'

Annie didn't miss a trick. Those faded blue eyes noticed everything.

'Just thinking about our meeting the first day. We didn't exactly get off on the best footing, given that we're neighbours.'

'So I gather.'

So he'd mentioned something to her about it. The idea of that made Sophie feel a bit weird in a way she couldn't quite put a finger on. Since then she'd not seen him once, only the curl of the woodsmoke rising from his chimney when she'd left for work in the morning, and the dogs playing in the field outside while presumably he chopped logs or whatever it was he did all day.

'Anyway,' said Annie, pausing on the sand parallel to the

path that led back towards the cottage, 'I had better get on and let you have your walk in peace.'

'Oh you don't have to,' Sophie began, but Annie raised a hand in farewell and started up towards the grass.

'I have my son and daughter-in-law coming round for Sunday lunch later, so I ought to get back and get started on the potatoes.'

Sophie's stomach growled. She hadn't eaten, and the sea air had given her an appetite. 'Lovely to chat,' she said, a bit lamely.

'You're welcome to join us,' said Annie, stopping suddenly and turning round.

'Oh!' Sophie looked at her for a moment, wondering if she was just being polite.

'I'm not just being polite,' Annie said, as if she'd read Sophie's mind. 'Quite honestly, you might be just the diluting agent I need to make the afternoon tolerable. I can't bear my daughter-in-law,' she added, with a cackle of amusement.

'Oh I couldn't possibly,' said Sophie, automatically. Back home she'd never have dreamt of it – she'd always tended to keep herself to herself, especially after – well, she'd had her fingers burned. That's what she always told herself.

'Perhaps another time,' said Annie, equably. She didn't seem particularly ruffled as she turned and started making her way up the slope of the sand towards the grass below the cottage.

'Actually,' Sophie said, surprising herself, 'If you really don't mind, that would be lovely, thank you.'

Annie's smile lit up her face. 'Well, that is splendid news.'

CHAPTER FIFTEEN

Annie's cottage stood foursquare and solid half a mile down a little bumpy track, which was flanked on either side by hip height stone walls. Outside the front door a shaggy climbing rose arched over a trellis, giving the house the look of an elderly walrus with a drooping moustache.

'Needs a trim,' said Annie, ducking underneath it as she opened the door and welcomed Sophie inside. She'd led the way in her little car, with Sophie following behind, trying hard to tell herself that this was exactly the sort of thing that she was supposed to be doing as part of Operation New Life. The rumbles of hunger in her stomach had been replaced by her habitual butterflies. She followed Annie through a brightly painted yellow hall and into a kitchen which was as warm and welcoming as its owner. A bunch of colourful tulips stood upright in a tall white jug on the table, and beside it a black and white cat.

'Have a seat,' said Annie, running a hand along the arched back of the cat who'd reared up in welcome, 'and you can make yourself useful by peeling these for me while we chat. I'll put the kettle on.'

She handed a hessian sack of potatoes over to Sophie, who'd followed her instructions and sat down on a wide bench which ran parallel to the table. A moment later the potatoes were followed by a potato peeler and a big cast iron saucepan, a knife and a chopping board.

'Forgive my manners. This is Eddie, by the way.'

The cat had padded across the table and hopped down to join her, rubbing his head on Sophie's arm in greeting.

'Hello, Eddie.' Sophie started peeling, watching as Annie took the kettle which had been sitting to the back of the old fashioned Aga range cooker, and lifted the lid to put it on to bring it to the boil, which seemed to happen in about a minute.

'I've never seen one of those in real life.' It was the sort of thing she'd drooled over in lifestyle magazines, but it would have taken up most of the tiny kitchen in their little flat back home.

'She's a monster. Guzzles oil like it's going out of fashion, is vastly temperamental, and I love her.'

She might be a monster, but certainly produced a nice cup of tea. Sophie sipped it, hands cupped around the mug, and looked around. The kitchen was old and worn, the décor unsurprisingly minimal – the cottage was clearly reflective of Annie's taste – and reminded her with its spider plants hanging on knotted macrame hangers and sleek Ercol sideboard of one of the design magazines Bea loved to read. It had clearly been very much in vogue in the 1970s and had come around full circle to be the height of fashion all over again.

'Is that you?' There was a black and white framed photograph of a woman with Annie's eyes, sitting with her legs tucked beneath her on a pile of sleek wet rocks.

'For my sins.' Annie laughed. 'Quite a long time ago, obviously.'

'You look very glamorous.'

'It was taken on the beach. Funny to think about what was going to happen that year.' She put a hand up, touching the picture with a thoughtful expression on her face.

Sophie sliced through the potatoes she'd already peeled and placed them carefully in the pot. The clock on the wall above the Aga chimed midday.

'I was just pregnant in that photo, not that you'd know it. Thankfully *he* didn't stay around, and I met my husband here in Applemore that summer.'

'Oh,' said Sophie, surprised. It was easy to forget that the older generation had their own share of complications in their lives. 'Was that – I mean it must've been –' she tailed off.

'A bit of a scandal?' Annie finished her sentence. 'Is that what you're wondering? Yes, being a single parent wasn't exactly the thing up here in the Highlands back in the early 1970s. As it happened, I wasn't on my own for very long and people soon forgot.'

Feeling the conversation veering dangerously close to a topic she'd rather avoid, Sophie concentrated hard on the potato she was peeling, turning it around and around and then placing the curls of peel onto the chopping board as if it needed every single bit of focus she could muster. She looked up eventually, feeling Annie's eyes boring into her.

'You have a daughter, yes?'

'Tabby.' Sophie nodded.

'I thought I remembered that correctly. Pretty name.'

Sophie felt her shoulders drop slightly in relief. Talking about Tabby was something she could do more than comfortably. 'I think so. She did get her share of teasing at school for it when she was younger, but she tells me she likes having a name that's a little bit different.'

The phone rang loudly, making Sophie jump in surprise.

'Hang on, hang on,' said Annie, locating it on the shelf of the dresser, 'Hello? Oh, hello.'

Sophie tried to look as if she wasn't listening. Whoever it was seemed to be cancelling, and Annie didn't look particularly concerned at the news. A few moments later, she put the phone back down on the table and gave a huge smile.

'Saved – quite literally – by the bell. That was my daughter in law. They've had some trouble with the car, can't get it started properly and it's not turning over. Anyway, they don't want to risk taking it out and getting stuck here so they've cried off lunch.'

'Oh, I'm sorry.'

Annie chuckled. 'I'm not. How lovely. Not that I'm not very fond of my son, I should add, and of course I love his children and my great grandchildren, but his wife?' She gave a shudder. 'No, thank you.'

Sophie glanced up at the clock. 'If you're not cooking lunch for them -' she said, about to push the bench back and excuse herself.

'- the roast is in the oven already. These will only take three quarters of an hour or so.' She took the pot from Sophie and filled it with water, popping them on top of the stove to par boil. Then she turned back, a hopeful expression on her face. 'If you can put up with my company I'd be very glad of yours.'

'Of course.' It's not as if she had anywhere else to be.

'Wonderful. I'm glad I'm not going to be subjected to the usual quizzing about what I'm planning to do with the cottage, and all the rest. I swear sometimes I feel like she's just waiting for me to pop my clogs so she can get her hands on the inheritance. I have a good mind to sell the lot and give it all to Janine's dog rescue place. She'd make better use of it and they could do with new kennels.'

Sophie's eyes widened in surprise. 'Sometimes I wonder what it would be like having family,' she said, laughing briefly. 'But you're doing a good job of reminding me why I'm better off on my own.'

'You blooming well are.' Annie took a saucepan out of the fridge and lifted the lid for a moment to check the contents. 'I'm sorry, that was a bit insensitive. I don't mean to pry, but –'

Sophie shook her head. 'It's fine. My dad died ten years ago – heart attack. He brought me up. I didn't know my mum. She died when I was only three.'

'Goodness, I'm sorry. I bet you miss your dad.'

'I do.'

'Was he a vet as well?'

Sophie laughed and shook her head. 'No, he was a taxi driver. We didn't have a lot of money but he wanted me to have a profession. He was so proud when I graduated.'

'I'm sure he was over the moon. What would he think of you ending up all the way up here in the Highlands?'

'I think he'd be stunned. I left university in Liverpool and got a job working in a practice with a friend from the same class. I don't expect he imagined me moving any further than maybe back to Lancashire, where I grew up.'

'Must have taken a lot of thinking before you made the decision.'

'Not much. I mean basically none at all.' Sophie watched as Annie peered into the potato pan, moving it slightly off the heat so it didn't boil over. 'It was a bit of a whim, really.'

'I think when the children leave home, women often have a bit of a wobble. I've seen it quite a few times.'

Sophie nodded. 'I'd spent all my time making sure everything was just right for her, and then she was gone and there was all this time left and nothing to fill it.'

'No young men?'

'No old ones, either.'

Annie looked at her thoughtfully, her eyes narrowed slightly. 'You haven't left a handsome chap pining for you back in England.'

'Definitely not.' And somehow Sophie found it all tumbled out. Afterwards, she couldn't work out what had made her open up to Annie, when she'd kept her secret so closely guarded for the last six years, ever since her dad died and she'd inherited the nest egg he'd saved over the years for his only daughter.

'I had a horrible experience. I met a – someone. A man who I thought was lovely and charming and kind. Got to know him slowly at the side of the football pitch every weekend while I was watching Tabby play. He told me he was a scout for one of the bigger teams, and that's why he was there.'

Annie pulled out the chair at the end of the table and sat down, resting her chin in her hand as she listened.

'He made me believe he was interested in me. He took the time to get to know Tabby, and make her think he wanted to be part of her life. I blame myself because Dad had died and I was grieving and I wasn't thinking straight.' She sat up, rubbing her cheek with the flat of her palm, feeling the rigidity of the muscles under the skin. Even now, after all this time, the shame of it still seemed to be woven into her cell structure.

'I don't think you should be blaming yourself, whatever happened. Grief is a long road,' said Annie, gently, putting out a hand and squeezing Sophie's arm briefly.

Sophie took a deep breath and continued. 'He moved into

our little house and then it began. He was setting up a restaurant business and needed money, was waiting for his sister who was going to be investing with him – he made me believe it all. In the end I re-mortgaged my house to free up funds because he'd found the perfect premises and it was being sold by auction.'

'I have a feeling this isn't going to end well.'

'Not exactly, no. Once he'd got the money in his account – literally the same day it happened – he vanished. A year later the police caught him in the process of fleecing someone else, but the money was gone. He went to prison for seven years.'

'And the after effects are with you for a lifetime. I'm sorry, that's a terrible thing to happen.'

Sophie readjusted the woven table mat beside her so it ran precisely parallel to the edge of the table, making minute adjustments until it was just so. Looking up, she caught Annie's eye and made a face. 'Luckily, as you can see, I'm completely unscarred by it all.'

They both laughed and it lightened the mood.

'Yes, so anyway, that's the short version. Fortunately I managed to shield Tabby from the worst of it – she was upset that he left, of course, but we'd always been such a strong unit that I think that helped her to weather it.'

'And now she's gone to America and you're here with the rest of your life ahead of you.'

'Something like that, yes.'

They ate a delicious Sunday lunch together, sitting at the table with the spring sunlight shining across the table and the Aga keeping the room toasty warm. Annie's roast potatoes were crispy and golden, and the beef was just the right shade of pink and melted blissfully in the mouth.

'I couldn't eat another thing,' said Sophie, when Annie asked if she'd like some cake for pudding.

'Nor could I,' said Annie, patting her stomach with a happy sigh. 'I was rather dreading this lunch and it's been a delight. I hope you've enjoyed it.'

'I really have.' Sophie picked up the plates. 'It's hard to find the enthusiasm to cook for one, I find.'

'It's the one thing I find hard about being on my own. It's why I often cook in batches and deliver some to Ben, because he's in the same boat. He has a daughter as well. I think you'd probably get on.'

'Mm,' Sophie said, in what she hoped was a polite but not interested sort of tone.

In the absence of anything suitable to say, she got up and started stacking the dishes beside the big white sink.

'I rather enjoy solitude,' Annie said, joining her by the sink after a moment. 'All those years of looking after a house and a child and all the rest. I know people find it odd that I live out here alone, but I've always enjoyed my own company. Now I can please myself,' she gave a chuckle, 'And generally, I do.'

Sophie looked at Annie for a moment, wondering if she'd outstayed her welcome.

'Present company excepted,' Annie added, putting a hand on her arm.

'Thanks.' Sophie returned her smile.

'I'm not trying to marry you off if that's what you're thinking,' said Annie, with a snort of laughter, picking up a dishtowel. 'Just suggesting that you might actually have something in common.'

CHAPTER SIXTEEN

Sophie thought about Annie's parting words often over the next couple of weeks as she found her feet at work and wandered through the village, getting to know Applemore. They popped into her head unbidden at the must unhelpful of times – when she was trimming the hair which had grown over the eyes of a pet Yorkie dog, or when she was cleaning the loo down at the cottage.

'You've got a lot of life ahead of you,' she'd said, with a meaningful look, as Sophie was heading out of the door to return home. She'd been carrying a parcel of sliced roast beef ('for sandwiches') and a neatly wrapped fruit loaf ('you can share it tomorrow at tea break') in a bag.

'I hope so,' Sophie had replied.

'Don't be afraid to let it in,' Annie had said, enigmatically.

Driving towards the Applemore Gallery for the first of her art classes, she still couldn't decipher what she'd meant. Did Annie mean let *life* in? And if she did, surely stepping out of her comfort zone into the unknown must be moving in the right direction?

'This is exciting, isn't it?' Mhairi said, turning to look at her and beaming happily. She'd changed at work and was dressed in a rainbow striped long sleeved top, a bright green corduroy pinafore and a pair of fluorescent pink Doc Marten boots on the end of black and white striped legs.

'At least you won't lose her,' Thea had remarked acerbically, as they departed.

'I'm not sure exciting is the word I'd use.' Sophie had been feeling decidedly unenthusiastic about the whole art lesson thing all week, and if it hadn't been for the fact that she'd agreed to give Mhairi a lift, she probably would have ducked out and had a long bath instead. It had been one of those days, to top it off – the waiting room had been crammed with what felt like the entire village population of badly behaved dogs who'd barked and yelped constantly for the entire duration, and to top it all that afternoon she'd lost a little dog under anaesthetic while she was operating to try and save her from pyometra. Everyone had blinked back tears and watched silently as the owner had left the surgery empty handed. It didn't matter how many times it happened, she never failed to find it heart-breaking.

Mhairi had looked over at her with her little face gathered in concern. 'You're still thinking about Dilly, aren't you?'

'I can't help it,' Sophie said. 'Doesn't matter if there was nothing I could have done, I still beat myself up about it.'

'Fiona said that the day you stop being sad about the animals is the day you need to stop working as a vet.' Mhairi stopped herself midsentence. 'Not that she stopped because of that, obviously.'

'Her situation was a bit different, she had to take a step back because of her mum.'

'Yeah, exactly. I can't believe she's still down there and hasn't come back.'

'She said on the phone she's hoping to be back next week. I think they're having trouble getting home care sorted, or something like that.'

Sophie indicated to nobody in particular on the empty road and turned up the driveway towards Applemore. The sunshine of the weekend had been replaced with leaden grey skies and a hazy sort of rain which didn't seem to fall so much as hover, waiting to attach itself to anyone who dared to walk outside in it. She'd returned from the little supermarket with her hair hanging in sodden tendrils which had dried all crinkly. Where Mhairi had glammed herself up for art class, Sophie's appearance – she suspected – illustrated perfectly just how unenthusiastic she felt. She'd pulled on a hoody left by a sales rep and ran a hand through her hair whilst looking at herself in the mirror of the surgery loo. She had no make-up on, eyebags – because she'd woken up about five times in the night, dreading the prospect of this evening – and a spot brewing on the side of her chin, which at forty-three felt like a bit unfair.

Still, here she was despite everything, driving to an evening class to let life in, as Annie had exhorted cheerfully on the doorstep when she left. If this wasn't letting life in, she thought, pulling up on the courtyard and turning off the engine, she didn't know what was.

'Ooh, it's busy. I'll run in ahead while you get your bag so we can get a good seat.' Mhairi hitched her bag over her shoulder and scuttled on ahead on her little legs, her huge boots looking comical. Sophie, who was tall and long-limbed, caught up with her a few seconds later and together they walked through the glass door and into the huge white space that was the workshop. Tables had been set out in a horseshoe formation and a group of women were giggling together in a corner. It was her idea of hell.

'I just want to know when the nude model's arriving.'

'I told you Dolina's only here for the naked men,' laughed an older woman with close-cropped red hair. 'Hiya Mhairi, I didn't know you were coming. You all ready for the floor show?'

'There's no naked men really, are there?' Mhairi's eyes were wide as she turned to look at Sophie, who shook her head with a snort of laughter.

'There will be no naked men,' said a male voice with a gruff and distinctly northern accent. Sophie recognised it immediately, and turned around.

Standing there, taller and more well-groomed than she remembered, was her neighbour. He'd clearly been to the barber – his hair was still thick, dark and stood in untidy spikes, but his beard was neatly trimmed now and he was in a red plaid shirt with a white t-shirt underneath, a pair of faded jeans, and heavy brown work boots which gave him the look of a lumberjack more than an artist. He pushed up the sleeves of his shirt, revealing muscular, tanned arms dusted with dark hair. Something disobedient deep within in Sophie's stomach flipped over in a way that she tried to tell herself was nerves.

'Evening all. I'm Ben, and I suspect you weren't expecting to see me here any more than I was expecting to be here. Unfortunately Mel, your erstwhile tutor, has had an argument with a pavement and she lost. So you've drawn the short straw and you've got me.'

'I thought you were the male model.' The woman with short red hair gave a chuckle.

'Watch it Joan, or you'll be expelled before the class even gets started.'

Mhairi glanced over at Sophie to gauge her reaction. Sophie – despite herself – was amused by Ben's Northern humour, which reminded her of home.

'Right then, let's get you lot working. Pick a table, and you'll find paper and drawing materials there. While you're getting organised, I'll strip off.' Ben's face remained completely deadpan.

There was a hoot of laughter and then a flurry of activity as everyone got themselves organised. Sophie chose a table and dumped her bag at her feet, looking at the selection of tools that had been left out for her to choose from. Alongside a stack of pieces of A3 paper there was a handful of different pencils, all sharpened to a neat point, some charcoal in varying thicknesses, and some fat, colourful felt-tipped pens.

Ben, meanwhile, had carried a selection of objects into the middle of the room and arranged them so they stood on various solid white plinths, each at a different height. There were tall glass vases with interesting patterns on the side, faded and milky with age, and cracked wooden packing crates covered in dust and cobwebs, which looked as if he'd dragged them out of one of the old farm buildings nearby. An enormous leafy plant with trailing leaves was placed closest to Sophie, and she cursed herself for ending up with the object in front of her which looked like it would be impossible to draw.

If Ben had recognised her, he gave no indication. He strode around the room while everyone got themselves organised, and then stood in front of them all with a completely unreadable expression.

'Right then.' He folded his arms and for a fleeting moment Sophie thought she saw the tiniest suggestion of a smile tugging at the corner of his mouth. 'Before you all get yourselves settled into position, I want you all to start by moving two desks along.'

'You said we had to get ourselves organised,' said one of the chief cacklers from earlier.

Ben's left eyebrow raised a flicker.

'I didn't say anything about choosing a table.'

'I don't know,' continued the woman, 'Is this something to do with modern art?'

Sophie hid a smile as she picked up her bag. She obediently shuffled two tables to the left, where the smile disappeared rapidly when she found that instead of the clean white paper she had a stack of rough black craft paper, a box of white chalks, some silver pens and a slender paintbrush next to a fresh tube of white acrylic paint.

The woman was still chuntering away to herself at the table beside her.

'Shush, Dolina,' said the red haired woman, smiling a hello at Sophie as she passed.

'I don't know, I signed up for this thinking we were going to be doing painting with Mel and now we're here doing something entirely different.' She turned to look Sophie up and down briefly and then nodded a greeting. 'You must be the new vet I've been hearing about.'

'And you must be Dolina,' said Sophie, earning a snort of laughter from the woman on her other side. 'I've heard all about you.'

'Have you indeed?' Dolina folded her arms above a capacious bosom. 'I tell you what, this village is just never ending gossip. Everyone has their neb in everyone else's business, if you ask me.'

'And you are a paragon of virtue, I suppose,' chuckled the woman with red hair. 'I'm Joan,' she said, putting out her hand for Sophie to shake. 'I've been meaning to pop my head in and say hello. And this – you're right – is Dolina.'

'Lovely to meet you,' said Sophie.

Dolina, whose reputation as the village gossip did in fact go before her, seemed to be completely unaware that Sophie had picked up her name in conversation. She narrowed her eyes in suspicion as she said hello and gave the distinct impression she was sizing Sophie up. Luckily Ben distracted her a moment later.

'Right. Now I want to start with a timed exercise as a bit of a warm up. We're going to get ourselves working across the whole of the paper, covering as much as we can, with five minutes on whichever subject you like, starting – now!'

Sophie looked at the tall glass bottles in front of her for a moment and felt frozen with horror.

'What do you mean covering as much as we can?' Dolina was holding a piece of charcoal at arm's length as if it was an unexploded bomb.

'Exactly what I say. You've got a huge piece of paper there, I want to see it filled up. What are you looking at?'

'Well it's a pile of books, obviously,' said Dolina, as if she was talking to a very small child.

Ben nodded at the blank page, then glanced at his watch. 'Four minutes thirty seconds now,' he said, 'I'd get moving if I were you.'

Sophie put a tentative line on the black paper and realised almost immediately it was wonky. She looked to either side for help or inspiration, but both Dolina and Joan were intent on their own paintings, and neither of them noticed her silent entreaty.

She'd just have to get on with it. She looked again at the bottle, trying her best to fill the page with her attempt to replicate it, and was completely caught up in the shading at the top of the neck when she heard a bell ring and Ben's voice saying 'Time's up'.

She looked up, realising that she'd been completely absorbed in what she was doing.

'Right, great, chuck that down on the floor behind you and take another medium – if you were using pen, this time use paint, or chalk, or something – pick one and five minutes again, starting – now.'

Sophie tossed the black sheet of paper behind her, thankful that it landed face down so she wouldn't have the humiliation of him examining it as she worked on the next drawing. This time she used the paintbrush and squeezed white paint out onto the little plastic palette, tracing the lines of the bottle more boldly this time and even starting to sketch in some of the plinth it was standing on before the bell rang once again and she looked up in surprise.

'Now chuck that on the ground and move one table to the left,' Ben said, and there was a ripple of surprise but everyone did as they were told and then started again, trying another picture but from a different perspective. Drawing with soft black pencil on crisp white paper brought Sophie right back to art class at school, which she'd always loved as a respite from the intensity of studying all three sciences and maths, desperate to get the grades needed to make it into vet school. She was so lost in her work that she didn't even hear Ben telling the class it was time up, and it was only when she heard a movement behind her that she looked up with a start.

She turned, stepping back in surprise when she realised that he was just at her shoulder. In that second she caught the slightest impression of a masculine, woody scent which made her heart jump unexpectedly.

'Sorry,' she said, bending to pick up the brush she'd knocked over in her surprise.

He gave a brief nod. 'I like that,' he said, and turned away. Sophie felt her cheeks stinging pink. Dolina leaned over to peer at her drawing.

'That's not bad,' she said, admiringly. 'You can actually see what it's supposed to be, not like mine.' With a wave of her arm she indicated the slightly wonky looking attempt at the plant she'd created.

'I can tell what that is!' Sophie said, tracing the outline of the leaves with a finger. 'I like the way you've done the shading there.'

Dolina beamed so widely that her eyes were almost hidden by round cheeks and feathered laughter lines. 'Och, away with you,' she said, looking pleased and giving Sophie a nudge with her shoulder.

Sophie looked up as Ben strode across the room, hitching a hip up onto one of the disused tables. He looked almost cheerful for a moment as he rubbed his beard, thick eyebrows quirking upwards.

'That was just an exercise that's useful for getting you out of your head and not worrying about what your work looks like,' explained Ben, his long legs stretched out in front of him, one heavy booted ankle crossed over the other. He looked around the class. 'Everyone, whether they're seasoned artists or amateurs, gets stuck on what they think a piece of art should look like, and what helps more than anything is to forget that and think about what it feels like.'

'It feels like I haven't picked up a paintbrush since I was at school and that's about fifty odd years ago,' chuckled Dolina. 'I don't think there's any chance I'll be making it onto the gallery walls,' she added, making everyone laugh.

Ben, though, was still serious faced. 'Just you wait,' he said, tipping his head in the direction of the blank wall behind him. 'By the end of the eight weeks we'll be having an exhibition so you can show your friends and family what you've been working on.'

'Don't say that,' said a woman with huge tortoiseshell glasses and short curls cut into a bob, 'or none of us will come back next week.'

'Oh,' said Ben, calmly. 'I suspect you will.'

He was, Sophie thought, the stillest person she'd ever met. It was as if he was a lion, waiting patiently for his prey before he eventually pounced. There was something quite unnerving about him.

'And now it's time for the blindfolds,' he said, lifting up a stack of pieces of fabric, making several of the women giggle.

'Once again,' he continued, an inscrutable expression on his face, 'this is about getting you to stop thinking about the look of what you're creating and instead to think about the feeling of it.'

'This is all very Fifty Shades,' muttered Dolina, as Sophie tied the cloth blindfold around the back of her head and then ducked down so Dolina could do the same to her. 'I don't know what I was expecting from an art class but it wasn't this.'

'Joan, can you give me a hand,' said Ben, calling her over to help position each student in front of their easel. 'I can't really manhandle people into position, so I'm going to have to borrow you to do it.'

The blindfold painting was the ice breaker that got the whole class laughing. Attempting to paint from memory with no idea what they were doing was enough to make even the most serious faced amongst them get a fit of the giggles, and when the time was up and they removed the cloths to reveal their daubings, it just made them laugh even more.

'Now we've done some warming up, we'll spend a bit of time working with whatever you like on whatever you like. Choose whatever medium you enjoyed most, and find yourself a space – you can move the easels around if you like, just make yourselves at home.'

'Is this alright?' The woman in the tortoiseshell glasses called Ben over, an anxious expression on her face.

'Anything goes,' said Ben, looking almost cheerful. Sophie's eyebrows raised heavenwards in amazement. Maybe he wasn't a complete bear after all.

Once they'd all finished and were clearing up, the class finally had a chance to chat.

'So tell me why you decided to come to class,' Ben asked them.

One by one, people explained that they wanted a chance to do something outside of home, or that it was something they'd always wanted to do but they'd never had the time, or –

'Well I always liked art at school,' Sophie explained when it came to her turn, 'But I was told that it wasn't a proper job, so there was no point in doing it.'

'Cheers,' said Ben, drily.

'Oh - I didn't mean –'

'Don't worry, I've heard it all before.' He looked at her for a moment and she felt the intensity of his dark eyes as they met hers. Well, that was another opportunity to smooth things over with her neighbour gone. He moved onto the next student, and the moment was lost. She tried to find the chance to apologise for putting her foot in it but he was monopolised once again while everyone was tidying up by the woman with the glasses, who Sophie could see was going to be *that* student in class. She'd probably turn up next week with a shiny red apple for him.

'Well, hopefully I'll see some of you back here next week,' Ben said, as he stood at the door watching them all depart. 'That's if I haven't put you off completely.'

Mhairi giggled as she gave him a wave goodbye. Sophie gave him a brief smile which wasn't reciprocated.

As they headed back to the cars afterwards, Sophie noticed the two liver and white spaniels were sitting in the passenger seat of his truck, alert and looking out for their owner.

'He's on his way,' said Mhairi, tapping on the glass as she

passed, so they stood up and started wagging eagerly. 'They're gorgeous, aren't they?'

'They seem a hell of a lot happier than they were the day we met,' Sophie agreed. It was more than could be said for their owner. He was clearly going to take a lot more winning round.

CHAPTER SEVENTEEN

'Should I be worrying that you've missed my call?' Esther said, her voice carrying clearly on loudspeaker across the kitchen.

Ben put a lid on the saucepan of Bolognese he was warming through on the top of the woodstove and went back over to the table where his iPad was propped up against a pile of books, and Esther's face could be seen looking at him quizzically from under a hard hat.

'Well?'

He shook his head, laughing. 'I forgot when I told you to ring at eight that I had the art class today.'

'Heaven help your poor students. Did you give them the full grumpy old bear treatment?' Esther bit into a sausage roll as she spoke, wiping crumbs away with the back of a gloved hand. She was sitting in the welfare van again, waiting for her shift on the motorway to begin.

'I did nothing of the sort.' He looked at his daughter with a blank expression. 'I was charm personified.'

Esther snorted.

'What?'

'Nothing. I just know you. Your sense of humour is so dry that it's like the bloody Sahara, and I bet it went right over the top of the arty farty types who turned up for your evening class.'

'First things first – it's not my evening class.' Ben reached across the table for the bottle opener and cracked open the beer he'd retrieved from the fridge when he got in the door. He poured it into a glass as he spoke. 'Secondly, how are we defining "arty farty", madam? Given that your father is one of the aforementioned?'

'Oh you know, living on another planet, can't get a proper job...'

'It's not too late to disown you, you know.' Ben took a mouthful of beer and wiped the froth from his moustache, shaking his head at Esther's grinning face on the screen.

'Seriously, how did it go?' She popped the last piece of sausage roll into her mouth and glanced behind her for a moment. 'Just coming,' she said to someone out of view.

'You know what? It wasn't bad. I even made them laugh. There's a couple who've got potential, as well. That new vet I told you about, she did a pretty good pencil still life of some bottles.'

'Oh yeah?' Esther perked up slightly. 'Does that make her go up in your estimation after your first meeting? I got the impression you weren't that keen.'

'Oh she seems nice enough,' he said, with a half shrug. 'I think she's only doing it because one of the other girls from the surgery dragged her along, that's what I gathered, anyway.'

Esther gave him a beady look. 'Is she pretty?'

'Didn't notice.'

One eyebrow shot upwards. Ben, who was used to his daughter trying to matchmake from a distance, shook his head warningly and laughed. 'Don't you be getting any ideas.'

'I'm just saying,' she began.

'Well don't. Don't you have a bridge to measure or some concrete to analyse or something practical like that?'

'As it happens,' said Esther, her Lancastrian accent suddenly more pronounced, 'I do. I'd better get on. I'll let you get back to your arty farty stuff.'

'Watch it, missy.' Ben gave a chuckle, and took another sip of beer. 'I'll give you a call at the weekend, see what you're up to.'

'I'm away sailing, don't forget.'

'Get you,' he said, with a smile. 'It'll be hunting and shooting with the posh set next.'

'You can talk, you're friends with the Lord of the Manor.'

'I'd hardly call Lachlan that,' he protested.

'But he literally is the actual Laird.'

Ben ducked his head sideways in a brief nod of acknowledgement. 'Aye, he is, but he's not like that.'

'Neither is Harry.'

'He just owns a boat. As one does.'

'As one does,' giggled Esther. 'Anyway, don't go getting ideas. We're just friends.'

'Hmm,' said Ben, giving her a wink as she waved goodbye.

'Shush, Dad,' said Esther, leaning forward to switch off the video call.

He sat back on the chair, putting his feet up on the rail of the fire, enjoying the peace and quiet after the business of the evening class. Behind the thick glass of the range cooker, the flames crackled brightly and the pot – sitting to one side so it would warm through gently – was emitting a delicious scented steam. His stomach growled. It had been ages since he'd eaten, and teaching had been far less of an easy ride than he'd expected. The class seemed a nice enough bunch, to be fair, and as he'd said to Esther, some of them seemed to have an aptitude he hadn't expected.

He finished his beer and wandered across the flag-stoned kitchen floor to fetch a bowl, followed by the dogs, who trailed behind him, hopefully wagging their tails in the hope of a treat. He reached up to the shelf on the big bleached wooden dresser and fished out a couple of gravy bones for each of them, tossing them in the air so they caught them, jumping up and then heading back to the warmth of their bed by the stove.

Shaking his head thinking about Esther's teasing, he dished out a plate of food and sat back at the table, thinking about what he had to do the next day and trying not to think about how he'd felt when he'd stood close to Sophie, the new vet, when he'd admired her drawing.

He'd stood there, taking in the tumble of dark hair and the unusual gold-streaked hazel eyes which had widened in surprise when she'd turned to see him standing there. They'd not exactly got off on the best footing, considering they were supposed to be neighbours. Maybe this art class would be the easiest way of creating some sort of détente between them. At least she could draw, that was something. He was hopeless at pretending, so if he'd had to try to compliment her work he'd have struggled. As it was, he'd wandered around the class looking on as the students worked. He wasn't a praiser by nature, being a man who chose his words carefully, but when the students had been expecting sunny, cheerful Mel it didn't seem fair to land them with what Esther used to call Mr Grouch. So he'd found something to compliment, and it had been surprising to see how everyone – even Dolina, the village gossip, who he'd never had any time for in the past – had seemed to transform with a couple of well-placed words of encouragement.

He paused for a moment as the barn owl hooted loudly outside.

'Leave it,' he growled at the dogs, both of whom had shot up into alert mode, ears lifting and their heads raising from their slumber.

Otto flopped back to sleep with a heavy sigh. Bear sat up and started scratching his left ear again, then gave a little whimper.

'You alright, boy?' He reached down to stroke him but Bear ducked his head away.

Later, after he'd cleared up, he took another couple of treats and bribed the younger dog to sit still so he could have a look and see what was going on. No wonder he'd been uncomfortable – his ear was warm inside and it definitely didn't look right. So much for avoiding the new vet… he was going to have to get in there in the morning and have her check him out.

He woke early and headed to the surgery for eight thirty, parking outside and peering in at the sign on the window. He could have sworn the place was open at half past, but there was no sign of life – and the note in the window said drop in surgery started at nine.

He sat back in the driver's seat, closing his eyes and listening to the news on the radio until a knock on the window woke him with a start.

'You locked out?' Fiona, the owner of the practice, was looking in at him with an amused expression on her face.

Otto shot up with a bark of surprise – he'd clearly dropped off too, lying sprawled along the back seat with Bear, who gave Fiona a vague wag of welcome but didn't move.

'Just wanted to get this one checked out,' he said, thankfully, climbing out of the car and picking up Bear's lead so he followed obediently at his heels.

'You're in the right place then,' said Fiona, with her usual brisk manner, and held the door open for him to go inside.

The waiting room already had three people waiting. Over in the far corner, a small dark-haired woman was sitting with a cat box on her knee and a defensive posture, as if she was concerned that her pet might be eaten by a marauding stray canine.

'Tibby MacAllister?'

That moment the examination room door opened and Sophie appeared, hair tied back from her face in an untidy bun, dressed in the green scrubs with the surgery logo on her breast pocket. She caught sight of him and seemed to jump in surprise, turning away quickly and smiling a welcome at the cat owner instead, ushering her inside without looking at him again.

'We'll be with you in a sec,' said Fiona, disappearing behind the desk to give instructions to Mhairi, who smiled at him cheerfully.

'Hello again,' she beamed. 'Who have we here?'

'It's Otto,' he said, as the dog tried to shoot across the room to sniff hello to a bearded collie who was sitting between his owner's legs. 'Think he's got a bit of an ear infection or something going on, so I thought I should get it checked out.'

'No probs,' said Mhairi, typing his details onto the computer, 'have a seat for a moment and we'll be with you as soon as possible.'

Fiona headed back out again, pulling on a black waterproof coat. So much for hoping she'd deal with Otto and he wouldn't have to encounter Sophie and her disapproval when he inevitably behaved like a twit in the examination room.

The radio was playing and Mhairi was humming along while she worked. Two of the vet nurses travelled back and forth between exam rooms, and the waiting room slowly filled up as the minutes passed. On the wall there was a display of photographs of the members of staff and their pets – if he hadn't guessed from the pictures that surrounded her desk, it was apparent that Mhairi was a cat lover from the photos up on the wall. Thea, the vet who'd taken over when Fiona had taken a step back from the practice, was pictured with her spaniel in one photograph and with her arm around the neck of a white goat in another. Fiona beamed out from behind an alpaca and a couple of furry Shetland ponies. No sign of the new vet, he noticed. Maybe she preferred being snarky about other people's dogs to actually owning one of her own.

'Otto?' Talk of the devil. He stood up, and followed her as she beckoned him inside.

'Hello again,' she said, bending down to the dog's level and scratching him on the chest, just where he liked it. Otto lolled his tongue and grinned at her stupidly.

Thanks for the loyalty, Ben thought, rolling his eyes.

'Shall I put him up on the table?'

'That would be great thanks,' said Sophie, stepping back to let him past. 'What brings you here today?'

She seemed to be addressing the dog and not him. He was tempted to say 'Well, I've got a bit of a problem with my ear' in a growly voice. He suppressed a grin at the thought and he noticed her giving him an odd look as he did so. He was making a right pigs ear of this. Meanwhile Sophie was gently running her hands over Otto who was wagging his tail and looking quite at home.

'I've noticed he's been scratching his ear quite a bit. I tried to have a look but he ducked away. Didn't want to upset him,' he said, but Sophie had already gently lifted his ear and was making a face.

'Oh love,' she said, 'that's a nasty one, isn't it? Let's check the other ear.'

She lifted his left ear and made a face. 'Not so bad, but it's not great.'

She said something to Otto and then as she straightened she looked up at Ben for a moment, head cocked to one side slightly. She really did have unusual eyes – striking hazel brown eyes which were flecked with green and gold, ringed with grey. She lifted her brows slightly as if waiting for him to say something.

He looked at her for a moment and she looked back at him, eyebrows raising further.

'I said does he swim in the sea often, but thinking about the speed he hurtled off towards the beach I'm guessing that's a yes?' Sophie rubbed Otto under the chin.

'All the time. Even when it's bloody freezing out.'

'That'll be it,' she said, with a brief nod. 'It's a bugger for causing ear infections. He's got a nasty one. It's a testament to his spaniel nature that you've not noticed before now, because they're so easy-going you'd never know they were in discomfort.'

'Poor Otto,' he reached over, patting him on the side and rubbing him just where he liked to be scratched behind his foreleg, 'I feel awful. I had no idea.'

Sophie shook her head. 'It's easy to miss if you're not looking for it. Anyway we'll get it sorted, don't worry –' she addressed this to Otto again, clearly finding it easier to communicate with the spaniel than him, 'Just have to give you a course of steroids for a week to get things under control a bit and then we'll wash them out and get it treated.'

'Steroids?' It was lucky he wasn't trying to impress her with his wit and charm. He must be coming across like a complete moron.

'Yep, I'm afraid you might have to deal with a few side effects – or rather Otto will. He might be a bit sleepy, and he'll probably be ravenously hungry, so don't leave anything out on the kitchen table that you don't want him eating.' She smiled then, and dimples appeared in her cheeks which were freckled from the spring sunshine.

'Right, so pretty much the same as normal?'

It made her laugh.

'Only more so. Like a spaniel on – well, steroids.' She cuddled Otto, wrapping an arm round his neck so he looked up into her eyes adoringly. For a fleeting moment Ben felt envious of his dog's uncomplicated, loving nature. He cleared his throat and Sophie stepped back.

'So I need to make another appointment for next week?'

Sophie nodded. 'I'm afraid you're going to be seeing a bit of me over the next few weeks,' she said, looking down at Otto. Ben felt a weird rush of blood in his ears as she looked back at him a moment later.

'Sorry about that,' she added, making a self-deprecating face.

'I think we can live with it,' he said, lifting Otto off the examination table. As he did so he brushed close enough to her to catch the light, floral scent he'd noticed on her when he stood by her side in the class last night. It reminded him of the freesias that would soon be flowering in his garden. Adjusting Otto's collar, he straightened up to see Sophie had turned and was tapping something on the keyboard. She turned back and gave a brief, professional nod, dismissing him.

'Right then, we'll see you next week. Two secs and I'll get Mhairi to sort out the prescription for you.'

CHAPTER EIGHTEEN

The rest of the morning flew past. Fiona had popped in briefly, spent an hour going over figures with Thea and then disappeared again, looking frazzled. Trying to arrange care for her elderly mother was clearly incredibly stressful – she'd seemed distracted and even more brusque than usual, which Mhairi had assured Sophie was perfectly normal. Sophie had spent the whole morning feeling vaguely stressed, not just because the place had been manic but also with that stomach-churning sense that she was somehow in trouble. She knew it was just the old anxiety talking, and that if she had a chance to get out at lunchtime and get some fresh air she'd feel more human again.

The surgery was a blur of people and noise, dogs barking outside and the nurses run off their feet between her exam room and Thea's in the room next door, as well as dealing with their own clients. Some days, she was learning, were like that. It was an experience learning the patterns of a new surgery after so many years working at the same one. Just like back in England, here in the little village surgery, Friday morning could be guaranteed to be packed, with everyone turning up in a rush to make sure that they were organised for the weekend. Other days mornings open clinic was completely dead and they had nothing to do but catch up on paperwork and tidy up the examination rooms. Today had been the complete opposite and when they closed the door on the last client at lunch Mhairi fanned herself in mock exhaustion. She rubbed her hands down her face in exhaustion and groaned, standing up from her chair and arching her back to stretch it out. Grace popped open a can of Coke and took a long drink, then puffed out a long breath of relief.

'What a morning.'

'I think we've had half the pets of the village in here today.' Thea pulled her tunic over her head, revealing a grey and white vest top. 'I need a shower after battling with that demon cat Angus. He was like a rubber ball, pinging from one side of the room to the other. At one point I genuinely thought he was going out the window.'

Everyone laughed. Sophie headed for the back room, desperate to sit down and take the weight of her feet.

'Just putting the kettle on,' she said, filling it with water. She'd make a coffee, she decided – vaguely conscious that the last thing she needed when she was feeling antsy was more caffeine – and then head out for a walk around the village in the sunshine for a bit of a breather.

'I'm nipping up to the farm shop while we're shut to get some bits. Anyone fancy lunch up in the café?' Thea pulled on a spare tunic, her voice muffled through the material.

Sophie opened her lunchbox and looked at the slightly depressed looking sandwich she'd cobbled together that morning. Getting out of the village altogether? That was probably an even better idea, thinking about it.

'Actually I wouldn't mind. I forgot to go to the shop last night and my lunch isn't exactly inspiring.'

'They've got new Pot Noodles in the mini-market,' said Mhairi, pulling one out of her rainbow striped rucksack and waving it in the air proudly. 'Sweet and Sour,' she added.

Sophie shook her head.

'That's my daughter Tabby's idea of heaven,' she admitted, 'But I prefer my food to be made of food, not chemicals, ideally.'

'This is food,' protested Mhairi, turning the plastic pot round to look at the ingredients for a moment. She frowned, her little face gathering in concern as she scanned the tiny writing. 'I mean look it's got lots of things that might be food...'

'You're alright,' said Sophie. 'Given the choice between your Pot Noodle and my depressed sandwich, I'll take a salmon and cream cheese bagel up at the café any time.'

'Want a lift?' Thea held her keys up, jingling them in the air. 'No point taking two cars, is there?'

'Go on then,' Sophie closed the lid of her lunch box and shoved it back on the shelf. 'Yes please. That would be lovely, thanks.'

She grabbed her bag and followed Thea towards the door. One of the things she'd learned in the sessions of counselling she'd had following what she'd learned to compartmentalise as *the incident* was that it was important to try and head off spirals of anxious thinking at the pass by doing something different. Years had passed and she still felt a horrible, gnawing sense of shame that she'd been taken in by Craig, but she'd – well, she was better at accepting that it wasn't her fault she'd been conned. She watched as Thea blipped open her Land Rover and let Eddie out of the back for a quick run across the road to the little strip of grass opposite. He had a brief sniff and lifted his leg on a lamp-post before she whistled him back into the car.

Grace headed out at the same time, bustling off to visit her elderly father who lived along the road in one of the tiny white cottages that looked over the shore. She turned back, her hair ruffling in the spring breeze.

'Can one of you pick me up a bag of potatoes and a bunch of flowers while you're there?'

'No probs,' said Thea, closing the door of her Land Rover and setting off. Her dog Ted, his stumpy tail wagging at a rate of knots and his head sticking out the window, was delighting in the fresh air.

'Actually do you mind if we just drop in on Janine at the dog rescue? We're passing anyway and I've got the flea treatments she ordered in the other day.'

'Of course not.' Sophie laughed as Ted barked in surprise as they drove past a field of sheep, their tiny lambs gambolling about in the spring sunshine. It was good to get out.

They headed out of the village and up the familiar road towards Applemore House and the farm shop, but took a right down a little path she hadn't noticed before. The gateway was overgrown with dandelions and nettles, and the gravel track rutted and bumpy. Ted slipped sideways and fell from his viewing spot.

'Sorry, old boy,' said Thea, looking back at him. He popped his head between the two of them, tongue lolling cheerfully, and Sophie gave him a pat. A moment later he burst into a series of excited growls and barks, hopping on the spot as Thea pulled up outside a modern bungalow with a battered old Ford Focus parked outside. A blue marl collie dashed out of a dilapidated outbuilding and raced towards them, barking as they climbed out of the car.

'You can stay there, you know what Sapphire's like.' Thea

closed the door on a disappointed looking Ted who flopped down on the back seat, obedient as ever.

'And you,' she bent down to ruffle the fur of Sapphire's chest and the dog stopped barking and rolled over in a display of submission, 'You are a ridiculous all mouth and no trousers hound.'

Sophie laughed. She looked around, taking in the surroundings. So far everywhere she'd seen in Applemore had been almost too pretty and picturesque compared to the streets back home, where big Victorian houses stood alongside tiny cramped rows of terraced houses with their plastic dustbins tucked onto tiny front paths. This bungalow, however, was definitely not picturesque. A heap of plastic crates were stacked untidily by the back door, alongside which a scruffy looking ginger cat sat on a woven mat, cleaning his hind leg and ignoring them with typically feline disdain. Across a weed-strewn yard with some burst bags of cement sagging on a wooden pallet there was a ramshackle collection of buildings, from which came a crash followed by some choice words.

'Janice?' Thea looked over at Sophie and made a face. 'Sorry, I should have probably pre-warned you, it can be a bit… chaotic.' She lowered her voice. 'And Janice is lovely but she'd talk the hind legs off a donkey, so be prepared for me to make a hasty exit.'

A short woman with shaggy hair which had once been blonde but was now a sort of pale, ashy grey emerged from one of the buildings with a bundle of wriggling puppy in her arms.

'Sorry, I was dealing with this menace. He sneaked out of the crate when I was cleaning earlier and he managed to get himself stuck behind the old bales round the back.' She spoke with a strong Glasgow accent which was much faster than the soft Highland tones of most of the villagers. Janice looked down at the fluffy creature with a chuckle, her short nose wrinkling as she laughed. 'Just as well you're cute, eh?'

'This'll be one of the litter from the old farmhouse, yeah?' Thea peered over. 'Looking good, and I'm guessing he must be feeling good if he's off adventuring.'

'I have to confess that much as I'll miss them when they head off to their new homes next week I won't miss the mischief the four of them have managed to get themselves into.'

'We've brought those flea treatments. This is Sophie, by the way.'

'Ah, you must be the new English vet.' Janice gave her a welcoming smile. 'I've been hearing all sorts of good things about you. I was doon at the shop in the village the other day and Murdo was singing your praises. That's something you dinna see often.'

'He was?' Sophie said, taken aback. 'Sorry,' she went on, giving a nod in greeting, 'I should say hello, it's nice to meet you too.'

'Don't worry, we don't stand on ceremony around here, there's no time for it. You two got time for a cuppa or are you off on a call or something? I could do with a wee break before I get to it. I tell you what I've been non-stop all week. We've had two new rescues come in – one of them was abandoned in the layby on the road down towards Ullapool, believe it or not? I tell you I don't know what this world's coming to. It's a crying shame.' She paused for breath for a moment and Sophie rubbed her face, hiding a smile.

Thea took the opportunity to jump in. 'Off to the café, as it happens. You're welcome to join us, if you like?'

Thea might mock Janice's chatty nature, but she was good at heart – Sophie had worked that out already. She looked at the puppy who was still wriggling in her arms, and reached out a hand to scratch him behind the huge fluffy ears. He looked like he had a bit of German Shepherd in him, alongside goodness knows what else. He tried to chew her finger with his needle sharp teeth and she pulled back before he had the chance to do any damage.

Janice laughed, noticing. 'Och, that's nice of you to offer. I tell you I'm gonnae go stark staring bonkers out here on my own if I don't have someone to talk to soon. No, I'd love to, but I've got five dogs here in need of a walk and only one pair of legs. I'm missing Bill.'

'Her volunteer,' explained Thea. 'What about the others?'

'Oh I've got a few that drop in and out, but Bill was a star for coming out in all weathers and getting the rescues out for some exercise and socialising.' Janice frowned thoughtfully. 'In fact now I think about it, you don't know anyone who might fancy giving me a hand? Maybe I should put a wee poster up in the vets?'

'That's not a bad idea.' Thea nodded. 'I tell you what, why don't I put a card up on our noticeboard?'

'That would be amazing. You are a wee angel,' said Janice, looking for a second as if (despite having a puppy in her arms) she was about to try and hug the decidedly un-effusive Thea. Thea, clearly sensing the same, recoiled slightly, stepping backwards onto Sophie's toe just as Sophie's mouth seemed to take over before her brain had engaged fully.

'I could do it,' she blurted out.

Thea's eyebrows shot upwards. Janice beamed with delight.

'I'm not exactly busy,' she went on. 'I mean besides work I don't really have anything on at all. It would be a good way to get to know the area, wouldn't it?'

'Oh aye,' said Janice, putting the puppy down on the

ground and nodding vigorously. 'There are some bonny walks around here and we're never short of dogs needing exercise. Normally I'd ask if you're used to dogs but I hardly think that's an issue under the circumstances.'

'You must be insane,' said Thea as they left. 'She has a heart of gold, but you'll be talked to death if you're not careful.'

'Don't worry, I'll have an exit route planned at all times.' Sophie grinned as they turned onto the Applemore drive.

CHAPTER NINETEEN

'How on earth are you going to avoid coming home with eighteen different dogs?' Bea said, laughing.

Sophie, who was sitting on the wall that edged the garden, looked out at the sea, watching the waves as they washed gently onto the white sand. The evenings seemed to get longer and brighter every day in the Highlands, and the rainy weather they'd had earlier in the day had been replaced with a surprisingly warm sun, the setting rays of which were warming her through her thick grey sweater as she sat outside with a cup of tea chatting to her best friend.

'Who says I want to avoid it?' She turned the phone so she could waggle her eyebrows clearly at her friend who gave a snort of amusement. 'I might become a mad dog woman.'

'Well, you've got the mad bit sorted, that's one thing.'

'Very funny.'

'When's your first walk?'

'Tomorrow. Janice rang earlier when I got back from work and said she'd give me a map to follow, then proceeded to explain the entire route through the woods tree by tree. I reckon I could probably do the whole thing blindfold already. At least I managed to get her off the phone sharpish, which is more than Thea thought I'd do.'

'I swear these people all sound mad. You sound like you're enjoying it, though. Mark reckoned you'd be home after a week, you know.'

'Cheek.' Sophie shook her head. 'In case you've forgotten, I rented the house out so I couldn't even if I wanted to.'

'There's always a room here for you if you want one,' Bea said, kindly.

'I know.' Sophie gave her a brief smile. She knew Bea meant it, but after years on the dating scene and having almost given up on meeting Mr Right, she'd met up with Mark – neither of them particularly enthusiastic, both at the point where they'd pretty much accepted that there was nobody out there. It had been love at first sight, and now they were happily nesting, utterly in love, and very definitely not in need of a fortysomething house guest. 'Don't worry, I'm absolutely fine. As Janice told me, it's perfectly normal to have a midlife crisis when your child leaves home and you realise you're going to be on your own forever.'

'She what?' Bea spluttered with horrified laughter.

'Oh yes, she explained that's how she ended up coming up here and starting the dog rescue place,' Sophie said, drily. 'And it's not just dogs now, she said proudly, she's had an owl with a broken wing this week and three ferrets who needed rehoming. It's all go at the rescue kennels.'

'Are you quite sure you don't need us to come up there and rescue you? I'm worried you're going native.'

'I am absolutely fine, I promise. I've got my evening class as well, remember, and Grace asked if I wanted to make up numbers at the village hall Pilates class.'

Bea did a facepalm gesture and groaned. 'It's going to be Scottish Country Dance classes next.'

'I give you my full permission to drag me back to Merseyside and shoot me if that happens,' laughed Sophie.

'Anyway, not glossing over the art class, how was it with your frosty neighbour from hell?'

Sophie glanced unthinkingly behind her, looking up the hill towards Ben's cottage. It was so strange that they lived within eyesight of each other and yet somehow she'd never seen him out walking with the dogs since that first encounter. It was almost as if he was avoiding her, not that she'd noticed. Or that's what she was telling herself.

'Actually he was quite funny, I was surprised. I didn't expect it.'

'Oh that's something, at least.' Bea rubbed her nose, and the screen went blank. A second later she reappeared. 'Sorry, knocked the phone flat with my elbow. Anyway, what were you saying about your mysterious artist bloke?'

'Nothing much,' Sophie tried to sound casual, knowing what Bea was like. 'He actually came into the surgery the other day with one of his dogs. I think maybe I got off on the wrong foot with him, he seems quite nice.'

'Oh yes?' Bea perked up, exactly as Sophie had suspected she would if given even the faintest indication. 'Nice like what? What's his name again? Have you done a Google stalk?'

'I have absolutely not, and I don't know his name. It's just Ben,' she said, casually.

'Hmm,' said Bea, beadily. 'Ben, Applemore, artist.' She pretended to write it down on an imaginary notebook. 'Just say the word. All those years online dating gave me some serious Google powers. You've got to do your homework, Soph, to make sure you're not shagging some sort of secret psycho.'

'I'm not *shagging* anyone,' protested Sophie, shaking her head. 'This is exactly why Tabby says her friends don't tell their mothers anything. You're like a mad stalker.'

'I am not,' said Bea, chuckling. 'Like I say though, just say the word if you need me.'

'There will be no words,' said Sophie firmly, 'And I will have no need.'

They said goodbye, and Sophie headed inside to have a hot bath and a chat with Tabby to see how her midterm exams were going.

Applemore Woods were almost too beautiful in the spring light as she set off with Vinny, a stocky, square-set staffie cross for their first walk the next afternoon. The surgery closed for a half-day on a Wednesday – which was so quaintly old-fashioned that it made Sophie smile every time she thought about it – and so, deciding there was no time like the present, she'd offered her services to Janice.

'I've had a ring already from one of the women in the village as well,' Janice had told her cheerfully as she handed over Vinny's lead. 'That was quick work. I only put a wee sign up in the mini market yesterday evening. Mind it's easy enough to get walkers at this time of year when the weather's so bonny, isn't it? It'll no' be so nice when it's pouring down with rain and the wind's coming in sideways off the sea.'

Sophie's eyes widened slightly. 'I wouldn't mention that to any volunteers that turn up,' she said, checking her pockets to make sure she'd got her phone and then heading decisively for the car, Janice following in hot pursuit.

'You can park down by the adventure place,' she said, for the third time. 'Jack doesn't mind people using the parking places. He's a Glaswegian as well. Did I tell you that?'

Sophie was about to say that no, she hadn't, then shut her mouth, realising if she did she'd be in for another ten minute explanation and if she wasn't careful – despite the lengthening Highland evenings – she'd be still standing here at dusk.

'In you pop,' she said, closing the door firmly after fastening Vinny's travel seatbelt into place. 'Right, I'll be off.'

'Oh yes, I've got lots to do,' Janice had said, nodding. 'I must get on and not stand here chatting.'

Sophie had said nothing, but simply smiled in a slightly frenzied manner as she put the car into reverse.

She let the extending lead spool out as she wandered through the tall pines, watching Vinny bobbing about with his little stumpy legs carrying him through the needle-carpeted floor of the woods. The sun filtered through the trees, and Sophie wandered along happily, looking at the bright acid green of the unfurling new ferns and the clumps of freshly sprouted wild garlic which filled the air with their unmistakable scent. The path sloped away and as they walked down the hill the pines made way for a mixed deciduous woodland of vast oaks and tall, slim silver birch, their leaves still fresh and new. Someone had clearly plotted out this path – there were patches of newly laid woodchip where it might otherwise have been muddy, and when she turned to walk back up the hill she saw a track which was signposted for mountain bikers. Heading back down into the glen, a peaty-brown stream splashed through the rocks to her left, tumbling away into a waterfall that dropped down into a pretty deep pool. She stopped to take it all in. It was like something from a Visit Scotland holiday brochure, and it was all on her doorstep.

'Not many waterfalls in Preston,' said a gruff voice, making her jump. She turned quickly, her heart thumping against her ribs.

'Sorry,' said Ben, 'Didn't mean to make you jump.'

'You didn't,' said Sophie, who was standing with her hand on her chest and – she expected – an expression of shock on her face. She dropped her hand and looked down at the ground, where Vinny was – oh no, not now – squatting and in the process of doing a very large deposit on the soft, fresh new grass.

She looked up. Ben's thick eyebrows quirked upwards slightly as he cocked his head sideways, a half-smile twisting beneath his beard.

'Well, someone seems to be quite relaxed, anyway. And to be fair he's a lot more well behaved than my two were when you met them first.' He gave a low whistle and out of nowhere the two spaniels hurtled to his side, both snapping to attention as if they'd been born to it.

'They look pretty well behaved now,' Sophie admitted. 'Hello, Otto. How are those ears doing?'

'Not bad,' Ben answered for him as she bent to give them a stroke. Vinny, having finished his toilet, rolled upside down in a submissive position. Sophie took out a poo bag and scooped up the mess.

'So is he yours?' Ben said, nodding towards Vinny who righted himself and shook himself so hard that he almost fell over. His surprised expression made them both laugh.

'No, he's a rescue.'

'Oh right, one of Janice's dogs.'

'Does everyone really know everyone around here, or does it just feel like it?'

Ben grinned. 'It does feel like it, doesn't it?'

When he smiled, the lines fanned out around his eyes and he didn't look anywhere near fierce *or* grumpy, Sophie noticed, surprising herself. She looked away, not quite sure what to do with that information.

'Took a bit of getting used to when I arrived up here,' he went on. 'I'm not exactly a social animal, so I thought moving to the middle of nowhere meant I could just mind me own business and get on with my work. Turns out that's the last thing you can do if you move to a place like Applemore.'

'Yeah, I didn't even know the people who lived next door back home, other than to say hello, and they'd been there years.'

'Exactly.' Ben rubbed his jawline. 'I'd been here five minutes before everyone knew more about me than I was happy about.'

She looked at him quizzically. 'Were you in hiding from the CIA or something?'

He gave a bark of laughter. 'Nowt like that.' He looked at her for a moment with his deep brown eyes, a thoughtful expression on his face. 'That's a familiar accent, though. What brought you up here?'

Sophie raised an eyebrow. 'Is this for your personal use, or are you gathering intel for the local village gossip notebook?'

'Touché.' His mouth twisted in that same half smile again. 'Alright, let's try that again. You heading down the walk?' He tipped his head in the direction of the footpath.

'Yes, I've been given very detailed instructions by Janice to make sure I don't veer off and end up down on the Applemore private beach, not that it's private, but –' she did a passable impression of Janice's accent, making him laugh.

'Come on then, if you can tolerate me and these two miscreants, I'm going in the same direction.'

They started walking, side by side.

'Is he no good off the leash?' Ben said, after a few moments.

'I don't know,' she admitted. 'It's my first time taking him out, so I daren't risk it. Imagine the scandal if I came back empty handed.'

'You'd be run out of Applemore,' Ben said, holding back to let her go ahead as the path narrowed for a moment to allow for a little wooden bridge which crossed over another tiny stream.

'So what did bring you to Applemore?' Sophie turned to look at him. 'I'm guessing it's the sort of place artists like because it's peaceful?'

'Something like that. Or – well, as we've established, not as peaceful as it might be. It's not that bad.' He made a brief gesture with his hands. 'It's home, now.'

'And home before was where?'

'I grew up near Preston. Not many mountains or moors where I went to school. How about you?'

'Ormskirk. Then I went to vet school in Liverpool and ended up living in Merseyside.'

Ben turned to look at her. 'That's a big leap, coming from there to here.'

'Same for you.' Sophie tucked her hair back behind her ear.

'Yeah. I suppose I'm forgetting that being a vet you'd be into all the countryside stuff.'

'Not really,' she said, tugging the lead slightly as Vinny stalled at a particularly delicious smelling rotted tree stump. 'Actually, I was never much of a country vet, funnily enough. I came up here dreading the idea they were going to find me out.'

'And you've worked out how to avoid all the cows and sheep?'

'Actually, no. Funnily enough I ended up going out on a call with Thea, the other vet, when I first arrived. She knew what she was doing – managed to sort of drop me in at the deep end by stealth.'

'Crafty. So now you're over your cow phobia?'

'Something like that.' She laughed. 'I think I'd built it up in my head into something bigger than it was.'

'Easily done.'

'Like art, I suppose.' She looked sideways at him, conscious of his proximity.

'Oh yeah, art's a big confidence trick. That and practice. As you saw the other day.'

Sophie grimaced. 'I dunno, I'd hardly say I'm in the running for the Turner Prize.'

'I'm impressed you know what the Turner Prize is,' said Ben, stooping to pick up a stick and throw it for one of the spaniels. 'That's a start for your burgeoning new art career. Oh hang on, as you pointed out it's not a proper job. Nearly forgot that.'

Sophie put her hands over her face for a second. 'Oh don't, I didn't mean it the way it sounded.'

He shook his head but he was laughing. 'Believe me, I've heard it more than once. My dad worked in a factory all his life. You can imagine his face when I told him I wanted to go to art school.'

'Mine was a taxi driver. I think he'd have had the same reaction.'

'A taxi driver?' Ben looked at her again, with a curious expression on his face. 'I assumed all vets were posh. I thought you'd have been to private school and grown up with ponies and Labradors in the countryside.'

'Hardly. A terraced house in Barnoldswick, actually.'

'And now here we both are, two Lancashire urchins, walking dogs in the woods that belong to the Applemore estate. We've gone up in the world, eh?'

'Is this Applemore land?'

Ben shook his head. 'Actually, no. Lachlan's dad sold this off years before he died, apparently.'

'Lachlan, as in the Laird? You know him?'

'He's a mate, yeah.'

'So you don't actually live like a hermit and have no friends.'

Ben snorted with amusement. 'No, believe it or not I'm actually quite domesticated. Table manners, social skills, the lot.'

'Your dogs put me off the scent when I first met them.'

'Oh, very funny.' He grinned. 'You weren't exactly the friendliest either.'

'I'd only just arrived and they came hurtling round the corner growling and barking like they were going to take my arm off,' she protested.

'Two spaniels?'

'Yeah,' she gestured with her hands outwards 'Okay, fair enough, you've got me there. I'd just arrived, I was feeling all at sea.'

Ben's tone was gentle. 'It's a big change. I get it. I was all over the place when I got here.'

They walked along for a while in silence, turning up the path back through the trees which led back in the direction they'd come.

'He's going to sleep well tonight,' Sophie said, as Vinny trudged up the path in front of them. He'd stopped pulling now and was walking rather than trotting, his tongue lolling. It had been just the right length of walk for him. Ben's spaniels, on the other hand, looked as if they were ready for a twenty-mile run.

'You all set for another art class?' Ben said, as they crested the hill and she saw the wooden cabins of the activity centre.

'Can't wait,' said Sophie, rolling her eyes.

'Oh come on, it wasn't that bad, was it?'

She smiled at him. 'No, it was really good actually. I completely lost track of time when we were painting.'

He gave a brief nod. 'That's what I like about it.'

'Does everyone say that when you're teaching?'

'Literally never,' said Ben with an angelic grin.

'Really?'

'Really.'

Sophie stopped for a second and looked up at him.

'I've never taught a class before.'

'Seriously?'

'Not once. You talk about getting out of your comfort zone dealing with cows? If someone had offered me the chance last week to spend a night in a pen with a frenzied bull I'd have taken my chances.'

'I really enjoyed it.'

'You know what? It wasn't bad.'

'Spoken like a true Northerner,' laughed Sophie. 'Master of understatement.'

'It's our stock in trade.' Ben tipped his head as they headed down the hill.

'I'll see you tomorrow,' he said, raising a hand in farewell. 'Maybe I'll bring in a couple of cows for everyone to paint, then we can both work on the old comfort zone thing together.'

Sophie stood by the car watching him as he strode off down the track marked PRIVATE. He was heading back towards Applemore House to visit Lachlan, he'd told her. Whoever Ben Lewis was, there was a lot more to him than first impressions had suggested. She didn't want to admit it to herself, and there was absolutely no way she'd admit it to Bea, who'd have them married off before she could speak, but she was definitely intrigued.

CHAPTER TWENTY

'I'm sorry,' groaned Mhairi at the end of the day, 'I just can't do it when I feel like this. I'm having cramps from hell.' She put a hand to her stomach and rolled her eyes dramatically.

'You need to go to the GP about that,' said Grace, coming up behind her and putting her hands on Mhairi's hunched shoulders. 'You shouldn't be having period pains that bad at your age. At any age, come to think of it.' She squeezed gently on Mhairi's shoulders then released them, just as Mhairi tipped up her head to give a grateful smile.

'I feel really bad, Sophie. I'm the one who dragged you along to art class. You don't mind missing this week, do you?'

Sophie loosened her hair from her ponytail and untangled it with her fingers, shaking her dark curls loose for a moment before she looped it back into the band. She glanced up at the clock on the wall above the reception desk, making a mental calculation as she spoke.

'You know what,' she said, casually, 'I think I might go anyway. It's not like I've got anything else to do.'

'Seriously?' Mhairi's little face lit up. 'Oh that makes me feel loads less guilty.'

'Don't feel guilty,' Sophie said. 'You can't help feeling grim. You need to get home and have a night on the sofa with a hot water bottle, some chocolate and a Netflix binge.'

'And some painkillers,' added Grace, returning from the back room and catching the end of her sentence.

'Yes, and some ibuprofen. And make a doctor's appointment.'

'I will,' nodded Mhairi.

'I'll lock up,' said Grace, looking over at Sophie. 'You get off and get organised for your art class. You'll be needing your beret and your little palette and all the rest of it.' She chuckled.

'Something like that, Sophie laughed.

She jumped in the car and headed home, peeling off her filthy uniform and scrubbing herself clean under the boiling hot shower, washing and conditioning her hair before wrapping it up in a fluffy towel while she dried herself thoroughly, taking the time to put on some of the nice Clarins body lotion that she'd bought herself a while ago as a treat but which she kept forgetting to use. A bit like shutting the stable door after the horse had bolted, she thought regretfully, squishing the podge of her stomach and watching as the stretch marks that Tabby's pregnancy had caused puckered up, ghosts of long ago. They were silver and faded now where almost twenty years before they'd been vivid red stripes – Tabby had been a huge baby, almost ten pounds.

Ah well, Sophie thought, wrapping the towel round her chest again and wiping the mirror with her arm to clear away the condensation, it wasn't as if she was going to be showing her body to anyone any time soon. Goodness knows where her train of thought was going. She made a face at herself in the mirror. Maybe she'd put on a bit of make-up, just to perk herself up a bit, and definitely not because she'd been thinking all day about how much she was looking forward to the class. When Mhairi had said she couldn't make it her heart had sunk before she realised that there was nothing to stop her going on her own. And there was nothing to stop her sticking on a bit of cream blush and some grey eyeliner and a swipe of – she reached into her bag – mascara.

There, that would do. She brushed her eyebrows upwards, because she'd read somewhere that doing so was like having a free face lift. It didn't make any discernible difference and she frowned at herself in the mirror then shook her head, turning away and heading for the bedroom.

Get a grip, she told herself. You are behaving like a teenager with a crush.

When she arrived – with only a few minutes to spare - at the gallery, the students were gathered in a huddle outside the glass door. Dolina turned on hearing Sophie's footsteps on the gravel.

'Did you hear about this?'

'About what?'

'There's a notice, look.' She waved an arm in the direction of the door as Sophie approached. Tortoiseshell glasses woman folded her arms with an expression of dismay.

'I saw Ben in the shop yesterday,' she said, her freshly painted mouth puckering into a little scowl, 'And he didn't say anything about this. I suspect it's not his idea.'

Change of location for tonight – head up to the Flower Farm and I'll see you all there. B.

THE WRITING WAS firm and precise, and definitely that of an artist. It looked like the sort of script you'd see on a posh birthday card. Sophie chewed her lower lip.

'What do you think we're doing up there?' Dolina looked up at her with a concerned expression.

'Well I should think it'll be some sort of drawing,' said tortoiseshell glasses, hitching her bag onto her shoulder and turning on her heel. 'We'd better get a move on, or we'll all be late.'

With a skittering of gravel under her feet, she shot off towards her car.

'I expect she's got an apple for the teacher in that bag,' said Dolina, acerbically.

'Shush,' giggled Sophie. Then, lowering her voice and laughing, she added 'I did think the same thing last week.'

'Aye,' said Dolina, nodding. 'There's always one, isn't there?'

'It does seem to be the case,' Sophie said. 'Do you want a lift up in my car? It seems silly all of us driving up separately. How far is it?'

'Och, that would be lovely,' said Dolina, beckoning a younger woman and her friend. 'Jenny, Sarah, come on, we'll all jump in the car with – it's Sophie, isn't it?'

'That's right.' Sophie shot ahead, trying to simultaneously look welcoming and scoop an armful of random tat off the back seat of her car, tossing it onto the parcel shelf and hoping they didn't have to make an emergency stop. 'Sorry, it's a bit untidy.'

'I imagine you don't get much time to get on with cleaning the car,' said Dolina, lifting up an empty crisp packet and two boxes of dog worming tablets that were sitting on the front seat and plonking herself down comfortably. 'Don't worry, every vet I've ever known has a car that looks like a midden.'

Sophie, who wasn't quite sure what a midden was but inferred that it wasn't something very tidy, smiled again.

'Which way?' She was assuming it must be right, because the alternative was heading back down the drive towards the road back into the village, and she hadn't spotted any flower farm type places on her journey.

'Just up the road,' said Dolina, turning round to make sure the other two were settled. 'This is Jenny, my daughter, by the way, and her friend Sarah. Jenny works in the farm shop.'

Ah, that was why she'd looked vaguely familiar. Saying hello, Sophie set off.

'Have you seen the big house?' Dolina was sitting bolt upright in her seat which was slightly unnerving.

'I haven't, no.' She'd been desperate to have a look, wondering what it could be like – she knew from the girls in the surgery that Lachlan Fraser had spent a fortune doing it up after it had fallen into disrepair, and that they'd worked hard to turn the grounds into a wild camping destination which was popular with both campervans and tent-dwellers alike. She'd had a look on Google Maps, but the road petered out beyond the entrance to the driveway so you couldn't use the little man to walk along and imagine you were there. When Ben had turned off down the path marked PRIVATE the other day it had only piqued her curiosity even more, so it was nice to have a legitimate reason to be there.

'All this was overgrown,' Dolina was explaining as they followed one of the other pupils up the track in their little red Ford. They were driving for some reason at five miles per hour. 'The place basically went to rack and ruin when the old Laird was living here. Remind me and I'll tell you the whole story one day of him and the inventor chappie that lived in the lodge cottage back down at the shop. That was Polly Fraser's place until recently,' she continued, 'But of course now she's moved in with Harry at the hotel – you'll have met them, yes?'

Sophie nodded. The red car in front had now inexplicably ground to a halt. She tapped a finger on the steering wheel as she waited for the driver to remember they were supposed to be heading in the direction of the art class.

'Anyway,' Dolina started up again. 'Ah here we go. Just around the bend here, you'll see the big house.'

Applemore House spoke for itself. It was a huge, beautiful old house – or was it a castle? Sophie wasn't sure what the difference was – with turrets and tiny windows, a huge wooden door and a neatly mown lawn studded by trees that stretched down towards a dip in the landscape, beyond which lay a picturesque wood.

'It's beautiful.'

'Isn't it?' Dolina looked up at it proudly as they passed. 'And Lachlan's such a nice laddie, and his – she's not his wife, because they don't go in for weddings, apparently – well, his girlfriend Rilla is very nice too. They've a little girl called Kitty who just started at the nursery school in the village where Sarah works.'

Sarah, who until now had been looking quietly out of the window, leaned forward from the back seat, pushing her light brown hair back from her face and nodding.

'She's very nice,' Sarah said. 'Not at all stuck up. She's not from money, of course.'

'Not that the Frasers exactly had much money until Lachlan struck it lucky,' Dolina pointed towards a tall sandstone wall over which long strands of greenery were growing. 'That's it.'

Sophie pulled up behind the red car which had parked against the grass verge. There was a little painted door in the wall, and Dolina led on, beckoning everyone to follow her.

CHAPTER TWENTY-ONE

Inside the walled garden Sophie was amazed to discover that every centimetre of the place seemed to have been put to use. Long beds, neatly dug over and with their grass edges trimmed, held serried rows of baby plants and tall shoots held in place with supports made from hazel cuttings. Turning she saw two huge beds of tulips, their colour just peeking out from beneath tightly closed buds.

'In here,' said a familiar low voice. Sophie's stomach lurched as she turned to her left, where Ben was standing, his tall, broad frame filling the doorway of an old-fashioned Victorian glasshouse which stood against one wall of the garden.

'Are you playing hide and seek with us?' Dolina gave a surprisingly skittish giggle.

'Mother,' said Jenny, looking at Sophie and Sarah and shaking her head. 'Honestly, I can't take her anywhere.'

'I was hoping you might all give up and go home and I could get an early night,' said Ben, stepping back to allow them to pass. Sophie flicked a glance up at him as she stepped over the threshold into the greenhouse, and he raised his eyebrows briefly in greeting.

'Nice to see you decided to come back,' he said behind her, closing the door and following her into the room. Once again she felt oddly conscious of his physical presence. She hastily rubbed her mouth with the back of her hand to take off the rose coloured gloss she'd reapplied when she'd arrived at the gallery. Last week she'd turned up with unbrushed hair and a scruffy work hoody, and today she looked like she'd made an effort, and the idea he might think it was for him made her feel strangely uncomfortable.

He'd clearly worked hard. All ten of the easels that they'd used last week were now standing in a semi-circle around a workbench which was stacked with massed tulips and bunches of colourful purple hyacinths and white daisies, neat piles of terracotta pots and rolls of brown hessian string. A ream of brown paper and an old fashioned ink stamp sat to one side.

'Hi, everyone,' said a tall blonde woman with a smile. 'Ben, I'll let you get on and I'll get out of your hair. I've left the kitchen door open so you can get whatever you need for your break time.' She looked at everyone as she unfastened a brown apron and untied it, tossing it on the table without thinking then looking concerned. She waved her hand over it and looked at Ben with a worried expression. 'Oh Ben, sorry. Is this okay here?'

'It's perfect.' Ben laughed. 'I'm not rearranging the place, I'm leaving it exactly as it is, you don't need to worry.'

'He said he wanted to use it for a still life,' the woman explained, turning to everyone again. 'Of course I've spent the whole afternoon tidying the place up because I didn't want you thinking it was a bomb site the rest of the time.'

'It's perfect,' Ben said again, and shooed her out of the

greenhouse. 'Now go and enjoy dinner. I hear you're being taken out.'

'You did?'

Ben nodded. 'Bumped into Jack the other day when I was over with the dogs.'

'They're all very pally,' said Dolina, in a whisper, as she leant over to Sophie. 'That's Beth Fraser,' she explained. 'She grew up here. Of course this place didn't look like this back then, it was a wilderness.'

'By all accounts,' said Ben, making Dolina jump, 'Beth did it all herself.' He caught Sophie's eye. Dolina's chest puffed out in surprise, but she said nothing.

Ben turned and thrust his hands in the back pockets of his jeans, widening his stance slightly as he waited for everyone to come to a pause in their chatter.

'Right, everyone, I thought we'd have a go at something completely different this week and throw you in at the deep end. So we've got an hour and a half or thereabouts, with fifteen minutes for a cup of tea or whatever you like in the middle, and you've got this whole scene in front of you to paint.'

'What do you want us to do?' Tortoiseshell glasses looked at him anxiously.

'Well,' said Ben, deadpan, 'You've got an easel, a set of acrylics, and a few brushes.'

'And what exactly do you want us to do with them?'

Ben didn't say anything, but looked at the woman for a long moment, his eyebrow very slowly lifting, almost imperceptibly.

Sophie ducked her head, thinking for a moment that if she caught Ben's eye there was a distinct possibility she might burst out laughing.

'Right, so just a painting of what we can see in front of us?'

'That's the general idea, yes.'

'How do we know if we're getting it right?'

'Hordes of angels will fall from the heavens singing and playing the harp, I expect.'

'Really?' The woman looked at him for a moment. 'Oh you're joking.'

'I am,' said Ben, then he seemed to soften slightly. 'Sorry, I'm only having you on.' His accent thickened slightly as he said that. 'Whatever you do, that's right. That's the beauty of art. Whether you like it at the end or not, that's another matter. But if you paint what's in front of you, that's generally a good start.'

He might have been dry and sarcastic to start with, but as everyone settled down to their work, Sophie couldn't help noticing that he took the time to move around the students, giving each one tips on perspective and shading, talking to them about what they could see and how they wanted to portray it on the canvas in front of them.

She tried to focus on her work and not on wondering why he hadn't come to look at what she was doing, only walking past and passing her by as he went on to make Dolina giggle girlishly as he leaned over her, pointing to a particular flower she'd been working hard on.

'I'll put the kettle on for a brew in a moment,' he said after what felt like minutes. Sophie looked up and checked the time on her watch.

'I didn't realise we'd been working for so long.'

'Well look at that,' said Dolina, admiringly. 'That's looking lovely.'

'The apron is impossible to paint, isn't it?' Sophie pointed to an indistinct brown shape. 'I wish she hadn't left it lying there.'

'Mine looks like something shed its skin,' said Sarah, giggling and pointing to her picture.

'The tulips are lovely though,' Sophie said, consolingly.

'Maybe I should have done you all a favour and moved Beth's apron,' said Ben, five minutes later as they stood around drinking tea and eating chocolate brownies.

'I see we're getting the treats this week,' said Dolina, wiping crumbs from her mouth.

'Yeah, I thought I'd wait and see if you came back before I put my hand in my pocket,' said Ben, with a short laugh.

'Or if you did,' said Jenny.

'That as well.' He rubbed his bearded jawline.

'How is Mel doing? I saw Greta at the shop and she said something about her going down to Ayr to see her sister?'

'Yeah,' Ben nodded. 'I think she was going mad sitting at home doing nothing, and Fi had loads of work on as the season's getting going with the holiday cottages, so she shipped Mel off to get out of her hair.'

'Does that mean you're stuck with us for all the sessions?' Dolina raised an eyebrow. 'And to think I heard Jack telling Lachlan you'd never stick it.'

Ben growled slightly. 'Yeah, I heard they put money on it. That means I'm bloody well going to see it through.'

'We better be on our best behaviour then,' Jenny said, with a giggle.

'You better had.' Ben looked directly at Sophie as he spoke, and she felt a bolt of something unnervingly like desire shooting straight through her. Shaken, she dropped his gaze and fiddled with her coffee mug, turning it around in her hands, admiring the hand-made pottery design.

'It'll be clay next,' he said, a moment later, noticing. She looked up.

'Pottery?' Surely not some sort of Ghost situation with a

potters wheel and everyone looking on as she tried to make something from a lump of clay.

'Oh aye,' said Dolina, waggling her eyebrows. 'I always liked that Patrick Swayze. Shame he passed away, he was a bit of a dish, wasn't he?'

'Freehand,' he added with a chuckle, 'Don't go getting ideas. It's not that sort of class.'

The second half of the class flew past. By the end of it, everyone had at the very least covered their canvas and made a passable effort at painting the scene in front of them, and in some cases they'd created something really quite impressive. Jenny, Dolina's daughter, clearly had a talent for painting. Sophie had done a decent job of the tulips and the terracotta pots, but the brown apron on the front of the workbench still looked like some sort of muddy splodge.

'I can't seem to get it to look like anything,' she groaned, as they wiped up their brushes.

'There's always something,' Ben said, gathering everyone round to close up the class. 'The biggest enemy of art is perfectionism. For most of you it's been years – some of you decades – since you painted.'

'You suggesting we're all ancient?' Dolina chortled with laughter at her own joke.

'I wouldn't dream of it.' Ben carried on. 'Good work everyone. I'll see you next week.'

'What are we working on?' Tortoiseshell glasses took out a little notebook and a pen and stood with an eager expression. Sophie had discovered at the coffee break that her name was actually Helen, but the nickname had stuck in her mind and she couldn't shift the association.

'Clay, didn't you hear?' Jenny said, looking at Ben for confirmation. He gave a brief nod.

'Oh good,' she said, noting it down and popping the book back into her bag.

'See you tomorrow,' Ben said to Sophie as she passed by him as they all trooped out. Dolina's ears perked up and Sophie could see she was making a mental note for later. No doubt that would be around the village grapevine in seconds if she didn't put a lid on it straight away.

'Do you want a hand with the cleaning up?' Helen paused for a moment on the step of the greenhouse, looking back at Ben, who shook his head, arms already full of paints which he was dumping back into a wooden crate.

'You're alright, thanks. Won't take long.'

It was still light outside and the long rays of the evening sun lit up the flower garden, warming everything with a pale golden glow. Everything seemed to be bursting into life, bright green and vibrant, just on the verge of flowering. It looked beautiful, but Sophie – who was not a gardener – thought it looked like a tremendous amount of work. Beth must be mad about flowers to want to spend all her time working here.

She opened the car and waited as Jenny and Sarah made themselves comfortable in the back.

'Oh aye?' Dolina looked at Sophie as she sat down in the passenger seat, an inquisitive expression on her face. She didn't earn her reputation as queen of the village gossips for nothing. She narrowed her eyes for a moment, but they were twinkling with amusement. 'What's all this. Are you having extra art classes with our hunky teacher?'

Sophie shook her head, laughing and hoping desperately that she wasn't going red in the face. 'No, one of his dogs is coming into the surgery. I probably won't even see him,' she added, trying to sound offhand. 'It'll probably be Thea or one of the nurses.'

She turned the key in the ignition and nothing happened. Dolina looked at her with an alarmed expression.

'Is that normal?'

'Oh, it is for this car,' Sophie said, trying again. 'It's a bit temperamental. It's been a while since it's been sticky, mind you.'

On the third attempt it burst into life and they drove back down to the gallery, laughing and chatting about their attempts to paint the flowers and wondering what next week would bring.

She drove back down to the gallery, and got out of the car while everyone climbed out and headed off to their respective vehicles. The Farm Shop was closed, but fairy lights glowed in all the windows, giving the place a magical air.

'Thanks for the lift,' said Jenny, touching her on the arm.

Sophie turned and smiled. 'No problem. See you next week.'

Dolina gave a cheery wave as she beetled off to get into her spotless little car. Sophie had just climbed back into the driver's seat when her phone rang. At this time of the evening it was only likely to be Tabby. She pulled it out of her bag.

'Hello?'

'Mum, I can't stop, just running into class,' Tabby said, breathlessly.

Sophie smiled to herself at the Americanism. She'd be losing her accent next.

'Hi darling, it's lovely to hear you. What's up?'

'I've been selected for the challenge cup team. Just had to call and tell you. Can you believe it?'

Sophie's heart swelled with pride. 'Oh Tab, that's amazing, well done.'

'Thanks! I better go, I'll message you later.'

'Love you darling,' she called, as Tabby said goodbye and the phone went silent.

She looked down at the blank screen. It really was true what they said about having a child. Part of her heart was thousands of miles away, running around a university campus in Atlanta, Georgia. But she had to admit that Tabby seemed to have settled and was living her best life over there – and up here in the Highlands, she owed it to herself to try and do the same. She put the phone back in her bag and started the car, ready to head home. It was strange how tiring painting could be.

The car, however, had other ideas.

'Come on,' she said, turning the key in the ignition again. It spluttered and then cut out. Sophie looked in the rear view mirror, realising that the car parking area was completely empty.

Right, she told herself, take a moment, let it sort itself out, take a deep breath. It'll be fine. She sat back and counted to twenty, then tried again.

After waiting five minutes, trying very hard to be patient and not panic, she closed her eyes and made a wish, then – with fingers, toes and everything else possible crossed, she tried one more time.

The engine made a feeble *phut* and then cut out.

'Oh come *on*,' said Sophie, banging the steering wheel with her hand. 'You can't do this now.'

'You alright?'

The car door opened, and Ben loomed over her, a curious expression on his face.

'I am,' she said, making a face, 'but the car isn't. It's not starting.'

'Hmm.' He looked thoughtful. 'Try turning it over again?

Nothing happened.

'Sounds like the battery might be flat. Let me move mine round, we can try it with jump leads.'

A couple of moments later, having manoeuvred his pick up into position and rummaged around in the back, Ben returned with a rueful expression on his face, rubbing his chin.

'I mean we could try it with jump leads, if I hadn't left them back at the house when I emptied this thing out so I could fit everything in to take it up to the Flower Farm.'

He dashed a palm to his head, laughing. 'Best plans, and all that.'

'It's fine,' said Sophie, picking up her phone. 'I'll just ring the AA.'

'Are you forgetting where we are?' Ben's eyebrows rose. 'We're not in Kansas anymore, this is the Highlands.'

'Oh.'

'Yeah. I mean there's got to be some payback for all this.' Ben waved an arm in the general direction of the pine-covered hills and the rolling moorlands bathed pale pink and gold courtesy of the sun which was setting in a cloud streaked sky. 'I can give you a lift back, if you like?'

'What about the car?'

'Leave the keys on the top of the front wheel, we'll give the mechanic a ring and he'll come over first thing.'

Sophie cocked her head sideways slightly in puzzlement.

'You say that like you have a mechanic just waiting on the end of the phone for your call.'

'He's a mate.' Ben beckoned her out of the car. 'Come on, I promise I won't bite.'

Sophie glanced over at him for a second. 'What about all the stuff you took up to the greenhouse?'

He shrugged. 'It'll wait. I can bring it back up tomorrow when I give you a lift up to get your car. If you want a lift, that is.'

He tossed a couple of boxes off the front seat and stepped back to let her in.

'Sorry it's a bit of a tip,' he explained, as they set off.

'Oh don't worry, Dolina's already remarked on the state of my car.' Sophie laughed. 'I expect it'll be noted down in her encyclopaedia of Applemore residents.'

'Sounds like you've got her number.' Ben slowed for a moment and pointed out of the window. 'Look at that.'

Three deer stopped dead in the woods to the side of the drive, pausing for a moment to stare at them in silence before turning and scampering off into the dark of the trees.

'We might not have the AA at our fingertips, but you've got to admit this place is pretty cool.'

Sophie looked at him as he drove along the narrow single track road, one hand resting casually on the wheel and the other resting.

'It is. Village gossips notwithstanding,' She pushed her hair back behind her ears and almost without thinking wiped a finger under her eyes, checking for smudged mascara. She shifted slightly in her seat, feeling very conscious of how close they were despite the broad armrest which divided them. His left elbow rested close to hers, the sleeve of his red plaid shirt rolled up to show off the muscular forearms she'd noticed before. He didn't look at all like an artist – or what she'd imagined one would look like. If someone had asked, she'd have expected someone slight and ethereal – whatever gender they were. Ben, though, was undeniably masculine, with the clothing and build of a forestry worker. He even had the woolly hat, she noticed, spotting a grey knitted hat lying on the dashboard. And now here she was sitting in his car on the way home to the cottage, desperately trying to think of something to say.

CHAPTER TWENTY-TWO

Ben stole a glance across at Sophie. She was gazing out of the window at the sight of Applemore, her legs tucked to one side, one arm sitting on the arm rest close to his. It wasn't often that he offered people a lift – to be honest, there weren't that many people that he could be bothered with. But there was something about Sophie – the way the freckles were sprinkled on her cheeks, the long hair with just the faintest threading of silver which she hadn't covered with colour – that he couldn't seem to get enough of. He'd stood watching her from the back of the room while she painted, the apron emphasising her waist and that deliciously plump bottom which…

He shook himself. What the hell was going on in his head?

He cleared his throat, making her turn to look at him. Her mouth was parted slightly, the pink stain she'd been wearing when she first arrived long gone. She had a habit, he'd noticed, of chewing her bottom lip when she was concentrating on a tricky part of a painting.

'I'd have asked Lachlan for a jump start,' he said, his voice gruff as if he'd not spoken for days, 'But he's down at Beth's place babysitting tonight.'

Sophie smiled. 'It's okay, it's really kind of you to offer me a lift.'

'Well, the alternative would have been you being stuck up there until we managed to get a hold of Jack from the garage and given it's dominos night down at the pub you'd be on a hiding to nothing.'

'When you put it like that…'

'Exactly.'

They pulled onto the road and rounded the corner, about to head down the hill towards the village, when a young lad in a dark boilersuit appeared, putting a hand up to stop them.

'Do you mind holding on a wee minute? We're just moving the cattle from one field to the other.'

'Course not.' Ben looked over at Sophie, remembering she'd mentioned she wasn't exactly a fan of cows. 'You aren't going to have a panic attack or anything?'

'Very funny.' She raised her eyebrows and made a face.

'I don't expect this happened much when you were living in town.'

They sat together, watching the procession of black and white cows. They took their time, bumbling across the road, stopping to peer at the car and splatter the tarmac with cow pats, making them both laugh.

'They don't exactly stand on ceremony.' Sophie was absently twirling a strand of hair in her fingers, looking up at him through long lashes as she turned to him and spoke.

'No, not really.'

An older man in a matching boilersuit rapped the bonnet of the truck as the last few cows skittered across the road, tails up in the air. He spotted Sophie and raised a finger to his forehead in a brief salute.

'That's us done now,' he said, giving a brief nod of thanks. Ben watched as he closed the gate securely and the two of them stood leaning over the top bar, watching the herd as they scattered in different directions.

'You've met Jimmy and Young Jimmy, then?' Ben put the car back in gear and they set off.

'Yeah, well, Old Jimmy, at least. He was part of my trial by fire in the first week.'

'How are you finding it?'

'Good.'

'Big change coming up here by yourself.'

'It is,' she nodded. 'It's the funny things you notice, though. Talking of which, I've just remembered – oh no, it doesn't matter.' She shook her head.

'Have you left something up at the car? Do you want me to turn around?'

'No, I've just realised I forgot about dinner. I was going to pick something up on the way home.'

He glanced at the display on the dashboard. 'The little shop's closed already – shuts at seven. What did you need? I've got milk and stuff.'

'Dinner, mostly. If the shop had been closed I'd just have driven the ten miles to town and gone to the garage. It's my own fault, I'm hopeless at feeding myself when it's just me.'

'I went through that phase when I first moved up.' The tiny germ of an idea was growing – was it too much to ask? He wasn't sure what the protocol was. It had been so long.

'Yeah left to my own devices I'd end up eating cereal and toast like a student. Then I decided even ready meals were an improvement, but I've been flat out with work and we had an emergency op that ran over last night, so I ended up not getting to the shop.' Sophie rubbed her nose. 'I'm sure I can find something.'

'You can stop at mine and have something if you like. I've got a ragu in the oven and there's only me. Saves me eating it for the next three days on the trot,' he added, then grimaced internally. Smooth, effortlessly smooth. He shook his head briefly.

'If you don't mind?'

He was surprised that she said yes. She seemed genuinely enthusiastic about the idea, in fact.

'Not at all. It'll be nice to have some company.'

They passed through the village and back up the other side of the glen out towards the croft. The light was fading now, and the hills had changed colour once again. It was like living in a series of beautiful landscape paintings.

He stopped at the gate and jumped out to open it, driving through and pausing on the track.

'I'll get it,' Sophie said, climbing out of her seat and fastening the gate securely. She climbed back inside, rubbing her arms. 'Ooh, it's colder than it looks, isn't it?'

'Always is.'

The dogs were waiting at the door, spinning on the spot with excitement. Otto recognised Sophie and jumped up at her delightedly.

'This is a warmer welcome than I got the first time we met,' she said, teasing them.

Ben took off his plaid shirt and tossed it onto the table, heading first for the wood burner. He'd stocked it well before he left, but the logs were running low.

'I'll just grab some wood from the yard.' He motioned to the chair closest to the stove, remembering she was chilly. 'Take a seat. I'll be back in a sec.'

When he got back in with the full log basket, he found her sitting perched on the end of the seat, knees tucked up, the dogs sitting on either side of her looking quite at home with their unexpected house guest.

'They don't often see anyone in here but Annie, so you're clearly approved of.'

'Either that or I've secretly drugged them,' she said, with a half-smile, running a hand down Bear's back. For a moment he paused, watching, then shook himself. Whatever the hell was going on, he needed to get a grip.

'Well, it appears to be working.' He took out a couple of glasses from the dresser. 'Can I get you a drink? I've got some wine if you fancy it. Half the bottle went in the ragu, we might as well have the other half.'

'That would be lovely.'

He turned away, trying to figure out what the hell he was feeling as he tipped the wine into glasses on the other side of the room. He'd shared drinks with friends, of course, and Annie had come round on occasion over the years, only ever having half a glass and then fanning herself and saying that it was going to her head before she disappeared into the night. But until now he'd drawn a line.

'Here you are.'

They sat in silence for a few moments sipping their drinks, the clock on the wall ticking uncomfortably loudly. Thankfully Otto took it upon himself to provide entertainment and decided that now was a good time to bum-scoot himself across the rough jute rug.

'Do we need to have words?' Sophie said, eyeing him and laughing.

Ben covered his face with his hands. 'You're ruining my street cred,' he said as Otto hopped up on to the bench beside him.

That seemed to break the ice. He filled a pot with water and put it on the stove to boil.

'This place is amazing,' Sophie said, looking around. 'Did you do it all yourself?'

'Pretty much. My daughter helped in the holidays when she was around.'

'Oh yes, Annie mentioned you had a daughter – '

He watched as Sophie unconsciously did a quick scan of the room, looking for signs of Esther. Her eyes lit on the photograph on the wall of her as a little girl.

'-How old is she?'

'Oh, she's grown up. She's doing a postgrad down in Bristol.'

'Ah.' She smiled, and he watched her long fingers cupping the bowl of the glass. 'I wondered if she was upstairs. I've got a teenage daughter at university, too.'

'No, she's not upstairs. Wish she was, sometimes.'

Where had that come from? He wasn't usually in the habit of giving anything away, and straight off here he was casually sharing information. He looked down at the dark red of the wine in his glass for a moment before taking a long draught.

'Weird, isn't it? I find myself getting up in the mornings and being disappointed the kitchen's still tidy.'

'Yeah.' He reached over, holding the bottle over her glass with a questioning look. She nodded and he tipped in more this time. 'She's only ever been with me in holidays since I moved up here, but she leaves a big gap when she goes.'

'So you moved up here when – did you – ' Sophie stopped midsentence. 'Sorry, I don't mean to give you the third degree.'

'You're not. It's fine. She – well, my ex and I split just as we were on the verge of moving up here. I'd got everything lined up, and I just decided to take the plunge. Esther was at boarding school anyway –'

Sophie's eyebrows raised almost imperceptibly.

'-I know what you're thinking. It was her mother's parents.

They'd a trust fund in place for it, wanted her to go to the same school her mother went to. Goodness knows why.' Thankfully she didn't turn out anything like her mother, he wanted to add, but didn't.

'So it didn't make a huge difference moving to the Highlands.' Sophie folded her hands, resting her chin on top of them and looking at him thoughtfully.

He gave a brief nod. 'Pretty much. She was at that age where parents are the most embarrassing thing in the world -'

'I'm glad that's over. It's the worst stage, isn't it?'

'-Awful.' He laughed. 'Anyway, now she comes up when she can, but she's off gallivanting round the place. Sailing this weekend, believe it or not.'

'Very posh. Maybe the whole boarding school thing did rub off.' Sophie gave a teasing smile and he shook his head at her.

'You can talk, with your veterinary science degree.'

'I told you I was brought up in a terrace.'

'You did.' He got up to check the water, which was almost coming to the boil, and tossed in some sea salt crystals.

'So your daughter – Esther – is she an artist, too?'

Ben gave a bark of amused laughter. 'No, absolutely not. She has no truck with what she calls 'all that arty farty nonsense'. She's a civil engineer, or she will be once she graduates. She's working nights on the motorways at the moment, doing some research project or other.'

'That's amazing.' Sophie was absent-mindedly caressing Bear's long, silky ears with one hand.

'And your daughter?'

'She's on a football scholarship in the states. Goodness knows where she got the sport gene from, because it wasn't me.'

He tipped some pappardelle out of the packet, taking it in

his hand and letting it slide into the now boiling water, giving a quick stir to create a miniature whirlpool in the pot. He couldn't stop himself from asking, hoping what the answer would be.

'Her dad, is he sporty?'

'He's not in the equation. We split up when she was tiny, and he moved abroad. He's not in her life.' Her tone was neutral, not bitter, he noted.

'Oh, sorry.'

'Oh no,' Sophie laughed, 'Don't be. He was a complete arsehole.'

'Well that makes me feel better. So you're not nursing a broken heart or anything like that?'

She gave him a slightly odd sideways look over the top of her wine glass.

'Definitely not.'

'I just wondered if that was the reason you –'

Bloody hell, he shouldn't be allowed out alone after dark. That had sounded like a chat up line when all he'd meant was he –

'- I didn't move up here to get away from the one that got away, if that's what you're thinking.' Sophie took a drink and put her wine back down, laying her palms flat on either side of the glass and sitting back slightly, as if putting her cards on the table. 'I – well, Tabby – that's my daughter – she was off at university in America, being bold and brave and making something of her life. And there I was stuck in the same dead end job I'd been doing since she was a baby and I graduated. I felt like I needed to put my money where my mouth was and show her I could do something as well.'

He was impressed. 'It's not an easy step moving up here.'

'You know it.' Sophie finished her wine.

He turned to the dresser which was just out of reach, picking up a second bottle.

'Shall we?'

'You're not saving it for a special occasion?'

'I live in the arse end of nowhere in the far north west of Scotland. What kind of special occasion are you thinking of?'

'When you put it like that,' Sophie said, pushing her glass in his direction. 'It's not like I have to drive home.'

'The dogs and I will see you right,' he said, twisting the corkscrew and opening the second bottle.

'There wasn't even half left in the other one anyway,' Sophie said, smiling a thank you as he passed her another – fuller, this time – glass. 'Although it's been ages since I've drunk anything. It feels a bit weird sitting drinking alone down there.'

'That's why I got these two.' He motioned to the dogs, who'd both now flopped onto the rug in front of the stove and were sleeping flat out.

'Maybe I need a dog.'

'Or someone to drink wine with.' He tipped his glass towards hers. 'Cheers.'

CHAPTER TWENTY-THREE

'This place is amazing.' Sophie got up from her chair, and wandered around the big kitchen, cupping her wine glass in her hand. Neither dog moved as she stood up, but Otto wagged a lazy tail in acknowledgement. Ben moved around the stove, preparing dinner.

The room was roughly plastered with simple whitewashed walls and a flagstone floor partially covered with a huge woven jute rug on which stood a long table of bare, waxed oak. A simple wooden worktop ran along the length of one wall, with a white stone sink and open shelving above it, on which stood neat stacks of plates and jugs, all in shades of stylish dark grey. She touched one of them, picking it up and turning it over.

'These are amazing. Did you make them?'

Ben turned back from the stove. 'Yeah.' He grinned. 'Allergic to Ikea, y'see.'

'I can tell.' She raised her brows. The place looked like something from a trendy house renovation Instagram account. It was understated and simple, and had the stamp of an artist all over it.

'Food's up,' he said, and she turned back.

'This is really kind of you,' she said, sitting down on the bench opposite him. He'd put a long tranche of wood on the table and on top of it placed the Le Creuset casserole in which sat the most delicious, deep-red ragu sprinkled over with a handful of fresh thyme and a slug of olive oil. A moment later he put another dish on the table, this one containing fat pappardelle pasta which steamed invitingly, and a pasta spoon.

'Help yourself,' he said, with an open handed gesture.

He'd warmed the plates, too, Sophie noticed, as she scooped some of the pasta on and topped it with sauce.

'I would've mixed it, Italian style,' he said, offering the black pepper grinder to her, 'But I got into the habit when Esther was little of serving it separately. She used to have this thing about food not touching.'

Sophie laughed. 'I was the same when I was a child.'

'And now?' He looked over the top of the dishes at her plate, a smile tugging at the corners of his lips.

'Now I'm mostly just delighted to be fed something so delicious,' she said, wiping a stray splash of sauce from her chin. 'This is amazing.'

'I'm just glad you're not a vegetarian or dinner would have been a bit more of a problem.'

'No, definitely not a vegetarian.' This meat was so melt in the mouth delicious that it would convert anyone.

'It was a present from my friend who's a gamekeeper.'

'You see,' she laughed. 'You don't really keep yourself to yourself.'

He rubbed the side of his face thoughtfully, fork in mid-air. 'You get to know people, true enough. I expect it'll be the same for you, especially being a vet. It must go with the territory. Did you leave loads of mates down south?'

She thought for a moment before speaking. 'Not really.' How to tell someone that over the years, life had shrunk for her? 'I – well, between work and being a single mum to Tabby, and all her football stuff – time seemed to get away from me.'

He nodded. 'I get that. It must have been tricky juggling it all. I can't imagine being a vet is exactly a nine to five job.'

'It depends a lot on the practice. This place is a lot easier because we don't have constant on call, because it's shared with two other surgeries. Means I can go to art class and have dinner with the teacher.' She looked at him and he met her eye for a moment before looking away. Don't make this weird, Sophie, she told herself. It was such an unusual situation. It had been so long since she'd been out with a man – not that this was a date, of course. But just being one-on-one with one outside of work was completely alien.

'Don't think I'm going to go easy on you next week,' he said, with a teasing look in his eye. 'In fact, I'll have to be twice as strict in case Dolina gets wind of anything.'

'She's not as bad as she's made out.'

'Aye, to be fair she's actually been quite decent in the classes. Until now I'd always thought of her as nothing more than the village gossip, but she's not bad at heart.'

'She's been nice to me,' said Sophie, who was still relieved that she'd been given the seal of approval.

'She was a bit off with me when I first arrived. I think she's always thinking the worst of blokes, because she had a bit of a bad time with her husband.'

'Oh really?' Sophie sat forward. 'How so?'

'Think he was in and out of prison more than once. Not that I'm gossiping about the village gossip, mind. Polly Fraser told me about it in passing one day. Anyway, after I heard that

I softened my opinion a bit. No wonder she's suspicious about people if she's had an experience like that.'

Sophie felt her eyes widening but said nothing.

'Anyway, enough about Dolina.' Ben reached over to tip some more wine into her glass then turned to toss another log onto the stove, twisting so his t-shirt rode up at the back revealing a back just as toned and muscular as his arms. She flexed the fingers of her left hand on the smooth wood of the table, for a fleeting moment imagining how it would feel to have his skin beneath her fingers. It had been a long, long time since she'd felt anything like this – if she ever had. He turned back to look at her and she dropped her gaze, concentrating on her food for a few moments.

'So you cut all the wood for the fire yourself?'

He looked up. 'Yeah. Well, I don't drag half an oak back from the woods – it gets dropped off. But yes, I process it all, log it up and stack it so it seasons. This stuff I'm burning is from a tree that came down a couple of years ago.'

'You're not living off grid though? I mean these lights?' She motioned to the wall lights which gave the room a warm glow. Outside the window the sky was darkening, the trees black against the skyline.

'No, that's common or garden National Grid. We'd struggle for solar power up here when it's winter. Summer too, come to think of it.' He laughed.

'That's a relief.'

'What is?'

'I was thinking with all the home caught beef –'

'-Venison.' He laughed.

'Oh no,' Sophie said, looking down at her plate, 'and we saw those cute deer on the way back as well.'

'You can be cute *and* delicious,' he said drily, looking at her with a blank expression on his face which made her laugh.

'Well, alright,' she felt her cheeks going pink. It must be the wine, she told herself. 'So you've got your home caught venison and your home chopped wood and you're living here out here in the middle of nowhere by yourself.'

'Well I was,' he said, dropping his chin into his hand and making a rueful expression, 'Until someone moved into the cottage down the road and started complaining about my dogs making a noise.'

'Very funny.' She wrinkled her nose at him. 'I thought they were going to have my arm off.'

Ben tipped his head in the direction of the sleeping dogs. 'I can see why you were concerned.'

'Well anyway,' she said, going to take another sip of wine and realising her glass was empty, 'Now I know they're not the Hounds of the Baskervilles I don't mind at all if you want to walk them down past the cottage.'

'That's good to know.' One eyebrow lifted almost imperceptibly.

'I mean I –' Why did he make her so tongue-tied? It was ridiculous. She shifted slightly in her seat, realising that the wine had gone straight through her and that she was suddenly desperate for the loo. '- You know what I mean,' she finished, and sat back in her chair, looking around.

Ben must have had a second sense because he pushed his chair back, and pointed in the direction of a stripped wooden door which was down a little step. 'I should have said, the bathroom's that way. Sorry.'

'Oh, thanks.'

The bathroom, predictably, was simple and stylish. A huge plain mirror hung over a simple white sink. The floor was wooden, and a dark grey towel was tossed over a huge heated rail which warmed the room. She was surprised to see a big freestanding bath as well as a separate shower. Looking at herself in the mirror as she washed her hands, she swiped at the smudges of mascara beneath her lashes and cursed herself for leaving her lip balm in the bag in the kitchen. Not, she told herself firmly, that she was trying to make herself nice for – oh, who was she kidding? She dried her hands on the towel, sniffing it to see if it smelled of the same whatever-it-was that made him smell so good, and – yes, it did. She glanced at herself in the mirror again. She had a flush on her cheeks which she could put down to wine and being in the company of an indisputably hot man – it was funny to think that the first time she'd seen him she'd thought he was some sort of unkempt bushman – but realistically she suspected it was down to being in her forties and not used to drinking much anymore. She sighed at her reflection. Far too old to be having ridiculous crushes on your art teacher, she told herself, as she headed back into the kitchen.

'I should probably walk you home,' Ben said, as she approached the table. He glanced up at the clock on the wall.

'Oh – sorry - yes,' she said, grabbing her bag so quickly that she spilled it across the table and had to hastily shove a stray tampon, a promo sample from a vet sales rep and her purse back inside. 'I'm sorry, I didn't mean to outstay my welcome.'

'You haven't at all.' Ben glanced at the bottle, which was empty, then directly back at her, his eyes holding hers. 'But if we don't get going now, we're going to have to open another one, and then neither of us is going to be in a fit state to make it down the track to your place and –'

Her stomach flipped over and she dropped his gaze, looking at the floor for a second before looking back up to see his eyes still fixed on her. Did he – was he feeling it, too? Surely not.

'Come on, you two. Call yourselves gentlemen?' Ben

nudged the sleeping Otto with the toe of his boot. The dogs sprung to life, tails wagging, suddenly excitable as they realised something was happening. Bear shot to the door and stood there, stock still.

'Contrary to popular belief,' Ben said, disappearing down a little passageway to the side of the kitchen, 'They are actually quite well trained.'

'I'm never going to live that down, am I?'

'Never.' Ben returned with a battered black wool coat. 'Here, you'll be freezing without it. Temperature drops really quickly at this time of the night.'

He wasn't wrong. Outside stars danced across an indigo sky, the moon hanging almost full above them. Ben opened the gate and stepped back to let Sophie through, closing it behind them as the dogs scampered ahead down the track towards the road, noses down and tails up as they tracked the scent of the evening's wildlife.

They walked along side by side in silence, Sophie wrapped in the warmth of Ben's coat. His hand brushed against hers briefly as they crossed over the road and she felt a shiver of longing. They stopped for a moment, watching the dogs as they ran up the empty road.

'Couldn't do that back home, could you?'

'They'd be flattened by a lorry in seconds. Or a boy racer.'

In the distance they heard the screech of a fox, and a moment later the beating of wings as an owl shot overhead.

'I was teasing, you know.'

She looked at the lines of his face, lit up by the moonlight. 'About what?'

'It's actually quite nice having someone down the road. At night when I let the dogs out I see the lights on in the cottage.'

Sophie swallowed, not quite finding words.

'That makes me sound like a stalker, doesn't it?' Ben

laughed briefly. 'Scratch that.'

'No,' she said, reassuring him. Unthinkingly, she put a hand on his arm for a second then pulled it away. 'No, I get it. I have to admit I keep an eye on your place just because it stops me feeling so alone out here in the middle of nowhere. I think I'd freak out completely if your croft wasn't in full view.'

'Even with Annie dropping by?' He turned to her and she could see – even in the darkness – the fan of lines crinkling at the outer corners of his eyes.

'I haven't seen her for a few days actually. Although she does keep popping in saying she doesn't want to be a nuisance but…'

'She's lonely since her husband died. And her family aren't up to much.'

'I nearly had the privilege of lunch with them the other day, but they didn't show up.'

'Happens more often than not.'

They started walking again.

'Really?'

'Yeah.' He whistled the dogs. 'I think the son's alright, but the daughter-in-law is just after the money. If it was up to her she'd have pressurised Annie into selling your place.'

'Then you might have ended up with even worse neighbours.'

They were at the gate to the cottage now, and Sophie pushed it open.

'I'm alright from here,' she said, politely.

'You sure?' Ben looked at her for a long moment, eyebrows raised in concern. The cottage was pitch dark. In the silence she could hear the wash of the waves on the beach and once again the unearthly scream of a fox somewhere in the distance. She didn't like the dark very much – never had. Since what happened, she'd worked hard to try to curb the anxiety that something terrible was waiting for her just around the corner. If she let them, intrusive thoughts would sneak in and keep her up at night. Living out here had been a bigger challenge to herself than she'd admitted to anyone. Telling Ben – admitting she wasn't as brave as she looked – that was a big step.

She squared her shoulders for a moment, then lifted her hand from the gate and met his gaze.

'Actually, if you don't mind,' she said, and before she could say anything more he'd opened the gate for her and was holding an arm out, motioning for her to pass.

'My pleasure,' he said, in his deep voice.

He waited while she opened the door and flicked on the light switch in the hall and turned back. Otto had slipped past and was sniffing inquisitively at the carpet on the bottom stair.

'Get back here,' he said, laughing.

'Thanks.' Sophie shifted from one foot to the other. She didn't want the evening to end. 'I feel like I should invite you in for coffee or something – '

His mouth twisted in an upside-down smile. 'And if I didn't have these two and we didn't have work in the morning I'd take you up on it. But I'm not sure Annie would be that impressed to find muddy paw prints all over her lovely cottage, and I suspect you'd curse me in the morning when you've got the delight of morning surgery.'

He was probably right. And more to the point, he was probably letting her down gently.

'Right then, I'd better get off.'

'Thanks, Ben.' The blood rushed in her ears as she said his name aloud.

'You're welcome. I had a good night.' He raised a hand in farewell as he turned to head back.

'Me too.'

She closed the door and turned away.

A moment later there was a rap at the door. Her heart hammering against her ribs, she pulled it open to see him standing there, a twinkle in his eye and a half smile on his face.

'Hello again,' he said, with a brief nod of his head.

'Did you forget something?'

'I think you did. Well, we both did. In all the excitement neither of us has remembered you've got no car and you've got work in the morning. I'm going to assume you'd like a lift, because if you're hoping for an Uber to turn up you'll have a long wait.'

Sophie put a hand to her mouth in surprise. 'I completely forgot. The car – I need to get it sorted.'

He shook his head. 'Don't worry. I'll drop Polly a text so she knows it's there, and give the garage a ring. They owe me a favour anyway.'

'Seriously?'

'It's no problem at all,' he said, gruffly. 'I'll pick you up at – what, eight? Eight fifteen?'

'Eight would be perfect.' She reached down to pat the dogs, aware that what she wanted to do was stand up on tip toe and kiss him on the cheek for being so sweet and thoughtful.

'Right then, I'm really going this time. I'll see you tomorrow.'

Sophie watched this time as he strode off across the grass and up the path that led along the fields and on to his croft. The moon had slipped behind a cloud and the darkness was deep and velvet black. Only once his tall shadow had disappeared into the darkness did she close the door. She leant back against the wall, closing her eyes and putting a hand to her chest.

CHAPTER TWENTY-FOUR

The next morning she got up at six thirty and had a long shower, then – feeling like a teenager – tried to apply enough make up that she looked appealingly fresh faced and youthful but not so much that she'd draw attention to herself at work, where she'd already fallen comfortably into a routine of dressing for practicality and not glamour.

She glanced at the clock. Two minutes to eight.

Outside the skies hung low, the cloud cover leaden and grey. Rain splattered against the windows of the kitchen and the sea – which yesterday had been a shining turquoise – was today a dull teal, with white horses dancing on the waves as they crashed against the shore. In the distance a white fishing boat rocked in the waters as it headed out to sea and the flash of the lighthouse on the distant rocks flickered in the low light. It was amazing how the weather could change so quickly.

Precisely on time, there was a crunch of tyres on the stones of the track outside and Ben's car swept round in a circle as she opened the door.

She locked the door and rushed over, Ben's coat in her arms.

'I forgot to give you this last night.'

He threw it on the back seat and she turned, realising the dogs weren't there.

'Left them by the fire,' he explained. 'They're fair weather walkers, surprisingly. It makes no sense to me because they'll leap into the sea twelve months of the year but neither of them can stand it when it rains like this.'

'It's like Manchester rain, isn't it?'

'Don't let a Mancunian hear you say that. You know what they're like, they're the only ones allowed to speak ill of the place.'

She giggled. 'Have you ever been to Manchester when it wasn't raining?'

'As it happens,' he said, turning to her with a grin. 'But I went to art school there so odds were I had to eventually see the sun shining.'

He dropped her in the village just as Grace was arriving for work. She stood on the doorstep to the surgery, waiting.

'I tell you it's lucky it's me spotting you jumping out of Ben Lewis's car and not Dolina, or you'd be round the village grapevine and married off by lunchtime.' She chuckled to herself as Sophie, feeling slightly embarrassed, followed her inside.

Grace seemed to pick up on her discomfort. Sophie leaned over the reception desk to read a note from Mhairi and a moment later a hand squeezed her shoulder. She turned around.

'I was only kidding you,' Grace said, looking up into her face with a kindly expression. 'Ben's a nice lad by all accounts.'

'Oh, there's nothing going on between us. He just gave me a lift in because my car was broken down –'

Grace gave a little nod. 'Well, he's single, you're single. There's no harm in it, now, is there? He's a good-looking man. I've never known why he hasn't been snapped up before now.'

Sophie gave a vague smile and muttered something about having to make sure the consultation room was organised before the doors opened. She headed into her room and closed the door, hooking her stethoscope round her neck and switching on the computer. The idea of anyone snapping up Ben Lewis when he was very clearly his own man made her smile. It was funny, he was so direct – almost intimidatingly so until you got to know him – but actually, behind the dry humour there was genuine kind heartedness. He'd insisted on walking her home last night, and this morning had told her as she climbed out of the car that he'd sort the repairs out as he had to speak to the guy at the garage anyway. Sophie suspected that wasn't actually the case, but – well, it was lovely to feel like someone had her back. Especially someone who looked like he did.

She made her way through morning surgery on autopilot, and checked her phone just before her final client of the day came in.

Car is sorted, Ben had written. Her heart gave a little skip when she saw his name on a notification.

Oh amazing, she replied. *Is it at the garage?*

He's dropping it off later. Should be with you at five.

The brevity of his text messages made her smile. They were exactly as she'd have expected them to be.

Sure enough, they were just closing up the surgery door late that afternoon when a little flatbed truck came trundling along the main street of Applemore with her car on the back.

'Delivery for Sophie Jones?' A young lad with sandy hair jumped out of the cab with a cheeky grin. 'We don't do this for all our clients, you know.'

'I-' Sophie felt her cheeks go pink with embarrassment. Mhairi had come out from behind the desk and was standing in the doorway with her arms folded, watching as Sophie's car was backed off the ramps.

'Hiya, Scott,' she said, with a little wave. 'Long time no see.'

Sophie noticed Mhairi putting a hand to her hair and ruffling it so it sat just right. She brushed down the striped dress she was wearing, tugging at the hem to straighten it.

The young lad lifted a hand and gave a half smile. 'Alright?

'How's it going?'

'No' bad. Haven't seen you in ages.' He passed the keys to Sophie, who thanked him and headed back inside to finish typing up some notes. Ten minutes later she emerged from her room to find Mhairi still standing chatting, twirling a lock of her hair and gazing up at Scott through lowered lashes. Scott seemed to be very much appreciating the attention, one arm crooked over the bonnet of the truck in a proprietorial manner, the other hand thrust in his back pocket, his stance open and inviting. It didn't take an animal behaviourist to work out that the two of them were clearly more than a little bit interested in each other. She hovered for a second, not wanting to get in the way.

'I'd love that,' Mhairi was saying.

'Cool, I'll pick you up about eight?'

'It's a date.'

Mhairi turned, giving him a coquettish little wave, and tripped happily back inside.

'Sorry,' Sophie said, knocking on the window of the cab as Scott was climbing back in the other side. The window slid open.

'How do I pay you?'

'It's sorted.' He looked distinctly pleased with himself.

'What do you mean?'

'Ben paid my dad earlier when he rang up.'

'Oh right thanks, I'll sort it out with him. Thanks again for dropping it off.'

'No probs.' He gave a brief wave. 'See ya.'

Sophie unlocked the car, which was gleaming and had clearly had a wash and wax while it was at the garage. Not only had they repaired the alternator and scrubbed all the dirt it had accumulated since the last time she put it through the car wash – which was shamefully long ago – but they'd hoovered and cleaned the outside, putting all the random detritus she had lying around on the seats into a neat pile. The dashboard gleamed.

She stopped at the bottom of Ben's drive, hesitating for a moment. Should she? Was it okay to just turn up randomly on his doorstep?

She took a deep breath. This was so far from the old Sophie that she didn't quite recognise herself, but – she rationalised, as she opened the gate to the croft – he'd paid for the repair, so she needed to find out how much she owed him, at least, and thank him of course.

She parked outside the long, low stone house and knocked at the door. There was no sign of him, or of the dogs. Feeling like an intruder, she peeked through the window of the kitchen – no sign there, either. Perhaps he was out the back, chopping yet more wood.

Round the back of the croft house she found the yard was stacked with wood, an axe balanced neatly by the side of the wall beside a freshly chopped bucket of pale kindling. A stone trough by the back door was crammed full of white tulips, underplanted with something else which was growing in and starting to climb down the sides.

Across the yard she heard a faint tapping from one of the stone outbuildings and headed towards it before knocking cautiously – and then more loudly – on the sliding wooden door.

A cacophony of barking told her that Ben was inside. A moment later the door slid open and she was set upon by the two spaniels, who jumped up at her, bouncy and over-enthusiastic, their long ears flying.

'Get down, you two.' A smile spread over Ben's face, making his eyes twinkle.

'Sorry,' she said, out of habit.

'Don't apologise. I wasn't expecting visitors.' He indicated his grey t-shirt which was covered in dust, and without thinking ran a hand through his hair, covering it in a fine layer of wood shavings. 'But it's nice to see you.'

'It is?' She was slightly taken aback. She'd always thought artists didn't like to be disturbed when they were in the middle of creating something.

'I'm trying to finish this off,' he explained, gesturing towards a wooden plinth, on which stood a huge horse's head. 'But I've been desperate for a coffee break and kept putting it off. You've given me the excuse I need. Got time for a brew?'

'I'd love one.' She followed him across the bare concrete floor to an ancient black woodstove which sat, squat and low, in the corner of the room.

'Won't take long.' He lifted a steel kettle onto the top and opened the front door, tossing in a handful of slim pieces of wood.

'You've got a wood burner out here, as well?'

He nodded. 'Wouldn't get much work done if I didn't, it's bloody freezing in this place.'

She looked around. The walls were stacked with paintings and canvases, some finished, some painted a single colour in what she assumed was a base coat of some kind. He showed her how he'd converted the old building, explaining how he'd cleared the place of decades of rubbish that had been left over from the elderly couple who'd lived there all their married lives, painting it and putting in huge skylights so that light spilled in all year round, whether it was sunny outside or grey, like today. Even on a miserable day the place had an atmospheric, arty quality that threw shadows on everything. She watched as he tipped instant into mugs by eye, apologising for it as he did so, then turning to pass her a steaming coffee. In the light his strong jaw, covered with the dark scruff of beard, looked almost as if he, too, had been sculpted.

'This is amazing.' She took a sip of the coffee, which was strong and bitter.

'The coffee?' Ben looked down at the contents of his mug. 'You must be really in need of caffeine.'

She laughed. 'No, this place. Your studio. I just assumed you worked in the house but you've got this huge space all to yourself.'

'Keeps me out of trouble,' he grinned. Then, looking suddenly bashful, he tipped his head towards the piece he'd been working on. 'Do you want to have a look?'

'It's gorgeous.' The main body of the horse's head had been carved from a solid piece of wood, and then driftwood of different hues created a flowing mane which seemed to hang in the air, suspended by almost invisible threads of fine metal. 'And you collected all the wood for this from the beach?'

'Not just your beach, no. I've got a few that I visit, depending on the tides. I feel like a magpie sometimes, wandering along picking up sea glass and random bits of tat that gets blown up after a storm. I need to do another trip out soon.'

'Every day must be so different for you. I can't imagine you ever get bored.'

Ben put his mug down on the side and leaned back against

the whitewashed wall, one long leg crossed over the other at the ankle.

'D'you know what? Sometimes I get up and I would rather do anything – clean the kitchen, get an office job – than actually get my arse in here and work.'

'Seriously?'

He nodded. 'Procrastination, you might call it. Or fear of messing up.'

Sophie cupped her mug between both hands, turning towards him. He looked at her with a rueful expression.

'You look surprised.'

'I just assumed you would be jumping out of bed desperate to get to work.'

'Oh, I love it when it's done, don't get me wrong.' He ducked his head for a moment and laughed briefly. 'It's just hellish in the execution.'

'All the time?' She was shocked.

'Not all the time. Just 90% of it.'

'Now you're teasing me.'

He lifted one shoulder in a half shrug and shot her a smile. 'Might be.'

'You've given me a whole new perspective. I'm imagining Van Gogh having to be dragged out of bed by his wife in the morning to get to work on his sunflowers.'

'He didn't have a wife.'

She let go of the mug and made a vague gesture with her arm. 'Girlfriend, partner, whatever.'

'Don't think his love life was a major concern given he went mad and shot himself.'

'Oh.' Sophie grimaced. 'Sorry, art history's not really my specialist subject.'

'Clearly.' He grinned. 'Anyway, poor old Vincent notwithstanding, I think when it's a job it's probably the same whatever you do. I bet you don't leap out of bed full of excitement at the thought of cleaning out a spaniel's grotty ears.'

I do when it means you're coming to the surgery, said Sophie's inner voice.

'Alright, you've got a point,' she said out loud.

'Anyway.' He rubbed his forehead, dislodging several wood shavings which fell from his hair, making her laugh.

'Oh, I'm sorry. You're trying to work and I'm getting in your hair.'

'The wood shavings are doing a good enough job of that.' He looked at her and lifted an eyebrow. 'I was just wondering what –'

'I came to say thank you for sorting the car, and to ask how much I owed you?'

He shook his head. 'Don't worry, it was nothing.'

'It can't have been nothing, he said it needed a new – alternator?' She was woefully clueless when it came to cars. 'Sorry, my car knowledge is on a par with my art expertise.'

'Yep, alternator.' He brushed some more sawdust from his t-shirt. 'I called in a favour, don't worry about it. Anyway if you want to pay me back,' he said, casually, 'you can always give me a hand at the weekend?'

'Sure.' Sophie's heart fluttered. 'I mean I'm saying sure, what are you doing?'

He indicated the horse's head sculpture. 'I was saying about collecting driftwood. There's a high tide on Saturday morning, so by lunchtime I'm hoping there'll be a decent haul up on the beach.'

She hesitated for a split second, trying to remember who was doing morning surgery.

'Only if you're not busy or anything,' he added, lightly.

'No, no, I'm not busy.' Now he thought she wasn't interested. 'I'd love to.'

'It's a date.' He stopped himself and laughed. 'I mean, it's – well, you know what I mean.'

Thinking of the easy, casual way in which Mhairi and Scott had arranged to go out, Sophie smiled. You'd think that two people in their forties might actually have it together and be able to communicate without stammering and tripping over their words, but apparently not.

'I'd love it,' she repeated.

'Great.' Ben's smile was broad. 'Okay, I'll pick you up around twelve? Is that okay?'

'Perfect.'

CHAPTER TWENTY-FIVE

Ben looked up as the door to the consulting room opened. Otto leapt to his feet, tail wagging furiously at Sophie who was dressed in dark green scrubs. She had her hair clipped back from her face, but tendrils had broken loose and hung around her temples.

'Don't forget you've got that call at four,' said one of the nurses, as she squeezed past Sophie, giving Ben a nod hello.

'Do you want to bring him in?'

She stepped back to let him and Otto into the room. On the table there was a plastic bottle and a package of cotton wool and some cotton buds.

'Up you come, young man,' she said, patting the examination table. Ben caught Otto around the chest and lifted him up so he was standing between them, a mildly alarmed expression on his face but his tail still wagging.

'Sorry, there's no fun way to do this,' she said, giving Otto a pat. 'Let's start by having a look at those ears, and see how they're doing.'

She reached over and picked up an otoscope. 'If you can just hold him side on, quite tightly,' she lifted an ear as he did so, 'I'll have a quick check and see how he's looking after a week on steroids. How's he been doing, food wise?'

Ben looked down at the younger of his two dogs with a laugh. Otto, normally more interested in what he could find outside in the fresh air than in titbits or scraps, had turned into a Labrador overnight as the steroids had kicked in.

'He's been mooching for treats every second he can get. You saw him the other night, he'd have had that pasta off your plate if he had half a chance.'

Sophie smiled back at him. 'Yes, they definitely make them more… food driven.'

'That's one way of putting it.'

'That ear's looking really good. I'm surprised it's responded so well. Switch him over, and we'll have a look inside the right ear.'

Otto shifted obligingly and Sophie examined him.

'Actually, that's looking great too. I think we'll get away with just cleaning them out today and leaving it at that.'

'Oh,' he said, without thinking, 'I thought we were going to be in every week.'

Sophie shook her head. 'No, I think we've been lucky.'

'Oh yeah, no, that's great.' It's not that he wanted his poor dog to be in discomfort just so he had a chance to see her. For goodness' sake, what the hell was going on with his brain?

'If you can just keep him close to you,' Sophie said, picking up the bottle, 'We'll give you a little clean up, Otto. I'll show you how to do it.'

She was so close to him that he could breathe in the soft floral scent he'd noticed before, and as she leaned over the neck of her loose scrubs slipped sideways, showing a glimpse of pale skin and the pale coffee lace of her bra. A breath caught in his throat.

'Okay?' She looked up at him through the dark fringe of her lashes. Her eyes really were striking.

'Yeah.' He cleared his throat and shifted his weight onto the other foot, holding a wriggling Otto still. 'I don't think he's that much of a fan of ear cleaning.'

'Not many of them are. It's a bit undignified, but it does tend to go with the territory with spaniels. It's these big floppy ears,' she said, addressing a relieved Otto as she motioned to Ben that he could let him go.

Before he could lift the dog down from the table Otto had leapt off and shaken himself off vigorously, making them laugh.

'I hope he'll forgive me,' said Sophie, putting the cotton wool in the bin and washing her hands.

'I'm sure he will.' Otto, as if reading his mind, trotted over to her and sat down on her foot.

'There you are. I'm out of the bad books already.' She leant down and rubbed the top of his head, tousling the fluffy mop which curled between his ears. 'I'll bring you some gravy bones as a treat on Saturday. In your current steroid-fuelled state you'll love me for that.'

'He'd love you anyway,' said Ben, meaning because gravy bones were both dogs favourite treat. But as he said it her eyes met his and there was a strange, fleeting moment of silence before she turned away, typing something on the keyboard.

'If you wait outside,' she said, turning back, 'I'll just get his prescription.'

The waiting room had filled up while they'd been busy, and Otto dashed out to the end of his lead before he could stop him, eager to investigate the contents of a cat-carrier box which was sitting at the feet of a long-legged teenage boy with spiky hair. He reeled him back in and stood by the weighing scale, waiting for a moment.

'Here you are.' Sophie handed it over. 'Every day for a week, and then you can let me know how it's looking and we'll take it from there.'

'Excuse me,' said an elderly woman with neat grey curls, 'Do you know when Harry's likely to be seen? I had an appointment for quarter to.' She looked pointedly up at the clock on the wall.

Sophie flicked a quick look in his direction and gave a half smile. 'See you later,' she said, ushering the woman into the consulting room.

Sixty pounds later, thinking that he was in the wrong business, Ben headed back to the croft. He'd just unloaded the dogs – Bear having waited patiently on the back seat outside the vets surgery – and was heading to the studio to package up the now-finished horse's head when he heard a familiar call.

'I don't suppose you've got time for a quick cup of tea and a slice of lemon drizzle in that busy schedule, have you?'

Annie, wearing an oversized red sweater and a bright pink scarf, a pair of faded grey trousers and walking boots, appeared around the side of the pick-up truck.

'You're looking very colourful,' he noted, watching as the dogs hurtled towards her with excitement.

'Just been for lunch with Joan up at the café,' she explained. 'I gather the art classes are going well?'

'You do?' Ben nodded in the direction of the house. 'Shall we have a cuppa in there? I suspect the stove's gone out in the studio.'

'Yes, please. You can fill me in on all the news.'

Annie gave him a knowing look which he ignored. He

stepped over a puddle by the back door, opening it – he never bothered locking the doors – and heading inside.

'I was going to pop in on Sophie at the surgery before lunchtime and see if she fancied joining me. Might be nice for her to meet Joan and have a chat with someone outside of work. I gather, though,' Annie said, craftily, 'She's been spending some time with you.'

Ben rolled his eyes. 'My life was a lot more peaceful when I lived in the city, you know. I went about my business without everyone knowing what I was up to.'

Annie sat down in the same chair that Sophie had occupied earlier in the week, her small bird-like frame taking up far less space. She folded her hands and popped her chin into them, looking at him with a focused gaze.

'I haven't a clue what you've been up to,' said Annie, innocently.

'I know you're lying,' Ben teased her, 'because your lips are moving. Come on, spill. What is it you think I've been up to?'

Annie leaned forward and started unwrapping the foil from the loaf of lemon drizzle cake. She lifted it up, smoothing the foil carefully and deliberately, tipping the stray crumbs into her cupped hand and then feeding them to a drooling Otto, who was sitting with his chin resting on her knee. He hoovered them up then returned to his post, sitting close by her in the hope that she might drop some more crumbs, or better still the whole cake. Sophie was right, the medication really had made him hungry. Hopefully now they could taper it down and he'd return to his normal, slightly less gannet-like self. Ben rolled his eyes inwardly, remembering the catch he'd had to make when he'd discovered that he wouldn't have an excuse to visit Sophie at the surgery every week. For goodness sake, he needed to get a grip. If he liked the girl, then he could man up and ask her out.

'Do you have a knife?' Annie broke into his thoughts.

'I'll go one better and get a plate. No expense spared.' He strode across the kitchen, conscious of her eyes on him. Returning, he passed the plates over. Annie cut two slices and put them onto the grey plates, sliding one back towards him as she spoke.

'Well for once the news isn't from Dolina, although by all accounts you're flavour of the month with her because you praised her painting.'

She wiped the crumbs off the knife and fed them to Otto. Ben gave her an admonishing glance.

'You're going to make him the size of a house.'

Annie cackled.

'As for Dolina, I have to admit she's not bad.' Given how many years it had been since she'd picked up a brush, she clearly had a natural eye. He still wasn't sure his future lay in teaching, but it had been an interesting experience so far.

'I wish I could be a fly on the wall when you admit to Mel you're actually enjoying yourself.'

'I wouldn't go that far.'

Annie's nostrils flared as she snorted.

'Anyway, to go back to my news. It was Jenny, Dolina's daughter, who was singing your praises. We stopped by the shop on the way into the café and she was full of beans, telling anyone who'd listen she'd been taking a step out of her comfort zone. I've never seen her so chatty.' She spun the cake plate around, her tone light. 'Oh, and Polly tells me that you rescued Sophie's car when it broke down up at the shop.'

He raised his eyes heavenward. Between Polly and the boys from the café, he'd suspected that the sight of Sophie's car being collected by the recovery vehicle would have got tongues wagging in the village. No doubt when he'd texted Lachlan and mentioned it, he'd told Rilla, who'd have told

Polly, and her sisters Charlotte and Beth, and… no doubt the next time he spoke to Mel on the phone he'd be getting the third degree.

He made a vague gesture with his hands. 'She broke down up there with no way of getting home, so I gave her a lift and then ended up inviting her in for dinner because she didn't have anything in.'

Annie's eyes widened. 'Well, that's news.' She looked pleased, her bright eyes sparkling as she smiled across the table at him.

'Oh, that hadn't made the jungle drums yet?' He dashed a hand to his forehead, but he was grinning as he did so. Oddly, he didn't really mind. It was nice to have a chance to talk about Sophie. Thinking about her seemed to be taking up an awful lot of his waking hours. He'd worked all morning with the thought of seeing her at front of his mind, and stopped work early to wash the wood shavings out of his hair so he didn't look like he'd been dragged through a hedge backwards when he took Otto for his appointment. He shook his head slightly. What the hell was happening to him?

'No.' Annie gave a little laugh. 'Don't you worry, I won't be gossiping. You know me better than that. I'm pleased to hear you've been keeping an eye out for her though. She's a lovely girl.'

He gave a brief nod. 'That she is.'

'She deserves a bit of kindness.' Annie lifted her chin slightly as she looked at him.

'What d'you mean?' He frowned as he turned to pour the water into the teapot, making it strong as Annie liked it. He could take or leave tea – not much of a northerner, his dad used to tease him – but he knew she loathed coffee, and so he tolerated it for her sake. He fetched the milk and a couple of mugs.

'Kindness?' He put the teapot down on the table and looked at her.

'Oh, just – ignore me, I'm talking out of turn,' Annie said, in a way that made it clear that whatever it was she'd alluded to wasn't up for discussion. She changed the subject. 'Joan reminded me that you weren't at the village meeting the other night, and she suspected that means you've got no intention of turning up to the May celebration.'

'She would be right.' He shook his head. 'I've donated a load of wooden decorations for the stall, and I'll buy as many raffle tickets as you like. Just don't expect me to turn up to a family fun day, or whatever it's called. You know it's my idea of hell on earth.'

'Are you busy on Saturday?' Annie took the mug of tea he'd poured her, sipping it with a sigh of pleasure. 'You do make a good cup of tea. It's always nice to have one made for me.'

'Happens I am.' He wasn't lying. Not that he'd any intention of going, even if he hadn't made plans to walk the shore with Sophie, looking for driftwood.

'Oh, really?' Annie sat back in her chair, mug in one hand. Her expression suggested that she thought he was being slightly economical with the truth.

He nodded briefly.

'So I can tell Joan you send your apologies.' She cocked her head slightly. Bear padded across the room and flopped down at his feet with an overdramatic sigh.

He snorted. 'You can tell her that if you like, it sounds a bit more palatable than the truth which is - as you know perfectly well - I'd rather be launched into orbit than spend an afternoon making polite conversation with a load of random do-gooders.'

'You are a curmudgeonly old horror,' said Annie, breaking a piece of cake off and popping it into her mouth. 'And if I didn't know you had a heart of gold I'd call you a miserable sod.'

'I am that,' he agreed.

'You're both.' Annie chuckled and fed another piece of cake to the dogs.

'But you know that already.'

CHAPTER TWENTY-SIX

Sophie poured herself a second cup of coffee, and headed upstairs to get ready. She'd stayed up late on Friday evening to watch Tabby playing in a match. Curled up on the sofa, she'd cheered her daughter on as she scored the crucial goal that took her university team ahead and into the next round of their league championships. *We're watching,* Bea had messaged her, sending a photo of herself and Mark with glasses of red wine held aloft. *Wish you were here.*

Me too, Sophie had written automatically.

After the match, she'd been brushing her teeth when the phone rang, making her jump.

'Hey Mom,' Tabby said, in a passable impression of an American accent.

'Don't tell me you've gone native.'

'Definitely not,' Tabby laughed, reverting to her usual Northern tones. 'I thought I'd call you while I'm waiting for Belle to finish fixing her hair. She takes ages.'

Sophie wiped her mouth and wandered through to the

bedroom, listening as Tabby chatted on nineteen to the dozen, high on a win. She'd been the same ever since she started the game - monosyllabic and silent on the drive to a match, delirious and overflowing with endorphins afterwards. If they lost, she was analytical, wanting to talk tactics and work things out in her head. She bubbled over with excitement, replaying the game verbally, asking Sophie what she'd thought of it all.

'Oh hello,' Tabby said, breaking off mid-sentence. 'She's finished at last. Hang on a sec, Mum.'

Sophie heard the sound of chatting in the background and Tabby giving a good humoured cheer as her new friend and team-mate Belle returned from the locker rooms.

'Okay we better get going,' she said, returning to the call.

'And I'd better get some sleep.' If she wasn't careful, she was going to turn up for her adventure with Ben looking like a vampire complete with dark shadows under her eyes and skin which looked distinctly similar in tone to the undead. Sophie had blown her daughter a kiss and wished her a good evening, pulling up the covers and wishing for sleep to come.

Looking at herself in the mirror that morning, though, it was pretty clear that she'd failed in her mission. Knowing she had something on the next day she'd done her usual and not been able to sleep, tossing and turning for hours – which seemed to be happening more and more, she'd noticed – and eventually falling asleep about five seconds before her alarm went off. She rubbed in some tinted moisturiser and dotted Touche Éclat beneath her eyes in the hope it might perform some sort of miracle feat, which it didn't. All she had to do, according to the super glamorous French Instagram person she'd watched that morning, was apply *le crème blusher like zis* (she rubbed it in, realised she looked like a doll, and wiped it back off with a bit of loo roll) and smudge some taupe shadow into ze crease of her eyelids. It made no appreciable difference. She put on some mascara, brushed her eyebrows and made a face at herself in the mirror as she ran a brush through her hair. This is a dog walk, not a date, she told herself, firmly.

It was something to do with being so far away from everything which made the difference. All those years had passed when she was back home in Crosby, and

after what happened, the prospect of ever trusting another man had seemed unthinkable. Thinking she was doing the right thing, Bea had tried to get her to sign up for internet dating – and of course it had worked for her in the end, and she was deliriously happy with Mark. The girls in the surgery had made innocent jokes, not knowing what had happened in the past, about sending in any good looking male clients to her consulting room. But until now she'd never felt… well, she'd never felt anything like this. The funny thing was that nobody here in Applemore had questioned her single status, seeming to just accept her for who she was. Maybe that made all the difference. She reached for a band to tie her hair back, then shoved it in the pocket of her jeans instead.

It was such a gorgeous morning that she took a cup of coffee outside and sat on the wall by the cottage, taking in the scenery while she waited for Ben to arrive. The grass beyond her feet had grown – she'd need to find the lawnmower soon – and was dotted with pink and white clover and yellow buttercups, on which the first bumblebees were feasting. The sun was warm on her back, shining in a sky which was periwinkle blue. Huge fluffy white cotton wool clouds hung over the sea, which was smooth and deep turquoise in colour. It could have been the Caribbean, if it wasn't for the craggy rocks in the distance, and the purple hazed heather of the moors that reached away into the distance. Strange to think that later that month she'd be on the other side of the world, visiting Tabby and baking in the heat of late spring in Atlanta.

A crunch of tyres on the track shook her out of her daydream and she turned, expecting the postman, but it was Ben, hanging out of the window of his pick-up, the dogs peering out of the back at her with tongues lolling and goofy spaniel grins on their faces.

Sophie cocked her head sideways in confusion.

'I thought you said we were going for a walk?'

'Jump in.' He leaned across and opened the passenger seat for her.

'I didn't explain,' he said, as he turned the car outside the cottage. 'I need the trolley to collect driftwood. It's almost impossible to get it over the rocks to the long beach, so it's easier to park up and walk down the track over by the castle.'

'Oh,' Sophie fastened her seatbelt and turned to pat the dogs. 'I haven't seen the castle up close yet.'

'It looks better from a distance. Last time I saw it there'd clearly been a gang of kids having a mis-spent youth moment up there.'

'In Applemore?' she laughed.

Ben turned left and headed north. In the far distance a rainbow arced over the pine tree forest, where the clouds darkened to a heavy grey.

'Yep. Even in Applemore, it would seem, you'll find teenagers drinking illegal beers around a bonfire. Pretty much standard behaviour.'

'We used to do it in the woods.'

Ben grinned. 'I am assuming you mean bonfires?'

Turning to him and seeing the teasing expression, Sophie realised what she'd said. 'Yes, bonfires. Nothing more exciting than that.'

Ben turned down a track between two fields. It was marked with a wooden footpath sign.

'Are we allowed down here? It says footpath.'

'Yeah, there's a patch down past the cattle grid where we can leave the truck.'

They bumped down the rutted track, the dogs slipping over and making them laugh.

'I reckon it must be pretty boring growing up here. I mean I love all the scenery and the quiet, but can you imagine being a teenager in Applemore?'

'I was thinking that the other day. Tabby's having the time of her life in Atlanta. I keep thinking that if she came up here to visit she'd be bored out of her mind.'

'You might be surprised.' They rattled over the cattle grid and Ben pulled the truck to a halt, switching it off and half turning as he continued. 'Esther really loved it from the first time she came. I think she liked the fact she could switch off and didn't have to deal with all the pressure they're under.'

'It's a lot, isn't it? Social media and all the rest of it.'

'So much. I'd have hated it as a teenager. Maybe growing up in Applemore gives you a chance for a bit of freedom before you go out into the world.'

They released the dogs and Ben lifted a four-wheeled metal trolley with a handle out of the back of the pick-up truck.

'I wondered what you meant when you said trolley.'

'Were you expecting me to arrive with a granny shopping bag on wheels?' He grinned.

Sophie pushed back a thick strand of hair which had whipped across her face, turning out of the wind. 'It had crossed my mind as we were driving up here, yeah.'

'Comforting to see that's how you think of me,' he said drily, but his eyes showed his amusement. He whistled the dogs, who had shot off in separate directions. Bear returned, a moss covered stick in his mouth.

'Where'd you get that from, boy? There isn't a tree for about three miles.' Ben took the stick and threw it overarm in front of them, sending the dogs bounding ahead.

'He's clearly got the memo about collecting driftwood.' Sophie fell into step beside Ben, who towed the trolley along behind him. It rattled as it bumped over the rutted ground.

'It's colder than it looks,' she said, turning up the collar of her sweatshirt.

'Always is up here. I wondered if I was making a mistake putting in a log fired stove in the cottage, but on average I reckon we get about two weeks where it's too hot and the rest of the time I get by.'

'I wouldn't give up the day job and start working for the tourist board if I were you.'

He shot her an amused look. 'I don't think people come here to get a suntan, though.'

'True.' She stepped sideways to avoid a dark puddle, the ground squelching beneath her feet. 'That's weird, it feels like we're in a peat bog but we're really close to the sea.'

'We are. It's covered over with sand that blows in off the beach. But if you look over there you'll see the reeds and –' he stopped, an arm directing her gaze 'it's called the blacklands – if you look you can see the way the land changes. In the distance there's the beach, then the dunes rise up and beyond them there's the strip called the machair – we'll come to that in a bit. And then it shifts, and the soil becomes richer.' He stopped and shook his head. 'Sorry, I'm mansplaining.'

'You're not at all. It's interesting.' They started walking again as if by mutual agreement.

'The crofters traditionally worked the peat soil close to their houses, and the moorland like that was shared as common ground. Back in the day, your place and mine would have been part of a township that worked together to produce food and everything they needed.'

'And now mine is a holiday cottage.' She felt inexplicably guilty.

'Yeah, and mine was falling apart when I bought it. I can't make the place work as a croft full time, but I can do my bit – that's why I do the stuff I do.'

'So you grow vegetables and stuff as well?'

'If you want kale,' Ben laughed, 'I'm your man. I can't get rid of the stuff.'

'That's because it's revolting.'

'You're telling me.'

'Why don't you grow something you actually like?'

'Well, I tried carrots but the rabbits got them. Then the dogs went mad for the rabbits so I had to put a better fence up to stop them disappearing on a wild goose – or wild rabbit – chase.'

'So now you've got a dog proof fence, at least.'

'And as much kale as you can eat.' Sophie bent to pick up a pretty shell which was lying on the grass, turning it upside down to examine the pink interior.

'What more could a man want?'

She looked up to see Ben gazing at her in a way that made her stomach drop. He looked away, clearing his throat and pushing a hand through his untidy dark hair.

'This is the machair I was talking about,' he said, a second later. 'It's famous for the wildflowers and birds you get particularly at this time of year. That's why we need to stick to the track and why – Otto, get here – we're supposed to keep the dogs close to hand. Bear's fine, but this one has a habit of scarpering given half the chance.'

Otto joined them, trotting obediently at his master's side.

A few moments later they were on the wide beach and Ben sent them off to play freely, laughing as they both headed straight for the waves.

'I think we might get lucky today,' he said, as they followed the dogs down to a long trail of seaweed that was tangled on the sand. The tide was already receding and along the gleaming white sand a treasure trove was waiting for them.

'So what sort of thing are you looking for?' Sophie stooped to pick up a twisted, bleached piece of wood about twelve inches long.

'That's exactly it. Small, big, anything you think might look interesting.'

'So what else do you make with them?'

Gulls whirled overhead, drowning out his words, making them both laugh.

'I never know until I start. Sometimes I think I'm going to make one thing, but halfway through it turns into another.'

'How does that work if you're given a commission? You said you had to make a second horses head for the people you sold it to?'

He nodded. 'That's the tricky bit. I don't much like making art to order, but needs must. I've got bills to pay just like everyone else.'

'University isn't cheap.'

'It certainly isn't. I'm still paying maintenance for Esther,' he said, tossing a battered looking piece of what looked like a fence post into the trolley.

'Even though she's doing a postgrad?'

'Even though.' He rubbed his chin as he turned to look at her, eyes squinting in the sunshine. 'I might not live with her mum but I take my job seriously.'

'That's nice.' Sophie felt her eyebrows raising involuntarily.

'You say that as if it's not been your experience.'

She shook her head. 'It hasn't. I mean there's only been me and Tabby all along. Apart from – ' she tailed off.

'Sorry, I didn't mean to pry.'

'You're not. I just don't really talk about it. I had a relationship when she was younger, it didn't work out.'

'Hard to juggle that stuff when you've got kids.'

'It is.'

They walked along in a silence which Sophie felt was a bit awkward. The only sound was the panting of the dogs as they galloped back and forth and the swish of the waves on the sand as the tide carried on rolling outward.

'I-' she said, eventually.

'D'you-'

They both laughed.

'Go on,' said Ben. He reached into his pocket and fed a treat to Otto. A jealous Bear thundered up a second later and threw himself at his master's feet.

'I was going to ask what made you move up here?'

He tossed a piece of dried out seaweed in the air, watching as the dogs chased after it, not speaking for a long moment then shrugged.

'Honestly? I'm embarrassed to admit it. I was in a relationship that wasn't working, thought if we came up here and changed everything it would make up for the fact that we didn't want to be together.'

'Esther's mother?'

'Yeah. For a long time I felt angry at her for pulling out at the last minute because she made me look like an idiot. Truth is, she had the sense to see it wasn't ever going to work. No amount of kale was going to fix things.'

Sophie burst out laughing. 'I'm not sure kale is the answer to anything, relationship wise.'

'I suspect you're right. Any road, I came up here, made the

best of it, and because I didn't have any distractions I actually started making decent money for the first time since I graduated from art school, which helped smooth things over with my ex.'

'And you lived happily ever after.'

'Something like that.' His eyebrows quirked upwards, a smile playing on his lips. 'Although I've started wondering of late.'

Sophie felt a shot of something like electricity which seemed to fizz through her body, the blood rushing in her ears. 'Wondering what?'

He made a vague gesture with his hands. 'I know everyone makes a joke about me living out here by myself with the dogs. But…'

Sophie looked at Ben as he rubbed his jaw for a moment, his eyes lifting to meet hers for a second and then darkening.

His voice was gruffer than ever. 'It's nicer doing it – this – with someone. With you.'

She opened her mouth to speak, heart banging so hard against her ribs she put an involuntary hand to her chest for a moment. 'It is,' she said, eventually.

'Uh-oh,' said Ben, a split second later. He spun on his heel as if with some sixth sense and cupped his hands to his mouth. 'Otto!'

Sophie followed his gaze. In the distance, hurtling up the far end of the beach and onto the dunes went the younger of the two spaniels, ears flying in the wind, tail low.

'OTTO!' Ben shouted again, turning back to Sophie and shaking his head. 'Rabbit,' he said, with a roll of his eyes.

'Will he come back?'

A long ten minutes later, having jogged to the end of the beach and up the track, Ben retrieved a bedraggled Otto, his white patches covered in black peat and his eyes slightly wild.

'That is quite enough excitement for one day,' said Ben, unhooking the lead which he'd worn clipped across his body and fastening it onto the still bouncing spaniel.

CHAPTER TWENTY-SEVEN

They wandered back along the beach, arms full of the driftwood they collected which they dropped thankfully into the abandoned trolley when they returned to it.

'Delinquent dog strikes again,' said Ben with a rueful grin.

'He can't help it,' Sophie laughed, 'It's not his fault rabbits look so exciting.'

She felt a vague sense of disquiet as they headed back along the shoreline, Otto still tugging eagerly at the end of his lead, looking for all the world as if he was about to set out on a walk rather than heading home.

'I bet you're glad the dogs you're walking for the rescue place aren't as naughty.'

'I'm heading there tomorrow, I'll report back.' Sophie said. 'Janine left me a message to say she's picked up a little terrier whose owner passed away, so I've said I'll take him to the beach for a bit of fun.'

'Let's hope the tide washes away any delicious rabbit scents.'

'Oh, I thought I'd just take him to my beach.' She stopped

herself, realising what she'd said, shaking her head and laughing. 'Get me. My beach.'

'You're getting airs and graces.'

'I'll be looking for a country estate next.'

'Going native.' Ben chuckled as they approached the car. 'Don't forget your northern roots.'

'Hardly likely. I know this place isn't permanent.' Sophie suppressed a sigh of regret.

'I don't think Annie's going to turf you out on the streets.' Ben opened the door and the dogs jumped into the back.

They drove home in silence, Sophie gazing out the window lost in thought. Ben dropped her outside the cottage with a brief wave goodbye, and she headed inside.

For a moment there it had felt as if there was – something. As if he was opening up to her, despite his bluff northern exterior, and showing her what he really felt inside. It had made her heart glow with something she hadn't felt in – well, forever. Hope. The possibility of something.

She switched on the shower, realising that despite the sunshine of earlier she felt chilled down to the bone.

The rest of the weekend whizzed past. She drove over to Janine's place, and spent longer than she expected playing with the rescue dogs and drinking tea and eating biscuits. Janine was clearly lonely up there on her own, desperate for someone to talk to besides the dogs – that was why she chatted the back legs of anyone who came near. Walking Zeb, the little terrier, on the beach, she found herself wondering if that was the fate awaiting her. She glanced up beyond the cottage on the shore and towards Ben's place, wondering if he was working hard in the studio, or sitting with his feet up by the stove. It was a windy, grey day, and she could see smoke rising from the chimney of his croft. A signal, perhaps. She shook herself back to reality. That comment he'd made about it being nicer doing things with someone – it had probably been something he'd said on the spur of the moment. It wasn't as if he'd mentioned it again, not even after things had calmed down and they'd recovered Otto from his adventures.

Each day as she headed for work that week she gazed up at the croft as she passed, telling herself she was just keeping an eye out. But he didn't pass by with the dogs for a walk in the long, light evenings. His pick-up truck was parked outside, smoke rose from the chimney, lights glowed late in the evening in the strange half-darkness as she headed to bed, but there was no sign of him. By Thursday, with Mhairi excited to return to the art class, she'd convinced herself that she'd imagined the whole exchange. She felt faintly sick at the prospect of seeing him again, and if it hadn't been for Mhairi needing a lift, she'd have cried off with a headache or some other excuse.

'You all set?' Mhairi shouldered her rucksack and looked up at Sophie as she switched off the computer.

'I am.'

'You still okay to get something to eat up at the café?' Mhairi applied some lip balm. 'I don't mind if you want to go home and get changed, I can always wait in the car.'

Sophie shrugged. Unlike last week when she'd spent ages making herself look good this week she'd thrown on a jumper and run a brush through her hair.

They earned a friendly wave and a greeting from Polly Fraser as they walked into the farm shop, and ordered something to eat from the boys in the café before sitting down at one of the window tables. Mhairi chattered away about her imminent date with Scott, and eventually after what felt like forever it was time to head over to the workshop, where the usual suspects were already starting to gather.

'All change today,' said Jenny, Dolina's daughter, who'd been working in the shop until a few moments ago. She was still wearing her black apron with the logo embroidered across the front.

'How do you mean?' Mhairi looked up from her phone, looking starry eyed.

Jenny inclined her head towards the door just as her mother bustled up.

'All ready for a bit of Patrick Swayze?' Dolina's laugh was contagious, making everyone smile. She gave her bottom a little wiggle. 'Maybe we can do a bit o' Dirty Dancing afterwards. That's if the teacher's not too busy giving you a lift home, eh?'

She elbowed Sophie in the ribs with a comedy wink.

'Oh did you not hear?' Jenny raised her eyebrows. 'Mother, you're losing your touch. We've got a different teacher tonight.'

Sophie's heart sank. Somehow she'd had a feeling something like this was going to happen. She tried to look casual, fiddling with her sleeve as they walked into the class and pretending not to listen as Jenny explained that someone else from the gallery was taking the class.

'Hi, everyone,' said a very tall, willowy woman with short hair tied off her face with a black scarf. 'I'm Magda, and I'm taking the pottery class this evening.'

'What happened to Ben?' Tortoiseshell glasses had appeared and was standing with her arms folded looking highly unimpressed. Her little mouth was pursed so tightly that it reminded Sophie of a cat's bottom, the idea of which amused her so much that she had to cough and bend down to pretend to tie her already tied shoelace.

'Oh we had a gallery meeting this week, and as the intro class has been such a hit so far it looks like ongoing classes are going to be feasible. I'll be teaching the ceramics course so it made sense for me to come in and give you a feel for what we'd actually be doing, rather than Ben giving you more of a general overview.' She wrinkled her nose and gave a little laugh. 'Ceramics aren't really his thing.'

Sophie looked at Magda through narrowed eyes. Ben's house was full of evidence that ceramics clearly were his thing – from the chic dark grey plates to the huge pot that stood in the middle of the scrubbed table, all of which made by his own hands, it seemed a bit of a cheek to put down another artist's work.

'Right then, everyone, let's get started, shall we?'

You were missed this evening

Sophie looked at the message on her phone for a moment, hesitated, then scrubbed it away with her finger on the delete button. Just because she had his number didn't mean she should start sending random and probably unwise messages after coming home from art class.

The next morning she was glad she hadn't. Driving up towards work she saw Ben and the dogs walking down the track towards the road. Her heart leapt and she raised a hand to wave hello just as he did the same. She paused for a moment, the engine idling.

'Alright?' He nodded, briefly.

'No rest for the wicked. Did you enjoy your night off from teaching last night?'

'Yeah.' His tone was casual and he lifted a shoulder in a hint of a shrug. 'Quiz night at the pub. I'd have got it in the neck if I hadn't made it.'

'Oh,' said Sophie, confused. 'I thought –' she stopped herself and gave a little laugh. 'Anyway, I better get off to work.'

'Have a good day.' Ben raised a hand in farewell and strode off with the dogs.

Magda said she'd chosen to take the class. He sounded like

he'd made a decision not to bother. It was nothing – because at the end of the day, it didn't matter to her whether he taught the class – except it was something.

She thought about it between patients and while she stopped for a coffee break. At lunch, she took herself out telling the others she had a bit of a headache and wandered down to the little bench on the green which looked down to the shore, watching a young family playing with buckets and spades, their waterproof coats piled up on top of a colourful picnic basket. It was the sort of scene that used to make her feel inadequate when Tabby was growing up – two parents, two children, everything picture perfect.

Why did it bother her so much? It wasn't that she cared that Ben hadn't turned up for the class – although she had to admit to herself that if Magda had been the teacher from the outset she wouldn't have enjoyed the classes anywhere near as much. Dolina had muttered sulkily on the way back to the car that it wasn't the same without him, and poor Tortoiseshell glasses had been on the verge of going into a decline. Sophie picked at her sandwich, eventually tossing it down for the young gull who had been circling in the hope of some left-overs. He grabbed it with a wide beak and flapped off to eat it, perched out of reach on top of the green painted lamp post.

It was the idea that he wasn't being truthful about something, she realised, eventually, heading back to the surgery. It might seem like a tiny thing to someone else – but after everything that she'd been through there was one thing that mattered to her more than anything, and that was honesty. If you can't get your story straight about why you're not teaching the class you've said you'll be teaching, Sophie thought, tossing her bag down on the chair in the back room, how on earth can I expect you to be truthful about the big things? Craig's deceit had left a long shadow. After everything that she'd been through, the one thing she knew she'd never stand for was anything other than 100% honesty – and that was something that everyone seemed to find impossible. Somehow because Ben was so direct, she'd imagined him to find it difficult to be anything other than truthful.

She stayed behind after surgery to get caught up on some admin. It niggled at her that she'd only been there a short while and had to take time off – but the trip to visit Tabby had been organised months before she'd agreed to take the job, and Fiona had been sanguine about it.

'Don't stress,' she'd said, in her brisk, matter of fact way. 'We've got a great locum who comes in to cover for holidays. She knows the staff and I'm more than happy letting her take the reins.'

Shuna, Mhairi had assured her, was amazing. Rather than take on full time work at a practice she travelled around doing locum cover to make money for the countless adventure holidays that she did the rest of the year. Mhairi had pointed out the colourful postcards of wildlife from all around the world which were pinned up on the notice board, explaining she'd been diving with Manatees in the Florida Keys on her most recent trip.

'You'll love her,' Mhairi had said cheerfully.

When the door clattered open, making Sophie jump, she looked up. Half expecting it to be the mythical Shuna arriving two days early, she was shocked to see Fiona, looking uncharacteristically pale and not her usual ruddy-cheeked robust self.

'Oh hello,' said Fiona. She put her bag down on the reception desk and pushed a hand through her short, greying ginger hair. 'I thought the place would be empty.'

She looked at the clock and frowned. 'It's almost seven, what are you still doing here?'

'I thought I'd get caught up,' Sophie said, motioning to the computer.

'Oh holidays, yes. Of course. Silly me.'

Sophie looked at the normally efficient Fiona who looked slightly lost, as if she couldn't quite work out what to do with herself.

'Are you okay?' Sophie went to stand up. 'Do you want –'

'No, no,' said Fiona, surprising her by putting her elbows onto the desk and sinking her head into her hands, where she remained for a long moment before looking up again, blinking hard.

'Can I get you a glass of water or something?'

Fiona rubbed at her face and then looked at Sophie as if she'd seen her clearly for the first time that second.

'Sorry. Didn't mean to spring myself on you, but I didn't quite know what to do and this place – well, it's all I've got, really.'

Sophie got up and moved towards her.

'I didn't know what to do,' Fiona repeated. 'It's mum. My mother. She passed away this afternoon.'

'Oh Fiona.' Sophie climbed out from behind the desk and round to join Fiona, putting a hand on her arm. 'I'm so sorry.'

A solitary tear gathered and then fell slowly from Fiona's right eye. She swiped it away, apologising.

'Let me get you a tissue. Do you want some tea?'

'No, no. I'm fine. Well,' said Fiona, with a damp smile, 'I will be. Not much else I can do, is there?'

'I'll put the kettle on.'

A cup of tea seemed to fortify Fiona, restoring her to her usual brisk state.

'Sorry about that. You're the first person outside of the home I've seen, that's all.' She put down the mug on the reception desk. 'I didn't know what to do. I don't have anything else – I mean, this place is – well, it's all I've got.'

'I understand.' Sophie picked up the two mugs.

'I've been so wrapped up in sorting things out and looking after her. Now she's gone, I – well, work is always there, isn't it? It's the one thing I can rely on.'

Sophie pressed her lips together thoughtfully. She wasn't about to tell her boss, who – let's face it, because she'd hardly been around – she didn't really know all that well, that the last thing she needed to be thinking about when her remaining parent had died was work. Grief was a weird thing, and people reacted to it in funny ways.

'Can I do anything else?'

Fiona shook her head. 'No, no, you get off. I'll close up here. Thanks, Sophie.'

CHAPTER TWENTY-EIGHT

Sophie drove down the road just as Ben was looking out of the kitchen window, half-thinking about the next commission he'd taken on. He had started the night before when he was supposed to be teaching. When Magda had insisted on taking the class at the Gallery meeting, he'd found himself in an impossible situation. How the hell was he supposed to admit that he'd actually quite enjoyed teaching, despite all his complaints?

'That'll be a relief,' Mel had said with a laugh, taking part in the meeting via a dial-in video call. 'You can get back to work, Ben, and not have to deal with – how was it you put it? Oh yeah, *a load of bored people who couldn't find anything decent to watch on Netflix*,' she'd finished, making everyone in the room laugh. He'd looked down at the floor, rubbing a hand across his face to hide the expression he feared might give away his feelings. The truth was he'd been looking forward to a reason to see Sophie again, and decided that he needed to just man up and ask her if she'd like to come round for dinner, or out for a drink – no, scratch that, if they went for a drink it would entail a million and one staring eyes from the village and the rumour mill going into overdrive. Dinner it would have to be.

He went through the motions at the quiz night, but his heart wasn't in it. Ducking out early, he headed home and worked long into the night on sketches, trying to get a handle on the piece he'd been asked to create for a sixtieth birthday present.

He watched as Sophie made her way down the track towards the cottage in her little car, climbing out and turning for a moment. For a fleeting second he thought she was looking up at him, then shook his head, heading back across the kitchen to open a bottle of wine.

On a whim, he picked up the phone to call Esther, not expecting her to answer.

'Hi Dad,' she said, sounding happy to hear from him.

'Didn't expect you to reply,' he said, tucking the phone under his ear as he put the bottle of wine between his knees, turning the corkscrew and pulling out the cork with a pop.

'Charming. Were you just ticking a box? Making sure you'd done your fatherly duty before you settled down with Netflix and a bottle of wine?'

'Something like that.' He shook his head, smiling despite himself. Esther always managed to knock him out of a mood, with her dry sense of humour and self-deprecating jokes. 'No, I just thought I'd ring my darling daughter, make sure she's behaving herself.'

'Funny you should say that,' Esther said, 'I was going to call you. Wondered if I could pencil a few days out on your busy schedule so we could come and visit.'

He took a sip of wine, taking a moment to register what she'd said.

'We?'

Esther giggled, which was most unlike her. 'Yes. We.'

He raised an eyebrow.

'Sailing weekend went well, I take it?'

'Very funny, Dad.' She paused for a moment.

'Am I to take it from this that we're knocking the whole "we're just friends, honestly" thing on the head?'

Esther cleared her throat. In the background he heard a distinctly male cough.

'You know I'm free whenever you want to come up,' he said, feeling a wave of love for her. 'Just say the word.'

'I'd love that. I'll give you a shout with dates – we can sort times, can't we, Harry?' He heard her calling across the room.

'You can tell him I'm not going bloody sailing,' Ben said, gruffly.

'You're on speaker,' Esther said with a giggle, 'so you can tell him yourself.'

'Sodding hell, Esther. I was only kidding. Sorry,' he added, to his daughter's brand new boyfriend. 'Not sorry enough to go sailing,' he added, a moment later, grinning to himself.

'How's the new neighbour?' Esther said, changing the subject, her tone arch.

'Sophie? Fine, I think. Why'd you ask?'

'Oh, just wondering.' There was a muttering.

'What was that?'

'I said yes, it's the new vet he's got a thing for,' Esther said, innocently.

'What on earth are you talking about?'

'You do, don't you? Come on, Dad, you can't be on your own forever. Plus think of the free vet bills. You'll be sorted for life.'

'I could go off you, madam,' he said, laughing again.

'You won't,' said Esther. 'We're about to have dinner, so I better go. I'll give you a shout with those dates in the next couple of days once Harry gets holidays sorted. Is that okay?'

'Of course, love.' He swallowed another mouthful of wine. 'I'll speak to you soon.'

'Oh and Dad?' Esther said, just as he was about to go.

'Yes?'

'You should go for it. You're only young once.'

'Go for what?'

'If you like her, and I think you do, you need to tell her.'

Ben groaned.

'Just because you're all loved up doesn't mean you get carte blanche to start pairing up everyone else in the world, you know.'

'That, my grumpy old dad, is exactly what I'm going to do.' And with a cackle, Esther was gone, leaving Ben shaking his head in despair.

It was all very well for her, he thought, wandering back across the room and looking down towards the shore. He'd pretty much accepted the rest of his life was going to be just him, the dogs, and his art, and then Sophie had come along and made him see things differently. He didn't even have a clue if she felt the same way. There was only one thing for it.

Draining the glass, he pulled on a jumper and headed for the door. The dogs, thinking Christmas had come early and delighted at the prospect of a bonus walk, spun round in circles, tails wagging furiously, as he opened the door and let them outside.

He picked up the bottle, almost as an afterthought, and headed back to work.

CHAPTER TWENTY-NINE

Nobody knew where the norovirus bug that knocked out the whole surgery later that week had come from. Fiona, trying to organise her mother's funeral and working all the hours she could as a distraction from her grief, seemed to be the only person in the place who wasn't affected. Sophie was struck down halfway through afternoon surgery, excusing herself midway through an examination of a puppy with a torn dewclaw to go and throw up in the loo. Grace had already been hit and headed home. Mhairi was looking distinctly green about the gills when Fiona, masked and gloved, waved Sophie out of the door.

'Shoo,' she said, firmly. 'I'll get someone to drop by later with some supplies. Get home, lots of fluids, get some electrolytes down you, you know the drill.'

Sophie rubbed her head, wondering where the blinding headache had come from.

'What about –'

'Don't worry, the cavalry is on the way.' Fiona motioned to a bright yellow Ford Ranger which was parked across the street. 'That's Shuna's truck. She's just putting her bags in my place and she'll be coming to take over.'

'I feel terrible leaving you in the lurch,' Sophie said, as a wave of nausea hit and her skin seemed to go somehow ice cold and boiling hot at the same time.

'Believe me, this is the best thing that could happen. Keeps me busy,' said Fiona, through her mask. She made a batting motion. 'Off you go. Shoo.'

Sophie made it home just in time, hurrying up the stairs to throw up before lying prone and miserable on the bed, half dozing, for a couple of hours.

She was just about to climb into some pyjamas and head downstairs when there was a knock at the door. Tossing the nightclothes on the bed, she made her way down into the hall.

Outside stood Ben, clad in a WWII gas mask. He lifted it from his face and waggled his eyebrows, making her laugh through the glass of the door.

'Emergency rations,' he shouted.

Sophie dropped her head into the palm of one hand and laughed through her misery. Despite her misgivings from the other day, despite how grim she felt, seeing Ben made her feel a million times better.

She pulled the door open cautiously. 'Don't come near me,' she warned, 'Or you'll be throwing up in about five minutes.'

He shrugged. 'I've got the constitution of an ox, don't worry. Fiona called and said you needed help, so I've been into the village and picked up some bits and pieces.'

'That's so kind,' said Sophie, taking the bag from his outstretched hand.

'Is there anything I can do? I'm aware you're the medic, not me, but –'

Sophie shook her head. 'I really appreciate it.' She shivered despite the warmth of the evening. 'I can't believe I'm sick and this is probably the only hot day we'll have this year.'

'Oh we should be due at least two more,' said Ben, cheerfully. 'You just need to make sure you're not out of the country when they happen. Oh, wait.'

Sophie laughed. She felt utterly grim, she looked like death warmed up, and yet somehow she didn't mind.

'As long as I'm better for the weekend, I don't care.'

'Is that when you're heading to the states?'

She nodded.

'And to think I thought you might be worried about missing my last art class.'

She darted a glance at him, remembering her misgivings from the other night.

'I thought you were quite happy to hand over the class to Magda.'

He twisted his mouth slightly and raised his eyebrows. 'About that,' he said, fixing her with his dark eyes.

'Your fan club was very disappointed you weren't there.'

'I have a fan club?' Ben's eyebrows steepled upwards.

'Oh Dolina was devastated,' Sophie couldn't help laughing. 'And tortoiseshell glasses – her name's gone, sorry – she just about set up a protest. I thought she was going to pack up her easel and leave.'

Ben shook his head. 'Well that's disappointing.'

'I thought you'd be glad you had a fan club.'

He looked at her for a moment. 'I'm disappointed at the membership.'

'Really?'

'Really.' He held her gaze. 'I was hoping – '

Whatever she'd felt the other day, her mind and her body – despite feeling utterly dreadful – seemed to be working on completely different planes. There was no part of the undeniable physical desire she felt for him that her brain seemed to have any control over.

'Were you?' She lifted her chin slightly, and folded her arms. Thank heavens she hadn't been in pyjamas or – braless – this would have been a much more uncomfortable conversation.

'Look,' he said, suddenly brisk. 'I know you're going to the states, but I wondered if you'd like to go out – well, maybe come for dinner – when you come back?'

'Dinner.' Sophie's stomach gave a slightly alarming growl. 'I'd love that.' Her mouth started to water. 'But I need to –'

'Oh – right. Of course.' He took a step backwards.

Sophie grimaced. 'Thanks.'

'Just going to leave now,' said Ben, 'Shout me if you need anything at all. I'm only two minutes away.'

Sophie, not trusting herself to open her mouth, raised a finger in acknowledgement, turned, and dashed up the stairs two at a time.

Three days later, feeling slightly hollow inside but very relieved to be better, Sophie parked her car at Manchester Airport after the long journey south and headed for Departures.

'You can leave it at ours and I'll drive you in,' Bea had said, as she'd called from the hands free speaker on the journey down past Glasgow.

'I'm coming to you on the way home,' Sophie had reassured her.

'I know but I want to talk to you in person.'

Sophie had glanced up into the rear view mirror, looking at her reflection for a moment. She looked tired and a bit pasty, but a million times better than she had.

'I'll be much better in person once I've had a week of Atlanta sunshine and a rest.'

'Alright.' Bea paused. 'Soph?'

'Bea?' Sophie overtook a lorry on the otherwise empty road.

There was a silence.

'You still there?' Sophie said into the silence.

'Yeah, sorry. It's nothing, don't worry. Text me before you take off, okay?'

'Will do.'

Sophie had made a face as she hung up. She'd known Bea long enough to know that "it's nothing" usually meant anything but.

Just checking you are checked in ok

Sophie smiled at the message from Tabby, complete with a photograph of her, tucked up in bed with her battered, much loved teddy bear from home.

Currently in your idea of heaven aka the shops. Any last minute requests?

There was a pause. Sophie watched the little dots and waited for her daughter to reply. It was so exciting to think that twenty four hours from now she'd be there in person.

Proper chocolate, came the reply. *I am so over the whole Hershey's thing.*

Done. Love you xxx

She headed for WH Smith and picked up some magazines, suspecting that Tab would love anything that would be a reminder from home, and for once took advantage of the proffered gigantic chocolate bars. The woman at the till looked astonished that someone had actually said yes and beamed as Sophie stuffed them into a carrier bag.

'For my daughter,' she said, proudly. 'I'm going to see her over in Atlanta.'

'I bet you can't wait, love,' said the woman with a kind smile. It was funny to be back in England where the accents that surrounded her were familiar. There were people everywhere, though, and more than once she found herself slightly overwhelmed with the crowds and chaos – Applemore had clearly had an effect in the short time she'd been living there. With the village in her mind, she sat down in the departure lounge, one eye on the flight boards as she tried to ring Bea back.

'Hey,' she said, leaving a voicemail, 'I know you hate it when people leave these. I'm trying to save my phone battery because I have the fear I'll get on the plane and not be able to charge it. Hope you're not working too hard and I'll text you when I land so you know I'm in one piece. Love you!'

She blew a kiss into the phone then put it safely back in her bag.

As it transpired, the plane not only had charger points but WIFI, which seemed utterly bonkers to Sophie. The whole joy of a plane was getting on and being cut off from everything and everyone so you could lose yourself in a book or watch a film... she did both, then closed her eyes and tried to get some sleep, aware that she was going to be bitten on the backside by jetlag when she arrived into Atlanta.

Her heart almost burst when she passed through arrivals to see Tabby – looking tall, tanned and athletic – standing with a decorated sign saying MUM.

'Oh I can't believe you're here.'

Sophie squeezed her tightly for a long time, taking in the smell of her familiar fresh perfume and running a hand down the long ponytail. 'I can't believe I am, either.'

'Belle's outside, she's waiting in the car park.'

'She is? I thought we were getting the bus back to the hotel?'

Tabby shook her head. 'I figured you'd be tired and Belle doesn't mind driving.'

'Lovely to meet you, ma'am.' Belle climbed out of the car as they approached, and went to shake Sophie's hand. Sophie gave her a kiss on the cheek.

'I've heard so much about you,' she said, as Belle and Tabby lifted her bags into the boot of the car.

'I can't believe I was worried I had too much stuff.' Her suitcases looked tiny in the back of the huge American car Belle owned.

'Everything is huge here,' grinned Tabby. 'Wait till we go to the ice cream shack. You won't believe the size of the waffles.'

Belle slid back into the driver's seat, flicking her long dark braids back over her shoulder and turning on the ignition. Country music blared out for a split second and she turned it down, apologising.

'You sure you're okay in the back?'

Sophie nodded. 'It's not exactly the same as the Citroen.'

Tabby giggled. 'We've got a teeny car back home,' she said to Belle, as they set off. Turning to Sophie, she pushed a stray lock of hair back behind her ear. 'We'll go to the hotel and check in, yeah? Then we can work out what you want to do. Are you tired?'

'Not too bad actually.' Sophie glanced at her watch. It was 4.30 pm Atlanta time. Back home the sky over the sea would be streaked pale pink, the fishing boats heading out for the night, slipping slowly out of view. She looked out of the window, surprised to see that the huge wide highway was flanked on either side by trees. Soon they were in the city proper, and old buildings jumbled with gleaming high rises as they pulled up outside their hotel. As they opened the door the hot air hit immediately, and she realised that jeans and a long sleeved top with a cardigan just in case was more than a little bit over the top. Tabby, in a vest top and cropped denim shorts looked far better equipped to deal with the weather

'This is a pretty cool hotel, Tabby,' said Belle, as they unloaded the bags. A man in a suit appeared out of nowhere, wheeling a luggage trolley.

'I'll take those for you, ma'am.'

'I could get used to this,' said Sophie, laughing. 'Everyone calling me ma'am

'Four nights here and then three nights in Athens.' Tabby bounced on one of the huge beds, the contents of her overnight bag spilling over the covers. 'I tell you what, this is a bit of a step up from the dorm.'

Sophie gazed out of the window and across the breathtaking view of the city. Trees and greenery were dotted between tall mirror-like plate-glass windows of high rise buildings which seemed to stretch out for miles. The sky was cloudless and bright blue. She turned to look at Tabby, who was now lying in a star shape on the bed.

'Shall we go and get something to eat?'

CHAPTER THIRTY

The week flew past. They played tourists and sat in the park eating ice cream and people watching, then after their time in Atlanta was over Belle – who seemed genuinely delighted to help out – drove down to the city and took them up to Athens, where Tabby showed her all over the campus, introducing her to her teammates. It was lovely to see her so happily unselfconscious about taking her mum all over the place.

'When I was your age,' Sophie said, as they sat by Lake Herrick looking out at the water, 'I would have died if my dad had turned up at university.'

It was the final afternoon they had together, and her heart ached at the thought of the loss to come. She put an arm around Tabby's shoulders, pulling her in for a squeeze.

'I've loved having you here,' said Tabby's muffled voice.

Oh, she wanted to wrap her in her arms and stuff her in her suitcase and take her home. That saying about having a child meaning your heart walked around outside of your body was horribly, brutally true. She squeezed her shoulders again, looking at the little birthmark by the side of her ear she'd kissed so many times when she was a tiny, sleeping baby. She swallowed, keeping her voice steady. 'You'll be okay when I go?'

She mustn't cry. She pressed her teeth together, pushed her tongue into the roof of her mouth, inhaled through her nostrils.

Tabby nodded and pulled away, a slightly wobbly smile on her face. 'Be brave, have adventures, all that stuff you said when I got the chance to come out here.'

'It can't have always been easy.' Sophie pulled a piece of grass from the earth, tearing it into pieces as they spoke. 'But everyone seems really lovely.'

'They are. And I've got you on the end of the phone. To be honest there isn't time to get homesick. If I'm not training, I'm studying and if I'm not studying I'm playing.' Tab had gathered herself, which seemed to give her strength.

'Ladies and gentlemen,' Sophie said with a little flourish of her arm and a laugh, 'My child, Tabby Jones, the prodigy.'

'Very funny.' Tabby took a piece of the grass from her hand and split it lengthways, examining the two pieces. 'You know I'm only the way I am because of you.'

'Hardly.'

'Seriously. You taught me to be brave. After...' she flicked a glance up at Sophie through her long dark lashes, then looked away, dropping the grass onto the earth. 'Well, after what happened.'

Sophie's heart seemed to skip a beat. 'With him?'

'Yeah.'

'I'm sorry, I blame myself.'

'You blame yourself because he ripped you off and took everything? Mum, don't be ridiculous.'

Sophie grimaced. 'Alright, I know, you sound like Bea. It's just – there was just the two of us, always. And I let him in.'

'He seemed nice,' Tabby made an open handed gesture. 'Everyone thought he was nice. It wasn't just you.'

Sophie looked out at the water, where three young girls of Tabby's age were laughing and splashing as they messed about on paddle boards. A bird flew past, landing on the wooden rail by the water and standing on one leg for a moment, turning to preen its feathers in the sunshine.

'You thought he was a good person because you're a good person. It's not your fault he took – ' she stopped herself and shook her head. 'He didn't take everything. He took your money.'

'Our money.'

Tabby shrugged. 'And look where we are now. I've got a full scholarship, and you've got an amazing new job. It doesn't matter that he's out of prison. Why would we let that pathetic man affect the way we live?

Sophie sat back, stunned. 'How did you – I –'

Tabby met her eyes, her voice steady. 'I know. I spoke to Bea just before you left. I don't know what made me think of it – maybe you being up there, and something you said. Anyway, I messaged her and said I wanted to talk.'

'She rang me when I was on the way to the airport.' That's why she'd sounded odd.

'I looked it up on the Liverpool Echo site to see what it said about the court case. It wasn't that hard to figure out that he must be due out round about now.'

Sophie swallowed back a bitter taste that rose in the back of her throat. 'Oh Tab, I'm sorry. You shouldn't have to be worrying about this.'

'I'm not. That's the point. When I thought about it, it all made sense. You knew I'd be out of reach over here, that's why you were all for me going away even though I could see you were really sad about it.'

'I was sad about it because I love you and I knew I'd miss you.'

'Well obviously,' Tabby flashed her a grin, 'But Athens Georgia is pretty much as far as you can get from Crosby, Merseyside.' She put on a Scouse accent as she spoke, then cocked her head sideways and narrowed her eyes. 'And the Highlands is pretty bloody far away as well.'

'Language,' said Sophie, shaking her head in mock disapproval.

'Don't change the subject.'

'Who is the adult here?' Sophie laughed.

'Me.' Tabby folded her arms. 'You can't let him ruin your life. Let's face it, he's already taken all your money, there's none left.'

'I hadn't thought of it that way.'

'Ha.' Tabby was endearingly sanctimonious. 'Look, Bea and I were talking about it. I know you're stressing about what happens when I come back in the holidays and I want to see my friends and stuff. I can stay at hers any time I want, you know that. But home…' she broke off, looking down at her lap for a moment.

Sophie watched as Tabby took a long breath in, then lifted her little chin with the look of determination she'd seen in so many football games over the years.

' – home's where you are. It always will be.'

Sophie lifted a finger to her daughter's face, brushing away the tear that had rolled down her cheek.

'I love you, darling.'

'Love you too.' Tabby rubbed at her face with both hands. 'Now we're both crying for heaven's sake, this is ridiculous.'

Sophie swiped at her nose with the back of her arm and

scrambled to her feet, putting her hand out to pull Tabby up to join her. 'Come on, let's go and get some waffles. I don't know what I'm going to do without them.'

'You mean without me?' Tabby fell into step beside her as they made their way through the trees and back towards the hotel for their last evening together.

'No, I mean without waffles.' Sophie nudged her with her shoulder.

'You won't need waffles, from what Bea tells me, because you'll be too busy hanging out with the hot artist.'

'Oh no,' Sophie groaned. 'What has Bea been telling you?'

'He looks quite nice, from what I could see.' Tabby's tone was mock-innocent.

'What you could see?'

'Oh come on, you don't think we had a look? He's got a website. And an Instagram account with his art stuff on it.'

'I thought I was moving to the middle of nowhere so I could live a quiet life. Now I discover you're Instagram stalking me from another continent.'

'I'm not stalking, I was just checking him out.' She broke into a run, turning after a few steps to jog backwards, ponytail swinging in the air as she laughed. 'I'm just telling you I think you should go for it.' She put her thumbs up and turned, dashing up the hill.

CHAPTER THIRTY-ONE

'Don't think I hadn't worked out why you decided to run,' Bea said, two days later. They were walking along Crosby beach, the afternoon sun casting long shadows from the Antony Gormley statues which stood, magnificent and enigmatic, on the sand.

'I didn't run,' Sophie protested.

'Alright, escape. Is that better?' Bea linked her arm though Sophie's and they walked along together for a while in silence. Out on the water the wind turbines spun silently and a tanker headed out of port, laden with vast colourful containers. She'd watched these sights a million times - they were comforting and familiar. Later that evening before she slept they'd have dinner in the little Italian on the High Street, then share a bottle of red outside on Bea's patio under the pergola she'd helped to paint and strung with fairy lights.

Her phone buzzed against her hip and she pulled it out, looking at the screen and frowning. 'It's Nick. Says if I have a sec, can I drop by the surgery.'

'Oh,' said Bea, her brows lifting slightly. 'Yeah, I mentioned to him you were going to be here today. He came into the café on Friday.'

Sophie looked at her sideways. 'Did he say what he wanted?'

Bea shook her head.

The surgery door was ajar. Sophie had left Bea and walked on down the High Street, her feet turning on autopilot down Grenville Road towards the little parade of shops, a strange feeling of apprehension rising.

She popped her head around the door.

'Hey,' said Nick, with a broad smile, coming out from behind the desk to greet her with a hug. 'Soph. It's good to see you.'

'You too.' She'd forgotten how sleek and modern the place was in contrast to the cosy muddle of the Applemore surgery. Since she'd been gone, they'd installed new screens along one wall and the computers had been upgraded. She smiled to herself briefly, imagining Grace's horror if she was presented with yet another new system to learn. 'So what's up?'

Nick sat back against the desk, extending his legs and crossing them over at the ankle. 'Well, the thing is this – I was going to ring you but it's much better in person. I don't know how you're getting on up there, but you're missed.'

Sophie reared back slightly in surprise. 'I am?'

Nick nodded. 'More than you might realise. I think we took you for granted – well, I did, anyway. You kept this place running.'

Her eyebrows - which had already lifted - elevated several more degrees.

'What about Claire?'

'Don't.' Nick shook his head. 'Look, you know me, it takes a lot for me to admit I've made a mistake.' He held his hands out. 'But I'm telling you now. I didn't think you wanted the extra stress. Got the wrong end of the stick.'

Sophie steepled her fingers, then ran her hands over her cheeks for a moment as if to rearrange her features.

'You said before you weren't keen on doing longer hours.' Nick picked up a pen and started twiddling it back and forth through his fingers.

'That was when Tabby was still at school.'

'I know, I know. I worked that out when you up and left.' He gave an apologetic shrug.

'I didn't up and leave, as you put it.' She leaned back against the wall.

Nick frowned. 'Oh come on, I gave the job to Claire and you handed in your notice. I'm not the sharpest but even I can make the connection.'

She sighed. 'I left because I was worried about Craig getting out.'

Nick stood up and started pacing the room. 'Oh, Soph. I'm an idiot. I – I didn't forget, I just – '

'Why would you remember. It didn't happen to you.' Strange that something that had been so huge to her was just something to be mentioned in passing now.

'He ripped you off.'

'It was a lot more than that.' She'd thought about it on the flight home, Tabby's words echoing in her ears. Had she run away? She'd given up the life she had – small as it was, with familiarity and friends on the doorstep – and taken herself to the Highlands to start again. Or that's what she'd told herself anyway. And now here was Nick, offering her everything she thought she'd wanted.

'I know you've rented your place out for a year – Bea mentioned it – but you can have the flat above here for the rest of the tenancy, if it helps. Then when your tenant moves back out you can go home and we can get back to normal. Only you'll be – well,' He tipped his head towards the door. 'I think your name should be out there on the door, don't you?'

'I can't afford to buy in and become partner.'

'We can work something out. Claire's moving on, you can have carte blanche to run this place the way you like, hire in some new blood…' he tailed off, making a rueful face. 'I'm sorry, Soph. I screwed up.'

She screwed her eyes closed for a moment as jet lag mingled with confusion.

Nick put a hand to her arm. 'You don't need to decide now, have a think and let me know. The offer's on the table.'

'I'd better go,' she said, suddenly overcome with exhaustion.

'Give me a call, okay? There's no rush.'

'Will do.'

Unsteady on her feet, she almost lost her footing as she stepped off the pavement and crossed the road, almost bumping into a grey-haired man in a faded black vest. 'Careful love,' he chuckled, 'Bit early for hitting the prosecco, isn't it?'

Sophie gave him a fleeting polite smile to indicate she got the joke, then headed back to Bea's place. She had a lot to think about.

CHAPTER THIRTY-TWO

It wouldn't take long to pack up the cottage. She'd jettisoned so many of her belongings before she left, putting the rest in storage and leaving the furniture for her tenant. She paused for a moment, standing by the bedroom window, looking out at the dazzling turquoise sea and the heaped grey rocks which encircled the little private beach she'd come to love. She'd kept the place deliberately impersonal, not putting her stamp on the place. She'd even chosen to leave Mino behind, and now he'd settled so well at Bea's place that his four little white feet were well and truly under the table. She turned and headed downstairs, picking up the phone.

'Fiona, it's me. Can we talk?'

Fiona had taken her by surprise, turning up on the doorstep ten minutes later. In her usual brisk manner she'd explained that she was just on her way out.

'Heading past in any case,' she'd said, stamping mud off her boots as she followed Sophie into the hall. 'Just been on a call. Jersey cow over at Little Strathan.'

Sophie's hand hovered over the kettle. 'Tea?'

Fiona shook her head. 'Awash with the stuff. I've been up there two hours and I think they gave me about five mugs. I'll be peeing like a drayhorse all evening.'

Sophie had tried not to laugh, asking Fiona to join her at the table. Butterflies had been crashing around in her stomach since she'd called her earlier.

'So what's all this about? You're not about to throw in the towel, are you?'

Sophie felt her eyes widening in surprise. 'I wanted to talk to you about the cottage.'

'This place?' Fiona looked around at the pretty, tidy kitchen. The only evidence that Sophie lived there was a loaf of sliced bread on the windowsill and a pot of dried basil she'd left sitting beside the hob before she left for America.

'I want to move out.'

It was Fiona's turn to look surprised. She raised her eyebrows and her chin dropped as she looked at Sophie over the top of her glasses. 'You do?'

'I do.' Sophie fiddled with the edge of the table mat then pushed it away to stop herself getting distracted. 'I think it's for the best.'

Fiona didn't say anything, but her face indicated for Sophie to go on.

She squared her shoulders and took a deep breath. She'd thought about it on the drive back, the little car eating up the miles as she mulled the idea over and over in her head until she knew it was the right decision. Things were going to change.

'I need to make a home here. I want to make a home here.'

There was a bang and a muttered swearing from the hall. They both turned towards the door.

'Hello-oo?' called a familiar voice. 'I couldn't resist popping in the second you got back.'

Of course. She'd been spotted by Annie, who she knew was desperate to hear all about the trip to the states. She appeared in the kitchen, brandishing a gingham cake tin. 'Ah, I thought you were back. Oh, hello, Fiona. Sorry to hear about your mother. It's a sad time.'

Fiona nodded acknowledgement.

'I won't keep you, I just saw the car and thought as I was passing – I'm on the way to the village for crochet club up at the hall – I'd drop this in. No doubt you've eaten your body-weight in junk over there in the states so I thought you might appreciate a nice fruit cake.' She winked at Fiona. 'Keep you regular. You've got to keep an eye on your bowels, you know.'

Sophie didn't know where to look. This whole situation had gone so much more smoothly when she'd rehearsed it in her head.

'Lucky you turned up,' said Fiona, turning to face Annie. 'This one's decided she wants to move out.'

'Of this place?' Annie's brow gathered in concern.

'Apparently so.'

'I thought you liked it here.'

Sophie felt her face going scarlet. 'I do. I mean I did. I love it. I've loved it.'

'Well that makes it clear,' said Fiona, acerbically. 'Did you get that?'

'If you love it,' said Annie, 'Why are you wanting to move out?'

Sophie sat forward, leaning her crossed arms on the table and looking at the two women who'd – in their own distinctly peculiar ways – done so much to make her feel at home here in Applemore.

'This was only ever temporary, while the flat above the surgery was being repaired.'

'Still waiting for Kenny to sort the plastering,' muttered Fiona, 'That reminds me I must give him a call.'

'I'm not worried about the flat. I want a place here that I can make my own. I want – ' Sophie cast around wildly, realising as she said it that yes, she did, '-I want a dog. And I want to bring my things up from Crosby and have my books on the bookcase and make it feel like home. It's beautiful, but it's been like playing house.'

'And what's to stop you having all those things here?'

'This place is yours. I assume you're going to want to rent it out again or sell it, or…'

'Or let you have it?' Annie folded her hands and looked at Sophie for a long moment. 'That seems like the perfect solution to me.'

'But you wouldn't – I mean would you mind me having a dog? What if it gets messy?' She thought of Ben's place and the muddy spaniel footprints all over the rug. 'Dogs and pale sofas don't exactly go together.'

'Get a throw.' Annie chuckled. 'Or don't. I couldn't care a hoot. We can sort an official tenancy agreement, if it makes you feel better, or we can carry on the way things are.'

Fiona tipped her head in agreement. 'Sounds good to me.'

'Seriously?'

'Seriously.' Annie pushed the cake tin towards them. 'Now I'd love to stay and celebrate but I've got a class to get to.'

'And I've got to get back to the surgery.' Fiona stood up and went to follow her out of the kitchen. 'Unless there's anything else?'

Sophie shook her head.

'Right, well, we'll see you bright and early tomorrow morning.'

Out of nowhere Sophie did a huge yawn.

'And get an early night. Jet lag is a bugger.'

She stood on the doorstep and watched the two women leave, their respective cars trundling up the track towards the road. A movement caught her eye up at the croft.

CHAPTER THIRTY-THREE

Ben stood by the gate, watching as Sophie – her hair blowing loose in the wind – marched up the hill towards him. He'd spotted her coming home earlier that afternoon, and suppressed the urge to head down with some spurious excuse so he could see her. Her absence had shown him one thing. He didn't want to be there by himself any more. He'd spent long enough alone, focusing only on work and his daughter. He grinned thinking of Esther's teasing the other day, and was still smiling as Sophie came into shouting distance.

'I'd like to point out that we have all been behaving ourselves,' he said, pointing to the dogs, who lay sprawled on the grass in the sunshine.

'I'm glad to hear it.' She'd caught the sun in America, freckles sprinkled prettily across her nose. She folded her arms on the top of the gate, her hazel eyes sparkling.

'I came to tell you I'm not moving,' she said, looking up at him. The light fabric of her shirt shifted in the wind, revealing the soft curve of her shoulder.

He tipped his head sideways, narrowing his eyes slightly

but not dropping her gaze. Sophie's mouth twisted in a cheeky half smile and he felt his heart thumping unevenly in his chest. Oh, hell.

'You're not.'

He felt his lips twitching in a smile to match hers.

'Nope.' A flicker of an eyebrow.

'Well, I'm glad to hear it.' He took a step closer and then they were standing face to face, only the solid wood of the gate dividing them.

'I hoped you might say that.' Sophie put a hand on the top of the gate, her fingers curving around the wood he'd crafted to keep his place secure and isolated. All he wanted to do now was rip it out of the way.

'Goodness knows who I'd end up with as neighbours next time,' he said, his tone deliberately light.

She lifted a hand to swat him on the arm and unthinkingly he caught it, and somehow a second later his fingers were tangled in hers. He looked down at them and then back up into Sophie's expectant face.

'About what I said. Before.' His voice sounded gruff, even to him.

She nodded, biting her lower lip and looking up at him.

'About dinner?'

And then he grinned. 'You can have dinner, if you want.'

'Now?'

'Have you got other plans?'

Sophie stretched out her fingers against his, then curled them back, her thumb brushing against his. 'Nothing that can't wait.'

He let go of her hand and unlatched the heavy gate, pulling her through the gap, drawing her close. Her soft curves seemed to fit against his body perfectly. His hand ran down the small of her back, pausing to span the curve of her waist.

His heart was banging against his ribcage and Sophie was looking at him with a smile on her face which seemed to light her up as she started to laugh.

'What's so funny?'

Her eyes were sparkling. 'I've just… I've been thinking about that for a while.'

'Oh, I think I can beat you there,' he said, pulling her towards him and tipping her chin up towards his face so he could feel him smiling against her lips before he kissed her. Somewhere in the distance the sound of a bird echoed over the hills and one of the dogs barked a warning.

'And you two can sod off,' he growled, making her laugh once again. 'You're not going to screw up my chances this time.'

Sophie woke the next morning, taking a second to realise that the heavy weight across her waist was Ben's arm, which curled around her as if they were designed to fit together. She ran a finger along the dark hairs that dusted his tanned skin, then shifted slightly, feeling the scruff of his beard catch for a second against her hair, and turned to face him.

'Hello,' he said, sleepy eyed and smiling. He ran a finger down her bare shoulder, making the hairs on her arm stand on end, crooking an eyebrow at her.

'Hi.'

He lifted her hair gently, tucking it behind her shoulder and rolling over to drop a kiss on her shoulder. 'Coffee?'

She made to move but he raised a finger in warning.

'You stay exactly where you are.'

He swung out of bed, pulling on a pair of faded plaid pyjama trousers, and headed out of the room. Sophie lay back against the pillows and closed her eyes for a moment, before opening them with a snap as she took it in. She was there – she really was lying in Ben's bed, looking out of the huge undressed window over the wild countryside that stretched down the hillside towards the cottage by the shore.

'Here you are.' He passed her a coffee and she cupped the grey pottery mug, feeling the smoothness against her fingers as the scent rose into the air, working its magic even before she took a first delicious sip. She'd pulled the covers up, suddenly conscious of her nakedness beneath them, and the unforgiving morning light.

'You look beautiful,' said Ben, surprising her with the tenderness of his tone. He climbed back into bed beside her, pausing for a moment to drop a kiss on her shoulder.

'What time is it?' She felt the warmth of his skin against hers as he shifted slightly, turning to look at her.

He shrugged briefly. 'Early?'

'I –' Sophie glanced over at the table by the bed. She'd left her phone in the other room last night when they'd made it inside, discarding it around the same time they'd both acknowledged that there wasn't going to be much in the way of dinner on the menu that night.

Ben caught on a second later. 'You've got loads of time. No curtains,' he said, indicating the long window, ' – it means I'm woken up ridiculously early in the morning. Not that I minded when it meant I could look down the hill and spot the pretty vet who moved in and improved the view no end.'

She looked at him sideways, meeting his eyes and returning the sleepy, sexy grin that was tugging at the corners of his mouth. She put down her coffee and turned back.

'I'm glad it's early,' she said, sliding a hand across his chest, feeling the tangle of dark hair scattered over the solid muscle. He caught her wrist, wrapping his fingers around it.

'Me too.'

A moment later any residual doubts she had about Ben's feelings towards her fortysomething body were forgotten, as was the coffee, which was stone cold by the time they remembered about it.

'I'll make you that dinner tonight, if you want to come round after work.' Ben pulled on a faded grey t-shirt.

Sophie picked up her clothes from last night, which had been discarded in a heap worthy of any teenager. She shook out her shirt and slipped it on, tucking a strand of hair behind her ear and looking up at Ben.

'Dinner?' She couldn't help but tease him with a cheeky smile. 'Aren't you supposed to play it cool?'

'Too bloody old for that nonsense.' His tone was gruff and the look of intensity in his eyes made her heart thump unevenly in her chest.

'I waited long enough for you. I'm not messing around.' Ben put out a hand to pull her upright and drew her once again into his arms.

'I'm glad to hear it.'

Sophie made it to work on time, but only just.

EPILOGUE

ONE YEAR LATER

The long table from the kitchen had been carried out to the garden. Esther, who'd come back for a visit with her boyfriend Harry, was decorating it with a centrepiece of flowers she'd collected from the meadow beside the croft. Daisies and meadowsweet were woven alongside golden buttercups and long sprays of pale yellow gorse flowers which scented the air with a faint hint of coconut, reminding Sophie of the first time she and Ben had gone searching for driftwood along the shore.

'What time are they supposed to be here?'

Sophie looked at her watch. 'Any time,' she said, putting down a tall glass jug full of Pimm's. Under the table, keeping cool in the shadows, lay Otto and Bear and alongside them Hallow, the scruffy little brindle terrier that Sophie had fostered to help out Janine. Catching her eye, he wriggled upright and jumped up at her legs, waggling his stumpy little brown tail.

'Hello, scruff,' said Sophie, reaching down to scratch behind his ears.

'He must be so glad you decided to keep him,' said Esther. She reached over, dropping a sprig of wild mint from the flowers she'd collected into the jug, then bending down to tickle a prone Hallow who was lying upside down with his tongue hanging out.

'I think we all are. I knew the second I picked him up there was no way I'd be able to hand him over to someone else.'

Esther scooped him up into her arms. He was tiny in contrast to the spaniels, a wire-coated bundle of love and enthusiasm who'd fitted in perfectly to her life from the moment he'd walked into it. She looked across the yard, watching Ben and Harry who were carrying a wooden bench towards them. Everything had fitted perfectly since she'd walked into Applemore, it seemed. She'd spent so long looking over her shoulder, waiting for something to go wrong, and then somehow the anxiety and fear had just fallen away.

'It's nice that we're here when Bea and Mark are coming to visit.'

Esther's voice broke into her thoughts. Sophie smiled across the table at Ben's daughter. It hadn't been a surprise that she'd been easy-going and friendly, but that hadn't stopped her feeling trepidatious before their first meeting almost a year ago. Now she'd moved out of the cottage and into the croft, and Bea and Mark were coming up with the last of her things which had been left in storage back down south in Crosby.

'It is,' Sophie agreed. She'd settled so well into life in Applemore and been accepted by the little community, all of whom had been delighted to discover that she and Ben were a couple, but there was still a quiet, residual sadness that Tabby hadn't managed to make it to the Highlands. She'd flown back out to visit in the autumn, but the longer that her daughter spent in the states the further away she felt. Having Bea and Mark here to visit now they were living together would somehow help to give their relationship a seal of approval from her old life.

'Alright, baby?' Ben caught her by the shoulders, surprising her. 'You look like you're lost in thought. Everything okay?'

Sophie nodded. 'Just chatting to Esther. She's helping get the table ready for –'

She looked up and realised Esther had slipped back into the house.

'She's probably back in there with Harry, checking on the bread. I told her it was far too hot to be putting on the wood burner but she's determined she knows best.'

Sophie caught his hand and pulled him towards her, feeling his warmth against her. 'Can't think where she gets that from.'

'Very funny.' Ben kissed her, drawing her close, so she could feel the heat of his skin beneath the shirt he was wearing.

'Where d'you want this?' Harry re-appeared with a bucket of ice cubes.

'Shove it on the table.' Ben stepped back, laughing, as his daughter reappeared.

'I'll just go and make sure we've got everything in the spare room,' Sophie reluctantly let go of Ben's hand.

'Again?' Ben grinned.

'I just want it to be nice for them.'

She headed into the house and made her way along the hall, smiling to herself at the display of framed artworks that were hung along the walls, taking pride of place. Ben had been touched more than he'd ever admit when – at the end of the art class – the students had got together and presented him with the pictures they'd worked on as a thank you. Now –

varying from the sublime to the ridiculous – they hung on the walls as a reminder.

'If I hadn't agreed to take that class...' Ben had said thoughtfully, hanging the last of the frames with the same consideration he gave to the most expensive artworks at the gallery.

'You'd have met me anyway, you sentimental old thing.' She'd put her arms around his waist and reached up to kiss the back of his neck. 'I can't believe you're such a softy underneath.'

'Shut up,' Ben had said, mouth full of screws and a wry smile at the corner of his lips.

'They're here,' shouted Esther through the kitchen door.

Sophie hurtled down the stairs, making her way back to the yard just as Mark's spotless grey Audi crunched onto the gravel.

'Oh, this is gorgeous.' Bea jumped out of the passenger seat, rushing over to give Sophie a kiss. 'Now I can see why you fell in love with the place.'

'I thought it was me she fell in love with.' Ben chuckled, strolling over to give Bea a kiss. 'How's it going?'

'Long drive.' Bea hugged him. 'But worth it to see you two in your natural setting.'

They'd been down to England to visit a few months before, spending a weekend at Bea and Mark's place, enjoying the chance to catch up but both delighted to return to the peace of the Western Highlands.

Mark had been greeted effusively by the dogs and then shook Ben's hand with a grin. 'Any chance of a beer for the driver?'

'Thought you'd never ask. I've got some in the fridge from my mate Lachlan - you can tell me what you think.'

Sophie smiled, watching as the two of them turned

towards the house. Bea caught her arm and she noticed Ben and Mark pausing for a second, turning towards her with an odd look on both of their faces.

'Soph, can you just give me a hand to get this stuff out of the back of the car?'

'Don't worry, we can get it later. I've made a jug of Pimm's.' Sophie waved her free arm towards the long table where Esther and Harry were now sitting, both looking at her with the same slightly odd expressions on their face.

'I just want to get this stuff now then we can have a drink.' Bea tugged her towards the car.

'Alright, alright…' Sophie pulled the door open and her heart leapt.

'Hello,' said Tabby, scrambling out of the back seat of the car and into her mother's arms in a matter of seconds.

'What – how?' Sophie squeezed her tightly, breathing in the oh-so-familiar scent of her hair and the sensation of her grown-up child in her arms, and felt tears running unbidden down her cheeks.

She looked up for a moment, seeing the faces of the people she loved looking at her with undisguised delight, and realised in that second that she'd been stitched up.

'How? I –'

'I had a flight home to use, and I spoke to Bea and she spoke to Ben and – well, here we are.'

'Oh darling, this is the most amazing thing. How did you get the flights sorted? How did you get from the airport?'

She pushed Tabby back to take her in, gazing with delight at her daughter, tall and tanned in a red t-shirt and jeans.

'Stop fussing, woman,' said Mark, laughing.

'I'll have that drink now, if it's still going.' Bea linked an arm through Sophie's.

They sat down together, drinking and talking and catching up on news.

'Did you ever finish that art class?' Bea said a while later, dropping her chin into her hand and looking over at Sophie with a mischievous expression.

'She did,' said Ben. 'Of course she only came in the first case because she had the hots for me, didn't you?'

'I did not.'

Esther giggled. 'You can talk, Dad.' She turned to the others, flipping her shiny dark bob back from her face. 'I used to call and all I'd hear was *Sophie, this Sophie that. I'm quite happy single*, he'd add.'

'Well I think it's sweet,' said Tabby, 'it goes to show there's someone for everyone out there, even if they are ancient.'

'Watch it, you,' said Bea, who was closest. She swatted her on the arm.

Hours later, with the plates cleared away and the shadows growing long, Sophie noticed a figure making her way up the path.

'Is that Annie?' Tabby peered down the hill, shading her eyes.

Sophie nodded. 'I invited her to join us earlier, but you know what she's like.'

'Bloody stubborn,' said Ben, standing up and giving her a wave.

'She does things her own way,' said Esther, peeling an orange.

'There must be something in the water,' said Bea. 'Anyway, I'm glad she's turned up, I've been dying to meet her.'

A few minutes later Annie – taking it steadily, leaning on her stick – made it to the table.

After the introductions, and with a glass of wine in hand, she sat down beside Sophie.

'She's very like you,' said Annie, smiling at Tabby.

'Everyone says that.' Tabby put an arm around Sophie's shoulder. Sophie reached up, squeezing her hand fondly.

'Didn't want to get in your hair when you're in the midst of a family gathering,' Annie said, looking at Ben and Sophie with a smile, 'But I thought you'd like to hear the news about the cottage.'

Sophie looked over at Ben. Since she'd moved out the cottage had stood empty for a couple of months, and they'd wondered what was going to happen to the place. Annie's son and daughter in law had continued their campaign to get her to sell up and hand over the inheritance early, to no avail.

'I've decided,' said Annie, with a slow smile, 'That I'm going to give in. I've been approached by a young couple who want to buy my place and turn it into a smallholding, so I'm going to give in. They can have the blooming money. It's no good to me when I'm gone, and goodness knows they've gone on about it long enough.'

Sophie felt her heart sink. She couldn't imagine Annie not being around. 'And you?'

Alice cackled. 'I've decided to take a leaf out of your book. I'm moving into the cottage by the shore.'

Ben smiled broadly. 'Well at least we don't have to worry about dodgy neighbours.'

'Exactly.' She gave a wicked grin. 'And you never know, Sophie, I might get lucky like you did and find a handsome young chap to share it with.'

Later that night Sophie and Ben wandered outside into the garden. The sky was clear and night was falling, the first stars pin-pricks in a sky that faded from pink to the palest blue. The moon was almost full and shone over a calm sea.

'If you listen, you can hear the crash of the waves from here.'

There was a roar of laughter from inside the house. They turned as one, looking at the figures that were silhouetted against the light of the kitchen. Bea was standing with her arm around Mark. Esther and Tabby were bending over the table, looking at something on one of their phones.

'It was a lot quieter before I turned up.' Sophie slid a hand under Ben's t-shirt, feeling the broad expanse of muscle.

'Bringing that lot?' He laughed, and pulled her close. 'Quieter, yes. Wouldn't change it for the world, though.'

She felt the heat of his body against the thin fabric of her shirt and her breath caught in her throat.

Ben was so close now that she could feel his smile rather than see it. 'Actually, I would.'

'You would?' She closed her eyes, waiting.

'I would,' he growled, laughing, before kissing her again. 'I'd tell them to bugger off so we could go to bed. None of them can take a bloody hint.'

'Excuse me, you two,' came a shout from the now open kitchen window. Esther and Tabby were hanging out, laughing. 'There *are* children present, you know.'

ACKNOWLEDGMENTS

This book is a thank you to everyone who works in the veterinary world - dedicated, unsung, often under incredible pressure and doing the job for the love of animals. (Please forgive any mistakes I've made along the way in writing Sophie's story!) It's an incredibly hard job with emotional, physical and financial challenges which people often don't realise. If you're waiting longer than you should be in the surgery when you're in for an appointment, it's probably because someone is going above and beyond for another client.

Thank you all for everything you do.

As always, a huge thanks to my lovely editor Hayley Webster and my brilliant cover designer Diane Meacham. Huge thanks also to my agent Amanda Preston at LBA who does such an amazing job along with the gang at ILA to sell my books abroad - it's so exciting to see the Applemore stories travelling around the world!

Love to my friends who cheer me on behind the scenes, and who don't mind my taking a week to reply to messages when I'm in the middle of writing.

The hugest love to Verity, Archie, Jude and Rory - all spreading their wings and doing amazing things while I feel a little bit like Sophie (writing about an empty nest as your nest empties is a little close to home). I am so proud of you and I love you all millions.

To my darling James - thank you for everything, really. We are lucky. I love you and our adventures.

Last of all, to my dear friend Jax, to whom this book is dedicated - thank you for always being there. Here is to writing your own happy ending, as I know you will.

THE WINTER COTTAGE

'Absolutely delightful - The Winter Cottage is romantic and fun' - Marian Keyes

Escape to the Scottish Highlands with this warm and funny second chance romance packed full of family, friendship, and love.

When Rilla Clark's reclusive professor dad dies she breaks her travel plans and heads to his cottage in the Scottish Highlands to sort out his affairs. She's got a plan: get in, clear up, and get out. The little village of Applemore holds memories for her, but looking back might just open up her heart, which she's kept well-guarded until now.

Lachlan Fraser isn't exactly wild about inheriting the title of Laird of Applemore. The castle is falling apart at the seams and he can't see why his three sisters love it so much. Gathered together at their family estate, the battle of wills over what to do with the house is just beginning when into their life walks Rilla, who they haven't seen for over fifteen years...

Old friendships and long-hidden emotions are rekindled as the romance of a Highland winter works its magic... will Rilla and Lachlan discover that home isn't a place, but a feeling?

Printed in Great Britain
by Amazon

21096525R00174